I0624794

FROSTARC

SECLUSION BOOK ONE

by ARTHUR McMAHON

Bald Crow Publishing

Copyright © 2012 Arthur McMahon

All rights reserved.

ISBN: 0615753922
ISBN-13: 978-0615753928

Cover illustration by Eran Fowler.
Book design and production by Bald Crow Publishing.

For mom and dad.

FROSTARC

CHAPTER ONE

Fear

The snow had ceased, and his truck was warming up. Inside his tattered cabin, Kozz prepared to leave on his monthly supply run. Staring into the bathroom mirror his fingertips brushed through a buzz cut of salt and pepper hair, then across the sandpaper stubble of his cheeks. Silver eyes and a strong jaw line gave youth to an otherwise aged face, and his block of a head balanced atop a spud-like body. Pale skin stretched tight around a growing waist where it once was pulled neat and fit around a warrior's physique.

"This mug ain't what it used to be, but I'll make it presentable enough to head into town."

After shaving Kozz walked into the main room and grabbed his belongings off the round table next to the small gas-fire stove. A change of clothes, a few meal bars, and his knife. He tripped over a stack of tabloid magazines, the same stack he told himself years ago he would find a better place for.

Kozz gave a last look around his home and felt for the

familiar cold metal surface at his side as he walked out the door. Sometimes Kozz could be forgetful, but he never forgot her.

The crisp sting of the air awakened his senses unlike any cup of coffee could, making the hairs on his body stand erect at its command. The air was calm, but its stagnant chill was ever present. Kozz reached inside his coat pocket and pulled out a fat stogie, then he lit it up. *The heat from the first puff warms my bones like drinking a cup of hot cocoa.* The smoke danced in circles and waves as Kozz exhaled.

The solitary man examined the clear view of white that stretched all around the horizon, meeting the blue sky with a clarity that only such a still day could bring. Most days were too dangerous to travel through the stark wilderness with the constant drapes of snow burying anything that stood still for too long. Only the warmers placed within and around his home kept Kozz from such a fate. The weathered chrome towers passed to each other a current of warmth which formed a bubble around the cabin, turning ice and snow into puddles.

The drive to town would take thirty hours on a good day and stopping for a rest was not an option. Kozz's rig would be engulfed by powder in minutes if a storm flared up while he was taking a nap. Checking on the integrity of his 200-ton H2O delivery truck one last time before leaving did not sound like such a bad idea. Kozz pulled in one final puff before tossing his cigar out into a drift of snow where it melted its way towards the soil. He walked down the steps that led away from his house and put his boot down onto the wooden tread where his foot broke through a rotten board that he had been meaning to replace. "Goddamn piece of shit," he cried as he tumbled to the ground.

Being taller than most and as broad as an oil drum, Kozz found that many conventional constructions were not built to accommodate his size. He sat there for a moment looking at the damage, more worried about the busted stairs than his sprained and scratched ankle. *This damn house needs some work, but it'll have to wait until I get back.* Kozz lifted himself up on his left foot, testing weight on his damaged right ankle. Pain shot up through his leg. Walking was not going to be easy. Kozz hobbled over to his large, ash-colored truck and grabbed a rag from under the passenger seat. He sat down and wrapped the rag around his ankle, filling it with snow to reduce the swelling. *Moe and the guys are gonna riot when they see me like this.* He stood up and limped his way around the side of the rig to check the energy cells. Large red lettering and symbols were faded along the behemoth's side, relics of a previous owner. Kozz reached the energy cell compartment and could hear their quiet buzz, then he opened the hatch and saw that the deep-blue electric glow of the two cells was healthy, the whirring buzz was another good sign. A slow walk-around showed the tires and treads to all be in good shape. The life-water canisters were full and secure. Kozz was satisfied.

He pulled his heavy body up and into the driver's cab. Two large seats rested behind the controls, and behind them was a small room filled edge-to-edge with a bed and a small shelf that contained a variety of editorial magazines alongside a slim selection of romance novels. Kozz threw his duffel bag on the passenger seat and felt for her at his side one more time before shutting the door and pulling back the gear lever.

Dials adjusted along the dashboard as the gears changed at Kozz's command. Digital displays danced along the windshield, several with faulty readings and one that flickered frustratingly at the crest of his vision despite his many failed attempts to disconnect the broken display. Numbers climbed as the speed increased, soaring upwards as the truck powered its way up the first few large snowbanks before it gained momentum.

The ashen truck was hauling over 150 tons of liquid water that Kozz had collected from the ice around his home, and the cargo was being delivered to a warehouse near Edgetown where it would then be sent abroad across the planet and to other worlds. Hydrogen had become a major source of energy, and water was needed on other planets. Erde was overpopulated, and Torris was dry. Frostarc served as humanity's fountain of life.

Water had been scarce in centuries past. Colonization of Frostarc was humankind's first attempt at spreading to another world, and the dire need of a dehydrated Erde outweighed the risks involved. The first colonists were memorialized as heroes.

The thirty hour drive was not necessary. Kozz could have chosen to live closer to the distribution warehouse and turn in more life-water at a faster pace, but he had chosen solitude over convenience. Most other harvesters had personal cargo-grade airships to transfer their loads more frequently and with greater speed, but Kozz did not want the money. He only needed something to occupy his time and enough cash to get by. The excuse to fire up his rig and tear through the snow drifts was enough reason to make the trip. The power was exhilarating, something he always thought a person could not feel properly without being connected to the ground.

The sun had only just risen as Kozz set off. The truck had taken time to power up to full throttle, plowing through the snow drifts and skidding across the glaciers. A retractable pilot mounted at the front of the vehicle wedged through the ice and pushed everything else out of its way. The self-righting propulsion system on the truck's underside allowed Kozz to turn in any direction at full speed without worry of capsizing. Cruising at a comfortable 287 mph, he grabbed a meal bar from his bag. *They'll never make this processed shit taste as good as the real stuff, but Lord knows it's what keeps me going out here.* Kozz flipped the cruise control switch, kicked his feet up on the dashboard, and flipped open a magazine entitled The Letterhead, continuing an article he had started earlier.

The attacks on the Insurrectionist Moon have accomplished nothing. Presider Conway and the Cooperation need to wipe out the entire world of rebel hooligans so that we, the people, can make proper use of one of the only known habitable locations in the galaxy. We must move forward on this issue.

Sure, twenty years ago the Presider's Enforcers were able to eliminate many of the highest crime lords that rule the planet, but what have they done lately? Our efforts have become ineffective and meaningless. The major threats we were able to rid ourselves of have been replaced and are now stronger than ever.

We cannot expect to live in a peaceful, unified society with a world of outlaws and dissenters living at our front door. It is time to end the petty attacks and negotiations. I call upon you Presider Conway, I call upon you the people of the Cooperation, because it is time for war! Let us use our might to end the threat of the Insurrectionist Moon before it grows any stronger. Let us end this now!

"Let's take over that godforsaken hellhole." Kozz growled as he flipped through the pages. *Every last one of those fuckers should be murdered,* thought Kozz, *every hovel they hide in destroyed. The organized crime and society built upon deception and greed that they have thrived on needs to crumble. The Presider has taken the issue seriously in the past, but his recent lack of effort has allowed their economy and crime lord hierarchy to rebound. We aren't doing enough.* Painful memories enraged Kozz's emotions, but before the thoughts consumed him he popped a couple of prescribed pills and they calmed him. He put the magazine down and shuffled about for something else to read, choosing a novel with a woman in tears on the cover as a man above soars away in an airship, titled My Passion, My Love, My War.

The further south he traveled, the more signs of life there were. The truck rolled through numerous paths in the deep snow left behind by animals and brown patches of shrubs became more common. At one point Kozz saw smoke on the horizon that he attributed to another harvester's fire-warmed home. The sun had set midway through the journey, but it would rise again before Kozz arrived at his destination. The short days of this small planet were something Kozz had never grown used to.

Small cabins appeared in the distance leading to a view of Edgetown along the horizon with reds and oranges coloring the sky as the sun began to rise over the sleepy tourist village. Few lights could be seen amongst the buildings, and the streets looked awfully quiet. *Must be due to the early morning hours.* Kozz's truck kept barreling along right past the town and towards Moe's Warehouse which resided another hour south.

Kozz arrived at the front gate to the complex and let

himself through, as usual. The building was a massive square of blue and gray corrugated metal which was topped with a high-peaked roof to keep off the weight of the snow. He drove over to the pumps near the front entrance.

Kozz stepped out of the truck and tentatively put his feet on the ground, feeling that the injured ankle had become stiff. The pain had subsided a bit, but he packed up another rag with snow and tied it around the swollen injury, then he pulled out a stogie from his jacket pocket and lit it up. The wind had increased and he needed the smokey heat to keep away the chill.

As expected, no one came out to greet him. Kozz limped around to the rear of his truck and hooked up his cargo to the warehouse pumps. As he neared the building Kozz felt a sound emanating through the wall like the muddled voices of a telepod left on in another room. The unintelligible sound echoed in his ear, its waves vibrating in his chest. *Either Moe's ripping into somebody or there's a party going on that I wasn't told about.*

Sounds of flowing pipe-water and the purr of the pumps faded as Kozz made his way over to the front door, his attention focused on the words coming from within the building. Ice had cracked the frame in several places and pushed the door away from its flush build. Kozz pressed the door latch, not aware that his other hand was feeling for her smooth surface at his side. The door slid open, and out blared a cascade of noise. Befuddled by the river of sound that crashed upon him, Kozz backed away from the door, clapping hands over both ears. Words blasted tremors through his body, some catching his attention: disease, dangerous, quarantine.

"...pending the status of your infection..."

"What the fuck? The hell is it talking about?"

Far enough away to shake off his daze, Kozz listened more carefully to the message. A female's voice read off a script, monotone and sterile.

Warning to all who receive this message. Warning. A fatal disease is spreading. This is a worldwide pandemic. The disease is extremely dangerous and highly contagious in numerous regards. It is recommended that all who receive this message avoid all others who exhibit strange behavior and move to one of the two quarantine zones. Quarantine zone locations: GRID ID 1128-34 located within Port Town, GRID ID 1189-09 located within the city of Quartz. You will be treated and released pending the status of your infection.

"Fatal disease...a pandemic." This is insane. *Moe and the others laugh their asses off and hop around like little bunnies in heat when they get me with one of their pranks, but this is too much, even for them.*

Kozz tore off a couple of strips of wet cloth from the rag around his ankle and stuffed his ears as best he could, dampening the sound a bit. He approached the entrance once more and the noise again pierced into his mind and the waves of vibrations shook his bones. Kozz walked in and saw no lights on within the entire warehouse. The doorway at his back allowed in as much daylight as it could, casting Kozz's shadow across the cement floor as his broad silhouette stood over the threshold. The place smelled of cold metal as it always had.

The minuscule amount of light was absorbed by the blackness of the building's interior, but with what little light there was Kozz could see stacks of fallen boxes that had strewn their metal bits, machine parts, and packing materials all about the floor. A second look made it seem as if they had not only fallen, but had been pushed over. It almost appeared as if someone had been rifling through the boxes, searching recklessly for what was within them.

Kozz tried to shout out the names of the people he knew at the warehouse, but even to himself his words were inaudible, engulfed and defeated by the roaring monotone voice.

"Warning. A fatal disease is spreading..."

I've got to shut this shit off. Kozz had been to the warehouse many times before and knew the layout well. His eyes could not see far in the darkness, so his memory placed the floor design at the front of his thoughts. Up above on the grated walkway sat some sort of control panel, probably what he could use to shut off the message and hopefully turn on the lights. He started walking forward to where he knew the stairway should be, but after taking a few steps something caught his eye.

In the corner of his vision, around the other side of some of the fallen boxes, was a horrid sight. A man, a corpse, lay eviscerated and disemboweled on the hard floor.

Images from Kozz's past overloaded his mind and made him vomit, the memories causing his heart to ache as if there were a hole in it. He ignored the pain, burying it deep within himself alongside all the thoughts of his past. Ten years of confined hatred and sorrow pushed on the walls of his mind, threatening to break loose and consume Kozz. The weight on his heart had grown heavier with each passing day, and the doctor was his only help. *Thank the Lord for those pills.*

Kozz shook his head, gathering himself. He recognized the dead man's face, but had never known his name. The murder weapon, a jagged piece of scrap sheet metal, was tossed away from the body. Kozz was familiar with death and murder, and he knew that this man had died recently, very recently. *Poor guy probably got axed not more than a day ago.*

He reached for her grip at his side and pulled her from the holster at his hip. Red. A scarlet six-shooter that Kozz had called his for most of his life. In a world where lasers had long ago replaced bullets, she was considered an antique, a collectable by most, but Kozz had kept her in working condition, as had his father before him. Her sunset shine coruscated in the darkness with the little bit of light that reached her from the outside.

He walked forward, keeping his senses alert while trying to defeat the blackness and deafening noise that surrounded him. He approached the lift assuming it would not work with the lights shut off like they were, and he was right. Kozz felt his way along the side of the elevator and across some metal beams until he felt the upward angle of the staircase railing. He climbed the steel-grated staircase, pain shooting up from his swollen ankle, until he reached the upper landing.

Kozz had never been on the grated walkway, but his memory from below guided him to take a right at the staircase and then an immediate left at the first intersection. He prowled his way along the path, trying to sense for anything out of the ordinary, holding the cold railing in his hand as he walked. The railing veered to the right, and that was where Kozz knew he should turn left. Just as he started down the next pathway he felt something move.

He did not quite see it, but he had sensed it nonetheless. Red was up somewhere in the darkness, pointing in the direction of the culprit. "Show yourself," Kozz bellowed, his voice again swallowed by the noise around him, but as if answering his roar two faint white lights lit up not too far down the path and they leaped towards him. Kozz fired, but the lights disappeared and he was not sure if his shot had hit. Then the thing jumped on Kozz. It was small and scrawny, but it felt like a man. The thing crawled over the top of Kozz and firmly clutched his neck with its boney hands. Kozz tore at the arms, but they would not budge. The pain in his left ankle increased with the extra weight on his shoulders. Still holding Red in his hand, Kozz grabbed behind his shoulders and gripped the thin man's under arms, then bent forward and flipped the man over and onto a solid object that he did not know was there.

A few reserve lights turned on within the building, sufficient to see with but not enough to blind Kozz after being in total darkness. The solid object was the control panel Kozz had been looking for, much closer than he expected. On top of the controls was Moe writhing in pain with old blood dried around his mouth and streaked across his arms, but he quickly gathered himself and launched again at Kozz. Now able to see, Kozz landed a blow across Moe's face and watched the man fall to the ground.

Kozz jumped on top of his friend and held him down. He could only see the whites of Moe's eyes with red capillaries along their undersides, and the surreal glow was still present. Moe strained and squirmed as he tried to free himself from Kozz's grasp, but the little man did not have enough strength. *This must be the disease.* Kozz leaned back as Moe growled and bit at his face. *No, this isn't a disease, this is a demon. Something evil has taken over. It can't be him any longer. This isn't Moe, this is some murderous beast. If I let him it go, it's just going to continue trying to kill me like it did that other fellow.*

Kozz let go of the creature with one hand and crashed the butt of Red across its face. "Wake up Moe!" He slapped again. "Get that thing out of you and come back!" The creature used its free hand to scrape and claw at Kozz's side. "Last chance, buddy." He delivered one more devastating blow across its face, knocking several teeth out of its mouth. The demon that was Moe started to laugh, gurgling blood as it did. *Wake up dammit! Come on Moe, snap out of it!* Moe's free arm grabbed the knife that was attached to Kozz's belt, but Kozz gripped the arm and snapped it at the elbow like a twig. The creature screamed out in pain as it dropped the knife, but the crying wails morphed into a wicked laugh and the creature swung its broken arm at Kozz's face.

That's it then. Goodbye Moe. Kozz planted his hands on the creature's throat and squeezed, the laughter becoming a squeak. Kozz pressed harder until no more sound could escape the creature's throat, but its face carried on as if it were still laughing. *Laugh all you want you damn demon, it's over for you.* Kozz put his weight into the force of his grip. The soft light disappeared from the creature's stare and the clawing hands stopped. Looking into the eyes as they rolled back into place, Kozz saw Moe. A look of fear and confusion glazed across his friend's face and Kozz released his hold, but it was too late. The demon had left and Moe's body went limp. Kozz had killed his friend. His heart lurched and the pain of it knocked him to the ground.

CHAPTER TWO

Ghost Town

Puffs of smoke billowed from the tops of chimneys, floating northward with the mild wind. The sun descended behind the valley plains to the west, fading the blue sky into carnations of pink and purple. Night approached and on flickered the warm and inviting lights of the tiny cabins and cottages that lined the main streets of Edgetown. Couples strolled the cobblestone paths as children chased each other around the ornate streetlights and under tiled benches. Aromas of ginger, cinnamon, and fresh baked bread wafted about, enticing the chilled to enter any one of the colorful shops for a hot meal and a cup of spiced tea. Candles glinted in the frosted windows, unshaded so that any passerby could see the little trinkets and wide smiles that waited inside.

Kozz parked his large vehicle on the outskirts of town and walked past the cute tourist villa that supplied Edgetown with most of its wealth. Several blocks behind the shops were the homes and byways of the local residents where the streets were either dirt or hard-packed ice. Most of the ramshackle homes were only slightly larger and better kept than Kozz's own shack out on the ice fields. Snow slid off the high-peaked roofs, creating large piles between the houses. Treading feet flattened the pathways, the roads by tires and plows, but everywhere else was claimed by the ever falling snow as it was considered too much hassle to maintain. Few homes had the money for outdoor warmers, and those that did only used them for gatherings and special occasions.

Across from the local mechanic's shop was Kozz's destination, McMick's Tavern. When Kozz walked in he was greeted by familiar faces, those that always knew when he would be coming in for his occasional visit. He took a seat at the bar. "Hey doll," he yelled to the bartender, "would ya mind fixin' me up a cup of hot cocoa?" Kozz lit up a cigar and yammered with his friends, trading stories and politics.

Linda, the bartender, filled Kozz's ears with the terrible tales of her tragic love life which she had experienced since his last stroll into town. Kozz could be patient when he chose to be, and women frequently told him that he was a good listener. He was her big teddy bear with a shoulder to cry on for the evening.

He stayed the night in town and stopped by the local drug store early the next morning. The young girls behind the counter always greeted him with a smile and had his prescriptions ready to go. The elderly pharmacist Todd was one to ask his regular customers for favors, and so Kozz, in no rush this way or that, was willing to shovel snow or lift some boxes for the ornery fart. He appreciated how silly it was for a business man to ask so much of his customers, but being the only pharmacy in town meant he could handle business however he wanted.

After lending a hand, Kozz walked over to the grocery story and grabbed as many goods as he could carry. The cashiers had stopped asking if he wanted help carrying his groceries to his vehicle once they learned he had to park on the outskirts. Bags upon bags hung from both of his arms as he trudged his way back to his rig. Kozz hefted the groceries up into his truck's cabin and placed them on top of his mattress.

This was how Kozz had spent his last trip into town and many of those before.

Hours were spent grieving his fallen friend and searching the warehouse for any clues as to what was going on. Kozz had fiddled with the computer systems as best he could and saw that all communication devices were inoperable. All he found were some power cables that had been slashed and ripped from their holdings. Unable to contact outside assistance, Kozz could not even offer Moe and the other deceased man the respectable closure they deserved. He could call for no one to take the bodies away, and the frozen dirt was impossible to dig through. Left unsatisfied and confused, he wasted the day away without anything to show for it. *I don't know if that demon that was inside you died, but at least you passed on without it in you, Moe. At least I had done that much for you.*

As Kozz approached Edgetown with the weight of his murdered friend on his conscience, he sensed an unusual stillness. Night was falling again and only a few faint lights could be seen amongst the assemblage of buildings. The houses looked cold without the smokey chimneys and soft candlelight that were the staple of the tourism-inspired main streets. *The city-folk nearly faint when they see this gingerbread village of a town with all the brown buildings and white trim.* Kozz drove into town, seeing that there was no one around the streets who would be bothered by his huge rig. *Looks like Edgetown closed down early tonight. Word must have spread about this disease, this damn evilness, and kept all the travelers home.* Kozz had seen Edgetown close down early before because of severe drops in tourism during the colder months of the year. *But this is different. This town looks dead, feels dead. Shit is going down. Maybe there is someone here to find, someone to tell me what is going on. Besides, I gotta get my meds.*

Kozz parked his truck and shoved open the driver door. The rig quieted as he stepped down into a knee-deep drift of white fluff. The town looked unkempt, taken over by the never ending snowfall. Streets were buried and snow drifts settled between the buildings, reaching as high as the lower edges of some roofs, the waves of white left untouched by man or machine. The warm and inviting shops and homes Kozz had known were now cold and lifeless, placid frost having crystallized across the windows that were once occupied by dancing candlelight. Not a single streetlight was lit and every one was wrapped in a sheet of white.

Kozz inhaled the cold air into his lungs and tasted stale bread. The crunching under his boots echoed and was the only audible distraction from his own breathing. Silence and solitude were his home, but feeling such seclusion in this part of town gave Kozz the chills. He walked down the road and found that plowing through the snow with a busted ankle was proving to be a pain. *But my truck's got too wide a load to fit through those skinny alleys the locals around here call streets.* He turned down a pathway and trekked through the drifts, dragging his sore foot through the snow.

The rustic and weathered houses hidden a few blocks back were no livelier than their main street counterparts and appeared to be abandoned like the rest of the town. Everything was succumbing to the snow. Without the stubborn persistence of people to fight for and protect their land, the town was quickly losing its battle with the forces of nature. Kozz could find no tracks in the snow, no movement in the windows or vehicles on the road to indicate the existence of life.

Kozz approached a house he was familiar with, Linda's place. Broken glass hung askew from the window nearest to the front door, most of it scattered on the sill and within the snow on the wooden deck. The door was propped open. *That broad is always in some kind of trouble or another. No vehicle in the driveway. Might be some guy roughed her up, or maybe she fled with the rest of them and someone robbed her while she was gone.* Linda was the usual bartender at McMick's. She was always getting herself involved with the wrong guys and Kozz had saved her neck more than once. She often repaid him with a free place to stay and drinks on the house.

Kozz stepped up onto the deck and opened the front door with one hand while the other gripped Red. Snow had blown into the living room, creating white trails that faded from the door and busted window into the shaggy brown of the carpet. A tall lamp which had stood near the window was now knocked over, but everything else seemed to be in place and it did not look like anything of value had been taken. The kitchen was a mess, but only in a way that reflected Linda's level of cleanliness. The bedroom held an unmade bed, an armoire with drawers all opened at various lengths, and a closet with a missing door. *Everything's still here. Clothes, jewelry— that girl must've been in a hurry to leave everything behind.* Kozz used her restroom and noticed that all of her toiletries were still there. He exited her home with more questions to answer.

The sky above was a deep orange with spotted gray clouds that faded to a dark blue in the east, and a soft snowfall drifted sideways in the light wind. Kozz continued down the road, but he stopped in front of Linda's neighbor's house where a large snow-covered lump sat in the driveway. Kozz walked over to it and brushed away the snow, revealing a red taillight. *Goddamn, first vehicle I've seen since coming here.* He pushed more powder away and found that the hood was open and bent back. *What the hell?* He dug out the snow that covered the energy cells and found them smashed. More digging exposed slashed hoses and torn belts. *What is this shit?* Someone had ripped the working parts of the vehicle to shreds and the rest of the vehicle was left undamaged. *Those power cables back at the warehouse, was that Moe? I don't know. Did another one of those demons do this?* More puzzle pieces filled Kozz's mind and he struggled to fit them together.

He turned to the house and saw more shattered windows. Red came out of her holster as Kozz began to fear the possibility that the town was not only empty, but dangerous.

He walked to the front door to see if anybody was inside and found that the door frame had been splintered by forced entry. He pushed the door open slowly, finding a room full of overturned furniture. His eyes fell on a cracked indent in a wall that was spotlighted by the sunlight which came through the doorway. In front of the wall was a tipped sofa with tan fabric that was streaked with dried blood. Kozz steadied himself and made his way to the other end of the room, eyes and ears open. He peeked around the edge of the sofa and found a bloodied man's body, frozen on the floor at the base of the wall. *Damn, it is them. It's here too. I've gotta get my meds and get the hell outta this place.*

Kozz left, not wanting to search the rest of the home. His years of bloodshed and death should have been behind him. He did not want the memories to surface, and he struggled to keep the thoughts of his son concealed from himself. He lit up a stogie and used it to calm himself. It was against doctor's orders, but a good cigar helped Kozz control his thoughts and settle his aching heart. Escaping the past was a daily battle for Kozz, one that he thought he would never win.

He picked himself up and blazed a trail down the road. The chill of the snow had worn through the thick layers of Kozz's boots and his feet began to go numb, the pain in his ankle subsiding with the loss of feeling.

Kozz turned a corner and saw a light on ahead a few streets

near McMick's tavern. *Maybe there is a soul left around here after all.* As he approached his destination Kozz realized that the source of the light was the drug store across the street from McMick's. With any luck he could get his medication and find someone to talk with.

Not a block away from the drug store Kozz passed by The Dawson Inn. Other than a couple of evenings spent at Linda's, The Dawson Inn was Kozz's usual stop for the night in Edgetown. The Dawsons never had a child, and so they treated Kozz like a son who visited home every so often from college. Mrs. Dawson always made sure Kozz had a good home cooked meal in him before he went to bed, no matter how much he may have eaten at the tavern earlier in the day. Mr. Dawson was full of extended tales that were adorned with life lessons and morals for Kozz to learn. Their inn looked like all of the other homely buildings off of the main streets, but inside it was quaint and full of smells that made Kozz feel like he was child again, back home with his parents in the good days. He adored the couple and was saddened to see that their home looked as empty and cold as the rest. The Dawsons, too, had fled town.

Kozz's hope to find life at McMick's was erased before he was even able to look inside. The sunken doorway had been completely entombed in snowfall. Trying to enter the tavern would require a lot of digging, and it was not worth the effort.

Light from the drug store escaped onto the snow-covered road and highlighted something Kozz thought was peculiar. The light created a shadow that ran down the center of the road where a dip had been created. *A path.* Kozz looked back at his own trail, a rough trench in the deep snow. *The recent powder may have softened it up a bit, but that's a person's path. That's for damn sure. Someone's been through here.*

Red in his hand, Kozz sneaked close to the window of the drug store and dropped down into a squat. He turned his head and looked back over his shoulder with Red gripped in both hands and hanging between his legs. Inside he could see that the light was coming from behind the pharmacy counter and that the aisles of assorted goods inside the store had been ransacked. Most of the shelves were completely empty and what was left had been scattered across the floor. *People must've bought up all the supplies they needed before making the trip east towards the city.* Another dim source of light appeared. Two small lights bobbed up and down in one of the aisles. Kozz almost jumped at the realization. They were eyes. *Lord! It's one of them. Another one of those damn demons.*

Kozz could have blasted it right then and there, but he did not know if they were all murderous. And then there was Moe. It seemed that Moe had returned to his normal self the moment before Kozz had ended his life. The man inside the pharmacy was hefty and balding, perhaps someone's father.

Kozz might be able to save him. Maybe there was a chance.

Kozz got on his knees and crawled under the window towards the front entrance. He then slid open the front door without making a sound and turned himself sideways, slipping through the entrance and stepping into the store. The floor was littered with odds and ends that were left behind in the evacuation.

Kozz stepped towards the man and put Red away to appear less intimidating. "Hey buddy, let's talk." The man's head popped up over the aisle's shelving, white eyes glowing. Kozz put his hands up palms-open towards the man. "No harm, no trouble." The man's head dropped and Kozz heard the fast thunking of the heavy body sprinting down the aisle. "I don't want to hurt you, friend." The body rounded the corner and charged, but Kozz held his ground. The demon-eyed beast hissed a throaty growl and leaped at its prey. The man was much larger than Moe and could do some serious damage, so to avoid taking the blow Kozz hunkered down low and used the man's forward momentum to lift the chubby body and hurl it over and behind himself. The man tried to latch onto Kozz and gashed three long fingernails across his cheek as it flew into the air. It crashed through several rows of shelves and was buried under the rubble, gurgling wet noises as it attempted to uncover itself.

"What's your name?" shouted Kozz. "Come on now. Fight

off that damn demon and give me your name!" Objects flew through the air as the demon-eyed man hurled the store's scattered goods at Kozz. He dodged a pair of pliers and blocked a couple pieces of broken shelf with his forearm, but a can of chili hit him square in his sprained ankle and Kozz yelled out with a cry of agony as he fell to the ground. The creature launched more objects at him and Kozz blocked what he could. "Fight that damn thing inside of you. Wake up and give me your name!" Kozz lifted himself into a sitting position with his arms and Red left her holster. A ceramic serving plate flew past his head like a frisbee and smashed into a wall. "Tell me now if there is a sane person in there or—" the body stood from the rubble, brandishing a long kitchen knife. The creature staggered over the mess and slashed the blade in Kozz's direction. Red found her aim. The demon found its footing and rushed forward.

KABLAM!

A hole the size of a fist exploded open in the possessed man's chest. The demon inside screamed at a glass-shattering pitch and its eyes beamed as if the light was steam released under high pressure, its face stretching out like a ghoul's to vent the explosions of light and noise. Kozz closed his eyes and plugged his ears. *Like a goddamn banshee!* He tried to protect his senses, but could not block its intensity, and he hollered back an unintelligible garble at the creature, doing all he could to escape the unearthly shriek. The body fell forward and landed at Kozz's feet. The howling light ended just as quickly as it had begun. The knife stuck into the floorboards with the dead man's grip still firm, but Kozz kicked the blade away and took in a deep breath.

When that thing died it didn't laugh like the one before. The glow in its eyes didn't escape, it was extinguished. That fucker didn't get away this time, I killed it. Kozz felt like he was going to pass out from the experience. His heart was pumping again and pain was starting to settle in. He tried to calm himself while marveling at what had just gone down. *This is wrong. They must know this isn't a disease by now. These people are possessed by something evil.* Kozz noticed Red in his hand, still smoking from the kill. *She's happy. She hasn't seen any real action in years, since before I ran away to this ice world. She's a canon, a magnum, a gun deserved to be called so. Pops taught me to take care of her and use her properly, told me to take my time and not waste my bullet. She's heavy. I can hold her true with one arm, most men would need two. She's pining for more.*

Kozz stood up to get away from the dead body. The can that had smacked his ankle caused more pain than damage, and other than a throbbing ache Kozz felt no extra grief from the impact. He walked over to the pharmacy counter to find his medication. The lone light was bright enough to see well behind the counter, but it would still be a chore to riffle through the shelves of medication to find his prescription. He remembered how the young pharmacists never went back to look for his pills, instead they always bent below the counter and grabbed a bag marked with his name. He checked under the counter and found a small brown bag, then turned it around and on it written in black marker was "Kozz". He opened the bag and inside the two small bottles rattled. One was for his depression, or so the doctor had called it, but he knew that it was more of a pill to control his anger outbursts. The other was for his chest pains, ischemia of the heart.

Kozz walked over to the restroom and washed the blood and sweat off his face, cleaning the three gashes that were cut across his left cheek. His eyes were cold steel. "You're one ugly dog," Kozz said to his reflection, "but you've got class." A small smile cracked the corner of his lips and he saluted himself. It was refreshing to see a somewhat normal face, one that was not stretched out of proportion or holding a murderous snarl.

He sat on the toilet to rest and he let out a slow sigh. Thinking of the faces of the two men he had killed over the past few hours soured his thoughts. *I'm sorry for what I've done, but I think I might've helped Moe and that other man escape their evil captors. Torn power cables and smashed cars, scuffled homes and an empty town. No way to get a hold of anyone. This is something serious. All I know is that whatever is happening is some freaky shit, and I'm sure I'll see a lot more of it if I keep going on. I could go home and ride this thing out on my little ranch. I can find enough food in this town to last me a while if I have to. I might be lonely, but I'm sure I would be safe from whatever the hell is going on, the disease or whatever it is couldn't survive the miles upon miles of frozen wasteland.*

And what about Priscilla? My darling Priscilla. That message said that this was a worldwide pandemic, but what if it has escaped to the other planets? What if it made it to Erde? I have to make sure she's safe from it. Ten years since I've seen her, ten years since those bastards stole my son away from me, ten years since I abandoned my beautiful wife, but I had to. There was no other choice, no other way for her to be safe, but now she could be in danger again and I have to find her. "I sought solitude for good reason, but now I've got to get out." *I'm going to die cold and alone on these frozen plains if I stay much longer. At one time that seemed like it was worth it, it was what I was looking for. I wanted to die alone. I wanted to never be seen again.* "Hell, it's been long enough."

So that's it then, I'm not going home. I might return one day, but that won't be for a good long time. Kozz fired up a stogie. *Sometimes a hard think is enough to send my ticker racing. The pain it brings is like a swift kick in the nuts. It'll make me drop to my knees and beg for mercy, something no person has ever been able to do, but I've been good lately. Between my medicine, the cigars, and some smarts I've had good control over it, though that might change soon. It may not be too good for my heart to get all charged up, but it feels damn good. I shouldn't enjoy this, but I am.*

CHAPTER THREE

The Boy

Kozz rummaged through the remaining goods on the drug store floor. He found a leather bag and loaded it with his prescriptions, several packages of dehydrated of food, a few meal bars, bandage wraps, and some other odds and ends, then he strapped it onto his shoulder and went out the door. Kozz welcomed the outside chill and set out for his truck, taking a new path back and cutting through the dip in the middle of the street. The direct route to the main streets took him through a thin alley, bordered on one side by a wire fence and the other by the back ends of homes.

Along the path Kozz spotted another light shining in the night. A back porch light hung from its holding by a solitary wire, still emanating a faint, frost-covered glow. The geothermal generator in the yard was still running and had kept itself warm and free of snow. White powder around the home sparkled as Kozz walked, reflecting the bulb's light like a shimmering sea on a moonlit night. He approached the back windows and looked inside, seeing that nothing was left but a hefty-looking table in the center of the house. Kozz moved on, the homes growing in size and decoration as he neared the main streets.

Thud.

A hollow sound in the distance. *It could be anything,* thought Kozz, *maybe a garbage can falling over or a door swinging in the breeze.*

Bam!

A small explosion out there somewhere, like a large firecracker. Kozz was not sure what was going on, but Red had found her way into his hand. The noise was far away and he did not feel an immediate threat, but the sounds changed and amplified as he approached the main streets. An extended scraping sound, like a rusty knife on sheet metal, made Kozz cringe.

He reached the street, exited the alleyway, and down the road he saw a sight that made his heart drop. *Shit.* Two bodies were tearing at his truck. He saw that many of the tires had been popped and the energy cell compartment was opened and bent back. "Get your asses off her you dirty freaks!" Kozz's shout caught their attention. A tall, thin man bounded through the snow towards Kozz, and not far behind was a child struggling to move through the deep snow.

"Tell me someone's in there you dirty bastard!" Kozz held

Red with one arm, straight like an arrow towards his assailant. The tall man ran through the drifts with ease and was soon close enough for Kozz to see the glow in his eyes. "Hey day-glo, is there anyone in there who can hear me?" The creature was unmoved by Kozz's words. It stomped forward and raised its hands like a carnivorous beast ready to pounce on its prey. The creature was close. "Last chance, buddy." It ducked its head forward and charged like a bull. Red shivered with excitement. Closer it came, the demon almost leaped from the man's eyes. Closer. Red braced herself. Close enough.

KABLAM!

Half of the man's face was gone, its remaining eye beamed like a flashlight in the night and it gurgled its scream through the blood that poured down its throat. The man's body fell forward and the demon's deathly howls were muffled by the snow. The boy followed the trench-like path the man had made and ran at Kozz. He was small with thin, shoulder-length black hair that reminded Kozz of a fistful of string. The boy crawled over the hills of snow as he approached Kozz, white eyes gleaming like the moon.

Shit. There's no fucking way I can kill a kid. The boy found a solid piece of ground and jumped into a sprint. Kozz noticed the screwdriver the kid held in his hand and Red dropped to his side, sliding back into her holster. *I've gotta do something. Doesn't matter if he might try to kill me, he looks too much like—* The boy lunged forward, hacking with the screwdriver. Kozz brushed him to the side, but the kid swung back and grazed Kozz's thigh with the tip, cutting through his jeans and a few layers of skin. Kozz bent down to grip the boy's arm and ripped the tool out of his hand, tossing it into the distance where it disappeared into the deep snow.

The boy thrashed about. Kozz pulled him in and wrapped him up in a tight bear hug, holding his arms so that only the boy's feet were free as they kicked in the air. Kozz squeezed, and the boy squirmed. The child grunted like an angry ape and whipped his head around, gaining enough stretch to bite down on Kozz's arm and rip off a piece of flesh. *Shit, what if it is an infection? This little bastard might have given it to me.* Kozz compacted his arms, his bulging muscles crushing the boy, suffocating him. Something popped, likely one of the boy's ribs. Kozz held for a moment longer and then threw the kid to the ground.

The fire-eyed boy arched in pain when he hit the hard street. He tried to recover, but Kozz dropped a knee on his chest, putting his weight into the knee and twisting it. The boy, the demon, writhed in pain. "Say goodbye, kid." Kozz grabbed Red and slowly motioned her towards the boy's head. "Your time is up." Kozz set Red between the child's eyes and a smirk appeared on the boy's face, widening into a devilish smile as Kozz's face went grim. "Burn in hell." Kozz's right forearm flexed as he tightened his grip, placing a finger on the trigger. The boy chuckled with the demonic double voice like Moe had, one soft like a child's voice and the other heavy like a diesel engine. Kozz put pressure on the trigger and started to pull it back.

The glow in the boy's eyes vanished, and Kozz saw a familiar fear and confusion in the child's brown eyes. Sweat and melted snow soaked the boy's forehead, causing his hair to stick to his head like a mop. His eyes darted all around, examining the setting. He focused on the gun that poked his forehead and the grisly glare of the old man that held it, then he became aware of the prominent pain in his chest. His lips quivered.

The shock of seeing the boy's transformation held Kozz in his position for a moment before he lifted himself off of the child and backed away, trying to show as best he could that he meant no harm. The boy scuttled backwards until he settled in a deep drift of snow. He panted and heaved, wincing at the pain he felt with every inward breath. The boy's world had abruptly morphed into a blackened twister of fear, confusion, and pain. Kozz was the first to speak.

"I'm not gonna hurt you anymore, kid. It was the demon that held you that I was after, and it's gone now. You're safe."

The boy's defensive posture did not change. He could not remember what had happened to him, but what Kozz was saying sounded right, even if it did not make any sense.

"As far as I can tell," said Kozz, "you and me are the only sensible people left in this town now. It was only me until I tricked that demon out of you." The boy held his chest with one hand and touched the center of his forehead with the other. "I held Red to your head, but she didn't thirst for your blood. One of your ribs is fractured. Maybe broken, but I doubt it. I'm sorry about that." He stepped towards the boy, but stopped short as the kid looked like he was about to bolt. "My name is Kozz. I once had a son about your age, his name is Jake. What's your name, kid?"

The boy tried to speak. "C-ca..." He coughed and cringed at the pain before working his way around it. "Caleb. I'm Caleb."

"Pleasure to meet you, Caleb." Kozz grabbed his leather bag and showed it to the boy. "I've got some bandages I just picked up from the store. Let's wrap you up and then head over to my truck. They'll help you heal better and I've got some aspirin for the pain."

Caleb examined the area, noticing the lack of lights and people. He saw the dead man down the street and then looked away. Something had happened that he could not remember. The town was different. He knew that Kozz had killed the man only minutes earlier, he felt like he should have a memory of it, but he had no other choice than to trust him at the moment. He nodded towards Kozz and tried to stand on his own.

Kozz took two of the rolls of medical wrap out of his bag and walked over to Caleb. The boy's muscles went stiff when Kozz neared. "This is gonna hurt, but it's gonna help. You'll pull through. Caleb's a strong name." Kozz wrapped the bandage around the boy's thin torso and over his bony shoulder. The child backed away as he was being wrapped, considering escape, but Kozz pulled Caleb close so that he could properly tend to the boy's injury. Kozz offered Caleb four aspirins and some water, but the boy only accepted the drink. Kozz put the pills away, impressed by the boy's toughness. He wrapped his bite wound and hoped that he was not going to turn into one of those demons.

Kozz helped Caleb stand up. Walking was excruciating for Caleb at first, but he quickly learned how to breathe and lean properly to avoid the sharpest pains. Kozz offered to carry Caleb, but the boy had none of it. "Grandma," said Caleb. "I want to see my grandma."

"Sure kid. We'll go find your grandma after stopping by my rig."

Kozz was dismayed as they approached his truck. Seeing the damage up close broke his heart. "My girl," he said. "What did you do to my girl?" Kozz walked over to the front of his truck and put a hand on her grill like he was feeling for a pulse. Several of the tires had been slashed, more than he had spares for. Everywhere the truck had dents and screwdriver-sized puncture wounds. The energy cell compartment was opened and bent back like the other vehicle he had seen, and inside the energy cells were shattered and many of the other parts had been ripped and torn. Kozz knew how to repair most of the damage, but his experience was limited and even if he had all the necessary parts it would take him days to get her back in operating condition.

Caleb did not know much about vehicles, but he knew that the truck was enormous and looked to be in bad shape. "Who did this?"

Kozz was flabbergasted. "You mean you don't remember doing it?"

Caleb stood wide-eyed, afraid of evoking Kozz's anger. He shook his head.

"Caleb, the demon that was inside you did it. That demon and the one inside that dead man back there." Caleb's first instinct was to deny such an accusation. "I only killed the man because his demon was going to kill me. That's why I had to hurt you, Caleb. Your demon tried to kill me too. I wasn't able to save that poor guy, but I saved you from the evil that held you."

Caleb's mind was racing, trying to recall the truth that Kozz spoke. It was there, but he could not access it. He felt like imploding from the disarray of his memories, the frustration of the emptiness in his mind. "I c-can't remember. I think it's true, but I can't remember. Kozz, I can't remember." The boy wept. Kozz balanced himself in the quake of the boy's sorrow, trying not to crack himself. He moved forward to hold Caleb, but the boy backed away. He may have felt the truth of the situation, but he still did not trust the man that had held a gun to his head. Kozz let the boy cry out his worries, his concerns, and tried to figure out what they were going to do now without a vehicle.

CHAPTER FOUR

Confusion

Caleb pointed in the direction of his grandma's house, noting that it was not a far walk. Kozz thought she may have left town like everyone else, but it was possible that she had stayed behind, wondering where her grandson was. His hopes were not high.

Only a couple of blocks away, the home was small and subdued, perched further back from the street than the other buildings. Soft light seeped from a side window. Caleb moved forward towards the door, but Kozz held him back.

"I'll make sure it's safe first."

"But Kozz, she's in there."

"Wait outside until I come get you." Kozz pulled out his knife and handed it to Caleb. "Use it if you need to."

Caleb did not have the breath to argue. Kozz opened the unlocked door and walked inside with Red ready to draw. The air was musty and cold. The furniture was neatly in place and untouched trinkets decorated every inch of shelf space, none having been packed and taken away. Thick carpet brushed ice and snow off of Kozz's boots as he crept about the house. He made his way to the hallway at the other end of the living room and saw the same soft, stagnant light under a doorway at the far end. He heard a low, unintelligible murmur coming from the room.

The hallway was thin enough that Kozz had to squeeze his way through. The noise became louder as he approached the door and he recognized the sound.

"Warning. A fatal disease is spreading..."

His body shivered at the remembrance of the deafening message. Kozz pushed the door open with his free hand, the other held his protector. The hinges squeaked like scurrying mice as they slid on their pivots. A small telepod displayed a gray screen with the warning message playing on a quiet loop. The muted light dispersed throughout the room and led Kozz's eyes to a horrifying mess on the master bed where a figure almost not recognizable enough to call an old woman laid battered and eviscerated on top of the mattress.

The mess was a dark red stain in an otherwise colorless room. Kozz would have considered himself faded to such a sight after living a life such as his, but a decade of gore sobriety had weakened his gag reflex. He backed out of the room and down the hall, half falling and half leaping onto the living room couch.

Kozz sat up and buried his face into the cushions, trying to erase the image and settle his stomach.

"Grandma!" Caleb called as he entered her home. "It's me grandma!" He ran to the telepod-lit hallway as Kozz sat up, shouting "Caleb, no!"

A short, high-pitched scream pierced Kozz's heart. The boy let out a few wails, then he stumbled back down the hallway and landed himself on Kozz's lap.

"I remember!" Caleb shouted, tears dripping and snot oozing. "I did it. I remember. I did it. I did..." He repeated the phrases until they turned into drooling sobs.

"You didn't do anything, Caleb."

"No!" the boy cried. "I did it. I killed grandma! I killed her I killed her. I remember! The thing inside me, it made me do it. I fought it, but it was too strong. I watched it make me kill her. It killed my grandma!"

The boy's confessions hit Kozz like a smack in the face. That was proof enough to him that this was no disease. A monster had taken over the little boy, the weak child that cried in his lap, and had made him murder his own flesh and blood.

"It wasn't you, it was that evil demon that was inside you. Caleb, you have to understand that this isn't your fault."

"But I did it—"

"No! The demons controlled you. They committed the crime. You fought them, you were brave, and your grandma would be proud of you for trying to protect her. You can't blame yourself." Kozz held the child and rubbed a warm hand on his back. "Caleb is a brave name. You were very brave to try and fight them off. There was nothing more you could've done."

The boy convulsed in his sobs, the pain in his ribs making it difficult to breathe between the wails, and Kozz just held him, giving Caleb something solid to hold on to in the chaos of everything around him until the boy cried himself dry. Kozz waded in the sadness of the moment and processed his thoughts. They had to move forward.

An hour passed before Caleb was steady enough to go on. Sad thoughts consumed the boy, but his uncontrollable cries had quieted. He mentioned his parents' home and told Kozz that it resided miles east of the town.

"How far of a walk would it be?" Kozz asked.

"I've only walked it once with my dad when we went on a hunting trip." Caleb mumbled. His energy had faded. He stared at the ground as he spoke. "Took us like five days but we camped a lot and moved slow when we were hunting the whitecats. Probably be shorter if we went straight there."

"With the two of us beaten up like the pair of eggs we are it'll take a week, I bet." Caleb huffed at the remark, letting Kozz know that he would have smiled if the situation were different. They limped their way back to Kozz's destroyed truck. A few days walk out in the frozen wilderness would kill them if they were not fully prepared, but as luck would have it Kozz had stowed emergency supplies in his truck cabin in case the behemoth broke down on the frozen plains. He grabbed a pair of rolled up sleeping bags, a few everlights, and the remaining food storage. Kozz held an assortment of bags on his shoulders, but Caleb insisted that he could carry something and so Kozz strapped the smaller of the sleeping bags and a small bundle of food to the boy's back. They walked eastward, leaving the rig behind them as Kozz pondered the likelihood that Caleb's parents were still around. The couple lived out in the country and may have missed the initial catastrophe that struck the town, much like Kozz had.

Caleb looked pitiful. Kozz had never seen a child so sad. "Hang in there, kid. She loved you, you know that. It wasn't your fault." Kozz felt a memory stab him in the chest. "It wasn't your fault. It never was."

"Yeah," muttered Caleb. The word oozed out of him like it was sludge. He wanted to believe it, but he did not.

The duo headed towards the end of town and Kozz scoured the landscape in front of them for any signs of danger, his instincts telling him to search every hole and shadow an enemy could hide in. He now knew that there was not a soul left in the town other than the demon-eyed zombies, and so he kept his senses open to anything that would catch his attention.

A face with glowing eyes flashed in a second story window. Kozz had seen it. "Run, Caleb." His voice was firm, but not harsh. "Run to the tree and hide behind it." Caleb looked ahead and saw the tree Kozz was pointing towards. A large pine stood at the end of the street, guiding tourists to their destination like a welcoming beacon of vacation and relaxation. The tree was the only one in the entire town. Planted long ago, it had been well tended by the townspeople. The pine had become the image of Edgetown, a monument that could be seen from miles away on the flat ice fields.

Caleb hesitated at the sudden command, but he saw Kozz's silver eyes staring at him through the darkness and understood the sternness in his voice. Caleb started to run, but a woman burst through the front door of one of the houses and sprinted straight towards the boy and Caleb froze in place. He pulled out the knife Kozz had given him and held it out, fully extended in the direction of the blood-covered woman. She clawed at the air as she ran towards him. Caleb heard Kozz's voice in his head, telling him again to run, but his muscles had seized up and he could not make them move. The woman's voice mixed with something deeper and grittier and together they screamed as she launched herself at the child.

KABLAM!

The woman's shoulder exploded in a flurry of flesh. She fell to the ground and grabbed Caleb's leg, her blood staining the white snow she sank into. The boy stood still with his knife extended and the woman pulled his leg out from under him.

KABLAM!

The woman howled into the snow as light spilled out of her body. Kozz walked over and pried Caleb's leg free from her dying grip, only then seeing the face of his victim. "Oh God," sighed Kozz, "Linda." The number of friends he had killed was increasing. *I had no other choice. She was going to kill the boy.*

"Kozz, behind you!" Caleb pulled on Kozz's coat and pointed down the street back towards the truck. Three more demons were bounding through the snow.

"Run Caleb! To the tree!" Caleb did not stall this time. He went straight for the tree as Kozz turned around and found Red in the air, eyeing her targets. *Aim true, Kozz. Take your time.* His eyes followed the barrel, landing square on the foremost threat. He saw the straight line that had forged between Red and the young man who charged down the street. If Kozz waited a second more, that line would be gone.

KABLAM!

All that was left of the young man's throat were a few slivers of clinging flesh. He did not scream, but his wounds poured blood and light like a waterfall. Next up was an older man with frostbitten fingertips. *Is Caleb alright? Did he make it to the tree?*

KABLAM!

The man fell. His knee had been shot through, the bone blasted to splinters. Kozz went to fire once more.

Click.

"Damn!" Kozz had not reloaded. "It's been too long. I must be way out of practice to forget this kind of shit." The third charging demon was a bulbous woman who was now upon Kozz. She tackled him and landed a solid head butt on his forehead that put him in a momentary daze. The glow in her eyes brightened with ferocity as she pummeled him with her fists, drool dripping and slinging all over Kozz as she gnashed her teeth and bit at him. He held her back with his forearm and landed a blow to her jaw. Blood mixed with drool as he hit her again and then a stinging pain shot up Kozz's leg.

The frostbitten man had crawled his way to Kozz, leaving a bloody path in the snow. The demon sank his teeth into Kozz's calf. He kicked at the glowing eyes with his other leg and landed a solid strike on the man's balding head, knocking him back and sending a swell of pain through Kozz's sprained ankle. Another direct hit with his good foot cracked the man's neck and Kozz heard him scream his death to the world.

The woman's weight crushed Kozz and made it difficult for

him to breathe. She attacked with her fists, landing blow after blow on Kozz's hardened face. He caught one of her punches with his right hand and bent her arm back further than it was meant to go, dislocating it with a pop. The woman shrieked in pain and bent forward to bite at his throat. Kozz tried to buck her off, but her weight was too much. As she went in for the kill, he grabbed her other arm and snapped it over her back, then he pulled at it hard and she rolled off of him with the flow of pain.

Kozz stood up and kicked her onto her stomach. He jumped on her back with both knees landing firm on her backbone, then he grabbed her head and twisted it.

The woman's body flopped around like a blubber-filled fish. She bellowed into the night, eyes and mouth shooting shafts of light into the darkness. When she died all was silent again.

CHAPTER FIVE

The Ranch

Heart pounding and aching, Kozz struggled to stay conscious. He numbed his bloody face with wet snow and wiped it clean, then heaved his mass from the ground and gathered the bags of supplies that had fallen from his body. *Madness. I've got enough of their blood and saliva on me to pass on any disease. I've got no chance if that's how it spreads.* Kozz walked down the street and checked behind the tree, finding Caleb crouched in hiding.

"I'm sorry I didn't help you." Caleb was carving a stick figure into the tree.

"You listened well. Best you hide and be safe from the danger."

"But you almost died! I saw. I could have got them with the knife." He pulled the knife away from the tree and looked at the blade. "I'm a hunter. I know how to use it, my mom and dad taught me. I was just surprised by that first lady. I could have helped you."

"Caleb is a brave name," said Kozz, "but I wouldn't have let you help. You need to be safe. You need to be away from the danger. I can't risk you getting hurt."

"But Kozz."

"No Caleb!" Kozz noticed that his voice was getting loud and he turned away from Caleb. "I'll do the fighting. You hide. If I lose you like I lost Jake.... You just listen to me and run when I say to. I'll protect you until we find your parents." He turned back and punched the tree, and then he punched it again. Caleb was scared. Kozz saw the boy's brown eyes well up and so he put his anger aside and tried to warm his frigid presence.

The lone eastward road continued across the flat ice of the high plains until it led down into a valley that separated two stretches of rolling hills. Kozz thought it might be best to stay off the main road, avoiding any houses that might contain more trouble. They trekked through the snow to the hills on the southern side of the road. Daylight had breached the horizon and from the tops of the highest hills Kozz could see the green forests to the south. The approaching day weighed heavy on the shoulders of the two exhausted and injured wanderers.

They never ventured too far from the road, always keeping it in their sights. Along the roadway there were many abandoned vehicles covered in snowfall. Some were buried deep under days or weeks of powder, but several seemed as if they had been abandoned recently. Kozz did not think it was worth the risk to try to find an operable vehicle amongst the junk. It was too dangerous.

Before they rested Kozz wanted to be as far from Edgetown as possible. He did not know how bad the trouble was everywhere else, but he knew that town was a hell hole. The sun began to set and the air became colder at about the time when Caleb was no longer able to hold himself up. Kozz decided to find a spot to rest for the night and they stumbled upon a small shack that looked as if it had been abandoned for years. It stood beside a large rock formation. The roof was missing many of its wooden shingles, and the siding was cracking in several places. Ice had crusted the door shut and Kozz slammed his body into it several times before it opened.

Inside was a single room with some dilapidated furniture and a haphazard stone fireplace that was pieced together by unprofessional hands. Outside Caleb slowly gathered fallen shingles, pieces of siding, and wooden molding, but a of couple armfuls was all his aching chest would allow him to carry. Kozz broke down the worn furniture and then started a fire, rehydrating a package of powdered beans to go with their meal bars. The shack did not hold the heat well and the breeze blew through the old walls with ease. As long as they stayed close to the fire they could keep away the stinging chill of the frosty night air.

"Kozz," said Caleb with his legs wrapped in his sleeping bag and his hands holding a can of warm beans, "where did you get your gun?"

"My pops gave her to me before he died."

"How did he die?"

"Him and my mother were in an accident when I was only a little older than you. I don't know exactly what happened, no one ever told me. Red, she's all I have left to remember them by. She's an antique though, you don't see many like her around these days with all those laser shooters that look like kid toys."

"My dad has old guns like that one too, but he never uses most of them. They just hang on the wall above our fireplace. He likes them a lot."

"Well when we get to your house your dad and I might just have something in common to talk about."

"Yeah. Maybe you guys will be friends."

"Yeah. Maybe."

It was difficult for both of them to sleep that night. Kozz had nightmares full of twisted faces screaming in the night. He kept seeing his wife and son walking like zombies with that demonic white glow in their eyes and woke up many times sweaty and angry. Every time he woke he heard Caleb's whimpers as the boy suffered through his own terrors. Kozz thought of waking Caleb to shake him out of the bad dreams, but decided to let him rest knowing that falling asleep with a cracked rib was difficult enough to do once a night.

The morning brought soreness and strain, but the morning was warmer than the last, making the trek ahead seem less daunting in their minds. The valley made a slow curve to the south where the wanderers soon found themselves facing a horizon of trees.

"That's where my house is," said Caleb, "right before you get to the woods."

As the hours passed Kozz learned that Caleb was staying in Edgetown with his grandma while he was going to school, seeing his parents several times a week and living with them during the off times of the year. The child cried as he spoke about his grandma, whom he loved and looked up to.

"How are you holding up, kid?"

"Fine, I guess."

"Don't say that. You can't be fine. She was someone you loved very much."

"What in the world happened anyway? What happened to me and all the others? What's going on? I wish I could just go back in time when it was all normal!" Caleb's face scrunched as he gritted his teeth and kicked at the snow as hard as he could. He winced at the pain in his chest. "Why did I do what I did to grandma!"

"I wish I could answer those questions for you, kid." Kozz put a hand on the back of Caleb's head. "Don't blame yourself, and calm down before you go and make that snapped twig of yours worse."

They later sat down for a midday break and built a small fire out of some brush that survived despite the snow. They settled in a small depression within one of the hills that was almost like a cave, resting on a patch of bare dirt and rock that had been left alone by the snow.

"So, um, you had a son?" Caleb remembered that the last time Kozz had mentioned his son he had become angry. He was afraid to ask, but he wanted to know.

"Yes." Kozz had been poking at the fire and stopped when he heard the question.

"What was he like?

Kozz stared into the small, dancing flames for a long time before speaking. "Jake was smart, funny, full of love. He was sad when he had to stay home from school. He always helped his mother make dinner and loved to eat everything he made. He wanted to be an airship captain when he grew up, just like he thought daddy was. He loved airships, built models of them that hung from his bedroom ceiling. There was this one time that he...." Kozz choked on his words and put his head down, hiding his watering eyes from Caleb. "He was a good kid."

"What happened to him?"

"Those are some difficult memories for me, Caleb. They hurt too much. Maybe another time."

Kozz stomped out the fire and he took his medication with the last of the melted snow water, then he put the pill bottle back into his bag and pulled out a cigar. *Not many left.* He lit it up and breathed in its heat, burning the sorrow out of his body and staying down wind of Caleb as they walked up the next hill.

Kozz spotted a person walking along the road, but the body staggered in an abnormal way, limping as if it were injured. The person looked into each abandoned vehicle it passed. Kozz and Caleb were too far away to see its eyes, but it was obvious that the person was not moving the right way, as if it did not know how to operate its body. Together they decided it would be best to not approach the person. They left the body to wander the valley road as they continued along their hill-strewn path.

"Kozz, I sometimes think I remember things," said Caleb as they walked.

"You don't have to think about what that demon made you do."

"No, like...like I remember when it first happened. Something was talking to me in my head, but I couldn't understand it. I think I remember it pushing me, bullying me. I told it to go away and tried to push back, but it was stronger.

And sometimes I see flashes, like memories of being able to see through my eyes when I wasn't in control. It's really weird."

"What did the voice sound like?"

"I don't know. It just made no sense." Caleb pondered his thoughts. "The last things I really remember is that the telepod was telling everybody to stay inside because there was a bad infection going around. School was closed for a few days and the police had caught a couple of people that had the sickness and they locked them up. I was with my grandma and then my head started to feel funny and then I woke up with you pointing your gun in my face."

"Do you remember what the date was when you were inside your grandma's house?"

"Like, the eighth or ninth."

"That's not even two weeks ago. It really hasn't been that long at all."

That night they risked entering a home that was more cozy than the rickety shack they had slept in the night before. Kozz scouted it out and found no one in the residence. The home was a large cabin, well maintained but completely abandoned and there were several soft beds for them to choose from. Night terrors still haunted them both. Sleep was more comfortable, but they had little of it.

The following morning Kozz had to rewrap Caleb. The boy

had squirmed around so much in the night that he had undone the bandaging. Kozz's ankle was stiff, but the pain was dull. He checked his own bite wounds and scrapes, all scabbing and healing just fine. He had no symptoms of the "infection" but decided to keep check on it in case he had to run himself away from Caleb. *Run away to protect him*, thought Kozz, *would it be right of me to run away again?*

The undulating hills decreased in size as they approached the forest's edge. They descended to a lower elevation, making their way down the glacier. The deep snow they had been traveling through gained a thin layer of crunchy ice spread across its surface. Caleb's light body stayed on top of the snow and he giggled as he watched Kozz's heavy bulk sink with every step. It was frustrating for the big man.

Blue skies were gradually covered by swirls of gray. Darkness loomed over the lands behind them to the northwest. Given the time of year, Kozz thought Mother Nature had one last ice storm to throw their way before she gave way to the relief of the warmer months. They were going to have to get to Caleb's house in a hurry.

"It's not that far," said Caleb as he and Kozz walked the descending hills at a brisk pace, "I think I can see it sometimes if I look hard enough."

They directed their path towards the road in order to make finding the home a bit easier. The blackened sky had gained on them throughout the day. Its low rumble reverberated through the hills, allowing Kozz and Caleb to feel it in their feet. The icy teeth of the dragon that consumed the sky would chomp down and swallow them if they were not able to find shelter by nightfall.

Caleb noticed a few land marks in the area and gathered a stronger sense of direction. A large pile of boulders meant they had to go one way, a meadow of turquoise tundra poking through the frost said they had to turn around a hill over there. The snow at their feet was now a dense layer of white ice, broken here and there by hardy, ground-hugging plants. Kozz followed Caleb's orders, but urged the boy to move faster.

The sun was engulfed by the darkness that hid the western horizon and rumbling clouds filled the sky sooner than Kozz had expected. Sprinkles of hail and wet sleet pelted their backs, the wind growing in strength with every step they took. The low rumble grew into a roar that sounded like the very earth behind them was being torn from its surface.

"There!" Caleb pointed towards a distant light in the field ahead. "That's my ranch. We made it!"

The patches of dirt and tundra beneath them would soon be blanketed in yet another layer of white. They hurried down the field along a wood and wire fence which outlined the property and arrived at a gateway with a sign that read "Northwood Ranch". The home was within plain view. Lights were on in all the windows and two people were seen running out the front door, perhaps to greet their son.

"Momma! Dad!"

Caleb hustled forward, but Kozz stood and watched for another moment. The parents did not run towards their son, they ran around the building, both holding objects. Then he heard the screams. They came from the woman, shrill and full of distress. She was being chased. The screams continued, her voice fading as she rounded the building and the cacophony of the approaching storm ascended. Kozz bolted forward, passing Caleb within a few strides. She was in danger and he had to help before it was too late.

A loud crash stopped both Kozz and Caleb in their tracks, and then another one followed. It sounded like thunder, but it came from the wrong direction. It came from behind the house. Caleb went to run forward again. Kozz grabbed the boy by the collar of his jacket and told him to stay put. Red appeared, fully loaded. Caleb shook his head at Kozz. He understood that Kozz thought there was trouble, but he could not let the man go at his parents with a gun. Kozz took a step towards the house and Caleb was ready to fight the gun from his hands. The woman walked around the corner of the home looking worn, disheveled, empty, and with a shotgun in her hands. Red rose up into the air. The woman hollered a sorrowful cry and dropped to the ground. Kozz and Caleb both ran to her.

"Momma!" Caleb yelled over the bustle of the storm. "Momma, what's wrong?"

"Caleb?" The woman raised her face from the cradle of her hands. "Caleb. Oh my—my Caleb!" She opened her arms and started to rise, but Caleb dove into her as she knelt on one knee. Kozz stopped at a distance and waited for the woman to make the first move. She eyed him in her wariness, holding her child like she had nothing else in the world. Mother and son embraced each other as if they thought they would never see each other again.

"Mom," said Caleb as he looked back over his shoulder, "this is Kozz. He's my friend. He saved me."

"Saved you?"

"Yeah, from the demons."

Caleb's mother's concern wrinkled her ageless face. She stood up, her short hair fluttering in the wind. She wore a long, brown dress that held steady in the turbulence with its thickness and weight. "Who are you?" she asked.

"A friend of Caleb's," replied Kozz.

She held her son at her side, considering the rock of a man that stood against the backdrop of an approaching storm. His face was stoic and scarred, but she felt a warm energy that emanated from him. "Come inside before we have to pry you off the ice."

She walked to the front door with Caleb held close. Kozz followed them inside. They had only just entered through the door when Caleb asked "Where's dad?" and his mother dropped again, succumbing to her emotions.

She tried to speak, but only one word escaped her sorrow.

"Dead," was all she said.

CHAPTER SIX

Moving Onward

Mother spent the night in her bedroom with her son. She told Caleb that she had shot his father, Harold, just before he and Kozz had arrived, and she said that his father had become sick from the disease that was afflicting the entire world, that he went mad and tried to kill her. She tried to talk to her husband. She tried to hold him back, but he was too strong. She tried to run, but had nowhere to go and there was no one to help her. She did everything she could, but in the end she had to protect herself.

Caleb confessed what became of his grandmother. Talk of murder and betrayal spat from the child's mouth. His mother's eyes widened. What was she hearing? She held her son tight, hushing his cries. "You would never do anything like that," she kissed his cheek, and then his forehead. "It wasn't your fault."

"That's what Kozz kept saying," admitted her son.

She squeezed her child. She felt nauseous. *Harold's mother is gone too? Caleb? This can't be happening.*

Their wails mixed with the howls of the wind. The storm unleashed its power throughout the night, shaking the home with its relentless force and pelting it with clumps of ice and snow. The noise drowned out the cries of of the broken family, allowing Kozz to gain some peace despite being surrounded by sorrow and thunder. He rested in a bed too small in a room too similar to one he remembered from his past. Inside Caleb's bedroom hung a dozen airships from the ceiling. The walls were stripes of bright blues, and the child-sized furniture sat neatly in place where his mother had put it as she had tidied up his room in his absence. The smell of the room was enough to bring Kozz to tears, its sweet clean scent masking the layers of dirt and adventure Caleb had brought into his home over the years. The weight of his memories caused Kozz's mental barrier to crack, and he let them pour through that night. As the wind cried and his neighbors cried, so too did he. The recollections of his past life hurt Kozz, but they did so in a gentle way, soothing his heart as much as they made it ache, massaging his muscles as they tensed, catching his tears as they fell. The storm carried on and the residents of the house shed all the tears they could. They all fell asleep to the swaying motions of the home and the bombarding sounds of the sky's icy tears.

The next morning Kozz woke to sunlight beaming in his eye and the aromas of a morning kitchen. Looking out the lone window in Caleb's room, Kozz saw that the blizzard had dumped a good foot or so of snow in its wake. There was a slight chill in the room, but when he opened the door he was greeted with the heat from the stove and fireplace.

Mother and son were quietly eating their breakfasts. Kozz saw the eggs and ham on the kitchen counter and he looked back over to the others. Luciele formally introduced herself and then motioned towards the food, signaling for Kozz to go and grab some while it was warm. He scraped a hearty amount onto a plate and joined the others at the dining table. He participated in the silence, but was drawn out of it when Luciele asked, "Is what my son says true? Was he one of the infected? You saved him?"

"All true," replied Kozz. Caleb looked up from his plate, telling his mom 'I told you so' with his eyes.

"Thank you. I owe you more than I could ever repay. The food and bed are the least I could do."

"I appreciate it all, but you owe me nothing. I saved Caleb because I wanted to, because I needed to. He's safe now and I'll be on my way soon."

"No. From the way you devour your food between your words I can tell you don't get many home-cooked meals.

You're going to stay and rest."

"Thank you," said Kozz with a piece of ham falling from his mouth, "but I need to be on my way."

"What you need is a bath and a change of clothes. Your face is a mess of wounds and your shirt is made of more blood than cotton. Caleb told me what you two have been through and there's no need for you to run away and see more of it all broken and exhausted like you are." Luciele stood up and walked to her bedroom. "Come. I'll grab you something to wear while I clean your stuff. You're a big guy, but I think some of Harold's baggy pajamas will fit."

"Mom only acts bossy like this when dad is in trouble," said Caleb. He looked at Kozz, then back down to his half-empty plate. "He's gone now, Kozz."

"I know. He'll be looking over you from above now, helping you when you're in trouble."

"Yeah. That's kinda what mom said."

Luciele emerged with a handful of garments and handed them to Kozz. He excused himself to the restroom to change. The pajamas were not a perfect fit, but Kozz was not uncomfortable. For an average sized man, Harold wore large and baggy night clothes. Kozz handed Luciele his stained shirt and pants, but said he would scrub his jacket himself.

Kozz sat himself next to the fire and admired the wall above where a dozen different guns perched, all from the gunpowder and metal era. Caleb brought Kozz a cup of hot tea. Kozz held the cup in one hand and Red in the other. Caleb sat in the chair across from him, wrapped in fresh bandages. He had finally taken some aspirin after his mother told him it was alright. Kozz spouted information about each of the different types of guns above the fireplace and Caleb listened, sharing the knowledge he held that was given to him by his father. The conversation led to the hunting trips Caleb had taken with his parents, a boy reminiscing about a man he loved, admired, and could not yet accept was truly gone from the world.

Kozz stayed for several days. His clothes were cleaned, but they still held their red stains and there was no other clothing in the house that would fit him. He helped Luciele dig through the cold ground behind the house and bury her husband. She planted a wooden tombstone at his grave and a funeral was held outside, wife and son grieving their loss while Kozz waited inside.

Luciele sat down and talked with Kozz the next day as the sun rose over the horizon. She asked him about who he was, about his past, about where he was going to go and what he was going to do. Kozz had little in the way of answers to give her. He held on tight to his secrets and only told her that he was heading to the quarantine zone inside Port Town where he planned on finding a ship to Erde. He told her about his life on Frostarc the last ten years, but she found that about as interesting as a bent nail. She explained how her family had moved to Frostarc from Erde when she was a child. She had met Harold in their younger days on a camping trip with mutual friends back when he was a big game hunter, and years later they decided to get married and settle on their ranch. She shared her story openly, hoping it would encourage Kozz to do the same.

"My past is full of pain," said Kozz. "I'd rather forget about it. Excuse me, doll." He left the room. Luciele sat where she was and stared at the armchair Kozz had vacated. Harold loved to sit in that chair and watch the flickering fire with a cold beer in his hand. His favorite dirty ball cap was still perched on top of the chair. She buried her face in her hands and let another wave of sorrow crash through her. Alone, she wept.

The day came when Kozz could wait no longer. Luciele and Caleb's tears only reminded him of his wife and his need to find her. He had to leave, but Luciele and Caleb did not meet him at the door to say their goodbyes. The morning when he was to head on his way, Kozz was met at the door by the mother and son garbed in their outdoor hunting gear and backpacks.

"What is this?" asked Kozz.

"We want to go with you," said Luciele, "to Port Town."

Kozz shook his head. "If out there is anything like Edgetown was, it's gonna be too dangerous. You're better off staying here until this mess is taken care of."

"We have no reason to stay." Luciele dropped her bags to the ground with conviction and used her arm motions for emphasis as she spoke. "Harold is gone from our lives. There is too much work on the ranch for Caleb and I to do alone. With Edgetown empty like you say it is, we have nowhere to go for supplies. We may be safe from the disease if we stay but we will still be in danger of starvation and loneliness. I have to do what's best for my son. We will be going to Port Town, to the quarantine zone. If you do not want us to travel with you then so be it, but it will be better for us all if we go together."

"Why don't you want us to go with you, Kozz?" Caleb spoke from behind his mother. She moved out of his way. "Is it because you're scared that I'm gonna turn into one of those bad guys again? I'm sorry. I'll fight it harder next time."

"No, Caleb. God no. I just want you guys to be safe, away from the danger. I thought that when I brought you home you would be safe here with your family." Kozz looked over the woman and child. They were so much like his family. He just wanted them to be protected, safe from harm. His past was evidence that he could not be the protection they needed, but the idea of them traveling alone in such dangerous circumstances, he could not even entertain the idea of leaving them to that. He had to protect them. He had to do better than he had done with his own family. "Let's get going then," he submitted. "I only hope my best is good enough this time."

The others did not know the meaning in those last words, but they were glad to be traveling together. Outside, Kozz was surprised to find two large pack mules fully loaded with supplies. Luciele tied on the last few bags which her and Caleb were holding. "My boy is hurt and you're not in great shape either, bucko. We'll need these beasts to carry our load. Gram had our truck." In truth, Kozz felt fine. His ankle was healed and his wounds were just itchy scabs at this point, but he did not argue since they had a long way to travel on foot if they could not find a working vehicle. Luciele lifted her son onto one of the mules and Caleb grabbed the reins, commanding the creature with ease like he had ridden it many times before.

They set off due south, downhill towards the forest. The consensus was that there was a greater chance of running into people, and the infected, along the warm belt of the equator, but it would also make surviving the forces of nature a much easier task. Luciele and Caleb stopped by Harold's grave one last time to say goodbye before they were off, then together they crossed to the other end of the ranch before reaching the forest, passing the herd of wooly cattle the family had raised along their way. "The herd will survive without us to care for them," Luciele explained to her son, "especially with the last of the winter storms behind us and the warmer months on their way."

Living far away from town, it was rare for Caleb to have a friend to play with, and so his comic books became his companions. He hung out with heroes and adventurers. They shared stories with him, taught him life lessons, and encouraged him when he was feeling down. The heartbreak of losing his father and grandmother was tragic, but all of the grand adventures in his comic books held some sort of tragedy. Caleb cried when he thought of their deaths, he was afraid that he would become infected again, but he knew that he was now on his own adventure. Already he had seen battles and death, escaped the evil that had captured him, made a new friend, and now he was traveling on the back of a mule to a far away city.

Caleb decided that if he was going on an adventure, he would have to be brave. He opened up one of his books and sought out his favorite speech at the end of one of the tales. He had always dreamed of having an adventure like the heroes in his father's bedtime stories or in his comics. Now he was seeing how difficult a real adventure could be.

> Go then young one, live life! Quit reading your books and watching your movies, instead go find your own adventure to tell. Do not focus on adding days to your life, focus on adding

life to your days! Before you reach the clearing at the end of the path, go and blaze your own trails through the muck and grime of life. Do not be afraid to get a little dirt on your boots.

Gather your bearings and head out into the unknown. If you have no goal in life, make one. If you do not have a destination, find one, and when you get there find another. There may be some scary things out in the world, but what is the use of feeling safe inside your own home if you do not know what it is like to feel true fear? Now I am not saying to go out and seek danger, but you need to not worry about running into difficulties on the road of life.

I say unto you dear reader, unto you traveler of words, journeyer of prose, adventurer of the pages of another's life, break away from your linear stretch of paved comfort and step into the squishy mud that few others dare enter. Play in it, stomp through it, pick it up and squeeze it and feel it ooze through your fingers and smell it and taste it. Use every sense you have on that mud and do with it what you cannot to the paved path. Create your own story for others to read.

Caleb put down his comic book. It was only the first night out and he had already gone through one of the few he had packed in his bag.

A full day's travel brought the group to the edge of the woods at the end of the ranch. They chose an area for camp that was sheltered by a few small trees which stood outside the wall of old growth. The twigs and branches Kozz had gathered held frost on the outside, but were dry inside. Luciele started a fire without any trouble.

"I don't know where we are going to go," said Luciele. "Caleb and I, we're like two pickles without a jar. Do you think the quarantine zone will be safe?"

"Depends," said Kozz, "on just how wide spread this outbreak is. Could be that they have a way to control it, could be that they don't."

"If only we had another choice. Harold and his mother were the only family I had left, and with them gone—" Luciele trailed off when she saw Caleb become upset at the mention of the departed. It was difficult for her to grasp that her son had become infected and in his state of delirium had committed such acts as attacking Kozz and murdering his own grandma. She still did not fully believe it, hoping that Caleb's sickness had created the thoughts in his mind. Kozz had not protested anything Caleb had said, but she did not want to believe it. *How could such a thing happen?*

Their first night out in the open together was uncomfortable. The lone tent they had was barely large enough to fit the three of them, especially with Kozz being as large as he was, and the ground beneath them was frozen and hard. In such tight and awkward quarters Kozz knew they would be forced to get to know each other well during their journey. The night was quiet and still, other than the sporadic 'haw' made by one of the mules.

The morning brought aching muscles, but everyone worked together to disassemble their campsite and made their way into the forest. The coniferous trees on the forest's perimeter had full branches all the way down to their trunks, but after breaching the first few rows the woods opened with only the roof of the forest harboring foliage. The edge of the forest was dotted here and there with stumps, trees that Luciele, Caleb, and Harold had previously cut down for firewood. There was no underbrush, only a thin layer of frozen ice that had entered the forest as light snow flurries landing on the undisturbed ground, succumbing to the winter chill and sinking down into a slab of ice. The air was quiet with not a single bird nor rodent to disturb the stillness.

Luciele took the lead, having spent a great deal of time in these woods with her husband and son. A good bit of the early travel was done on the trails the family had carved throughout the years. The barren forest was easy for the large mules to walk through, but it could be disorienting to a person who did not know the area well. Kozz was grateful to have Luciele as a guide.

The deeper they delved into the thickening spires of wood, the more the sunlight and ice dwindled. Generations of pine needles covered the forest floor. When Caleb was not on his mule he scuffed his feet along the ground, kicking away the layers of frozen needles and uncovering the cracked earth below. "The roots under these old trees run deep," said Luciele, "and you won't find much else sprouting from the ground in this neck of the woods. With nothing but acidic needles to eat it's near impossible for any little critters to survive. Whenever we hunted in these woods we had to reach the southern or eastern ends before we could find anything worth tracking. A few wandering predators will pass through from time to time, but only to get to somewhere else."

The forest thickened like a soup that was set aside to cool. Their pace slowed as they worked to get the mules through the tightening packs of trees. "Get a move on you old heifer," Kozz pushed one of the mules from the rear, wedging it between two large evergreens. Caleb turned around and giggled at the sight. His mother sighed.

"First off that isn't a she, it's a he," said Luciele. "Secondly, he is not bovine. And thirdly I'm surprised he hasn't kicked you square in the jaw by now, get your hands off his behind already!" She hurried over to the front end of the mule and rubbed its head. "I'm sorry, baby. He doesn't know any better. I ain't sure what was going through that thick head of his." Luciele grabbed its reins and backed the mule out, guiding it around the trees with ease. "Follow my lead and you won't be getting him stuck again, Kozz."

"I was!" he huffed. "We were following your steps but then

that damn horse went off on its own way and got itself stuck."

"Isn't a horse, and it won't go off thataways unless you make it go thataways. He knows how to follow quite well. You ever even worked with a mule before?"

"Animals never been quite my thing, darlin'." Kozz took the reins from Luciele's hand. "Go on, we'll follow."

She gave Kozz a fierce glare, but smiled when she turned away. Caleb buried his giggles into his shoulder.

They walked downhill into a large crater where small underbrush and saplings barely clung to life. A mostly frozen pond filled the bottom of the natural well, seeping between the trees like a marsh. They climbed to the other side of the dip and spent the night in a small clearing where one tree had fallen and taken a couple of others with it. A small patch of night sky poked through the pine-strewn roof above.

Caleb made the fire and Luciele warmed up some of her home-cooked leftovers before they spoiled. She set her packs aside as she cooked, and Kozz finally got a good look at the shotgun she was carrying. He asked if he could hold it.

"Mmhmm," replied Luciele. She handed him the weapon.

The double-barrel felt cold and dirty in his hands. *The way it probably made Luciele's heart feel when she used it last,* thought Kozz. He looked it over, ran his hands along its surface, dismantled it, and then inspected the insides. "How did you land your hands on this beauty?"

"Harold is the collector," she replied, "and he paid a good bit for this one. He had a bunch of firearms, what he calls his old guns. You saw some of 'em above our fireplace. I decided to leave the rest behind with him, except for this one." She grabbed the gun from Kozz and put it back together. "I didn't want to leave this one near him, the one that took his life away. It may have saved mine, but it killed my better half. My Harold."

Luciele excused herself to the tent. Caleb drew in the pine needles on the ground with a stick and Kozz asked what he was drawing. Caleb told him that it was his father sitting in an airship, he was flying his dad away into the air to protect him from the infection. "My mom says he's up in the sky somewhere right now, watching over us and protecting us as best he can. Maybe I'll be able to fly up there sometime and I'll get to see him again."

"It takes strength to believe." Kozz looked over the fire to the small boy on the other side. He could only marvel at how well Caleb was handling such tragic circumstances. "I'm sure he would like that, Caleb."

Luciele called her son to bed. Caleb kicked away his drawing and said goodnight before entering the tent.

Kozz sat with the fire by himself for a time and thought about his family. He had grieved for his son for so long, suffering through every element of sadness and anger a human mind could go through. He tortured himself with guilt and held the blame against himself for all of the years since his son had died. He had let his fear and self-hatred take over. He had abandoned his wife and tried to forget the entirety of his past life. He wept at the thoughts.

Caleb is so strong, he thought, *and I am so weak.* The boy and his mother were bringing up all of the memories Kozz had fought back and locked away over the past decade. Their questions, their stories, their familiarities were all keys that were unlocking the rusted seals in his mind. He cared for his new friends, but they swelled an anger inside of him. They brought up all of the flames of pain that he thought he had extinguished. He knew he was blessed to have their companionship, and he knew he had to deal with the pain. He could not fight it any longer. He needed to find his wife, he needed to see her again, he needed to be sure that she was alright after all of these years. A tsunami of memories flooded his thoughts, consuming him, drowning him. His mind was racing from one thought to the next, he felt like he was going insane, like he was going to die, like his brain was going to crack.

Kozz stood up and ran away from the campsite, his thick boots thudded on the ground and his breaths came out in grunts like a bear. His large body bounced between the trees and his jacket snagged on twigs and ripped them from their branches. Snot dripped from his nose, and he spat out the mucus pooling in his throat. Kozz tripped on something and fell forward, rolling down a hill. He came to a stop at the icy edge of the pond where its waters had frozen around the bases of several dead trees. There he cried in a way that only a man who had held in a lifetime of horrors could cry. Caleb and Luciele heard him in their half-sleep, the sound of such a strong man in such a state of despair was both heart-breaking and frightening. They felt sorry for him in the same way that they were sorry for themselves. This night was Kozz's window to forgiveness. The pines heard his wretched unraveling, they witnessed his convulsing sobs, and they gave to him the serenity and spiritual surrounding he needed to unleash his own personal demons. Kozz let it all out. He suffered, he apologized to his wife and son, he begged for forgiveness, he prayed, and he screamed out all of his anger, beating his self-loathing into the crispy pine needles with his fists. Kozz fought with himself through the night, eventually succumbing to mental and physical exhaustion.

He crawled his way back to the campsite and rested next to the fire where he fell fast into sleep. Luciele quietly exited the tent to put a thick blanket over Kozz and a pillow under his head. She stoked the fire and made sure he was safe from it. They all slept well past dawn the next morning.

Kozz awoke in a daze, his mind fogged over from the forces

exerted on it the night before. His face felt heavy and his entire body was sore. Luciele exited the tent and her son came back from somewhere beyond the camp, zipping up his trousers. Caleb was about to say something to Kozz, but his mother hushed him before he could speak. Kozz ignored it, knowing it was going to be about his episode last night.

That morning they crossed through the dense section of woods and entered a much more open forest. Thin shrubs scattered across the forest floor, dotted with small patches of broad-leaved ferns. A subtle din of birdsongs littered the distance, occasionally broken by the squall of a raptor on the hunt. Sprinkles of blue and thin rays of light broke through the green top of the forest.

After hearing his sadness the night before, both Caleb and Luciele were surprised to see that Kozz looked even stronger today than he had been in the past. His shoulders were no longer slumped forward, but held back with pride. His chin was raised just a bit higher than usual, and each step forward he took was planted with firm determination. *Something happened last night*, thought Luciele, *something has changed in him*. Though it was apparent from the moment they met Kozz that he was a substantial man with great power and skill, his presence seemed to have multiplied by the way he was now carrying himself.

"Kozz," began Luciele, "why are you—"

"I've been forgiven," said Kozz before she could ask her question. "Priscilla and Jake, they told me they had forgiven me a long time ago. They spoke to me last night and we all told each other how much we love one another. They told me I had to forgive myself. I told them I couldn't do it, not alone. They said they would help me, and they did. They shared their love with me, and I forgave myself for what happened. I forgave myself for what I've done and what I didn't do. I forgave myself for it all.

"Everything I've kept away, all the weight that was on my shoulders has been lifted. I can actually feel it. I'm lighter, less sluggish, and even my heart feels less restricted. I can feel it pumping harder than it has in years. I feel young again. I feel happy.

"Now we're on our way to Port Town. You, Caleb, and me, and we'll be there for each other the entire way. Then I'm off to find my wife, my lovely Priscilla. Nothing will stop me from reaching her."

Luciele walked over to Kozz and put her arms around him. "I'm glad you found what you needed," she said to him. "You're a good man, Kozz." She reminded him that he had saved her son, that he had gone out of his way to help her bury her husband, and that he had allowed them to accompany him on his journey.

"No," said Kozz, "you welcomed me into your journey. I

don't know if I would have survived this trip on my own. You and your boy have done more for me than you could imagine. I haven't felt this good in a long time, and it's all thanks to you two. All I needed were a couple of friends to give me a guiding hand. I still have a long way to feeling more like the man I used to be, but something snapped in me last night. I forgave myself, and that was the first step."

As the day passed they traveled into thicker underbrush and warmer air. The trees were still mostly pine, but a few deciduous oaks broke the monotony. Kozz was never one for remembering names of creatures and trees, but Caleb and his mother were wizards at it, naming every type of living thing they spotted along the way. It was a game for them, something to pass the time.

They camped that night and shared stories from their pasts. Kozz left out tales of his wife and son, opting to tell more about his childhood. He told them about life on Erde with his parents, about his mother's delicious double-baked pies, about the pool hall and shooting range he went to with his father, and about the family trips he took to the few nature reserves on the planet which were not overrun by tarred streets, concrete, and skyscrapers. Kozz explained how his mother was a schoolteacher and his father was a military man, how they lived a good life until his parents died in a vehicle accident. He spent some time in foster homes until he escaped them and decided to live life on the streets.

Caleb had fun talking about school and playing card games with his grandma and her friends. Luciele shared a few laughs about her high school days and some of the pranks she and her sisters liked to pull on boys.

"Sisters?" asked Kozz. "You have family out there?"

"Well...somewhere," admitted Luciele. "We had a falling out after mom and pop passed away. My sisters didn't like Harold. I haven't talked to either of them in years."

"That's too bad," said Kozz. "Do you know where they are?"

"Not a clue. They both moved back to Erde after mom passed. I haven't heard from them since, and that was before Caleb was born. They could be anywhere, and I don't really care where."

"Must have been a rough falling out."

"I'd rather not talk about it. In fact, I have this one story you have got to hear. Caleb, remember that time you were out at night chasing blinker bugs and ran back in the house all excited to tell dad and me about the warm pile of mud you found behind the barn?"

"Mom!"

A week had passed since Harold's death and this was the first leisurely night they had together as a group, putting aside their troubles for a few hours to laugh with each other and play games.

By noon the next day the air was mild and they all had to shed their winter coats to keep from sweating. The forest was cut off by a rock-faced bank with a steep slope. Small trickles of water dripped from the forest to the gray, slate surface and part way down the trickles merged to form a thin, clear stream. The few plants which lived on the smooth stone held onto cracks and small trenches scattered across the surface. The stream grew deeper farther down the slope as it weaved through its carved path between the boulders, and in the deeper sections of the stream was a species of enormous salamander, some as long as six feet and looked to weigh at least a hundred pounds. The harmless creatures took little notice of the group's presence.

The water made for a slippery descent down the hillside, but the many large rocks and fallen trees gave everyone solid holdings to grab on to. The mules had the most difficult time making the descent. Luciele grabbed the reins from Kozz's hand, intending to guide the animals herself. Kozz held the reins tight for a moment, but then let go with a huff. "I'm not used to being second in command, doll."

"Second?" Luciele cocked her head to the side. "Who said second? My son could handle all of this better than you if he weren't hurt. Heck, he probably can anyways, and stop calling me doll!" Kozz did not look pleased. Luciele smirked. It was almost too easy to get Kozz all riled up. "My woods, my mules, my rules."

"Hey momma," said Caleb, "why don't we get Kozz to carry some of our bags. The mules are looking awfully tired."

Kozz turned his attention from Luciele to Caleb. He stared at the boy, no emotion showing on his scabbed face. He would have looked menacing if he were not the butt of their joking.

"Great idea," said Luciele. "Kozz, why don't you?"

"Bah!" Kozz adjusted the sack on his shoulder and marched forward. He hustled down the hill and nearly slipped on the wet rocks.

"Like a grumpy old toad," said Luciele. "Isn't he?"

"Like a wart on the butt of a grumpy old toad."

At the base of the cliff the stream merged with several others and formed a small river. The forest floor was now dense with underbrush, mostly young trees and bushy ferns that were easy to push out of the way, and it was teeming with songbirds.

Descending the slope brought aching backs and sore legs. They made camp early that night and Kozz set out to teach Caleb how to use the knife he had given him, just in case, but Caleb argued that he had experience skinning and gutting game with a knife and did not need any lessons. "Attacking and defending with a blade is a completely different ball game," said Kozz. He placed Caleb's hands on the grip and lifted the boy's arms. "First thing you gotta know is how to hold it. You've gotta be threatening. It's your first line of defense. If you're scary-lookin' enough you might frighten them off, if you're lucky."

"Okay," said Caleb.

Kozz held the knife in his hand with a firm grip and slashed at a tree with clean swipes, then he stabbed it with determination and left the blade stuck point-first into the tree. "You see how that bark sliced off?" asked Kozz. "It was like butter. Go on, grab the knife and give it a go."

"Alright," said Caleb. He yanked the blade free from the tree and gripped the handle just as Kozz had shown him. Caleb had a hard time putting force into his swipes and could not get the blade to slice away sections of bark like Kozz had.

"Gotta get a tighter grip." Kozz grabbed Caleb's hand and squeezed it.

"Ow! That hurts!"

"That's how strong your grip has to be when you need to use that knife. You can't just hold it, it's gotta be a solid part of your arm. If you're not digging your fingers into that thing like your life depends on it you're not gonna have any force behind your attacks and the knife will just get knocked away from your hand."

"My arm's getting all tired already."

"Well you'll be needing bigger muscles then." Kozz punched at his biceps. "We're talking about fighting for your life, here. You'll be using all the energy you got."

"Guess I'll be needing to do some push-ups then." Caleb punched his own arms. He rubbed the pain out of them after Kozz turned to look at the campfire.

They ate a hearty dinner of beans and some forest critters Luciele had snagged along the way. Kozz wanted to start shooting practice with the boy and was surprised to find that Caleb had brought along his own small laser pistol. It was a thin metal device with a digital screen and a handle. They set up a range with a fallen log and a few empty food cans. Kozz cracked open an everlight and tossed it near the targets.

Caleb went first and took his time with each shot, knocking down all three cans without a miss. Kozz laughed at the sound it made when it fired.

"That thing sounds like my electric razor when it hits a rough patch of stubble!"

Caleb frowned. "Well it might not sound like an airship engine backfiring like yours, but at least I don't have to worry about forgetting to reload it." Kozz's deep laughter was cut short and he looked to Caleb's eyes. Luciele stood up with a sudden bout of worry, but then both Kozz and Caleb broke their stern faces and let their laughter escape simultaneously.

They walked through the forest for several more days until they came to an expanse of green grass being cropped by grazing cattle. The wind blew waves across the across the plains, causing them to shimmer in the sunlight. In the distance was a small, white house in the shade of a large red barn.

Caleb darted out of the forest's edge and down into the field where he jumped into the grass and rolled around, feeling the warm prickles on his skin. Though not fully healed, his rib did not appear to be causing him much grief. Kozz and Luciele walked down to where Caleb laid in the grass and looked across the fields to the house that waited in their path.

"I think we should go see if someone is in there," said Luciele.

"I agree," said Kozz. "If there's any trouble we should be able to handle it."

"There's a good chance that someone is still home and doing alright," said Luciele. "Everything looks so nice and tended to, not like a place that's been neglected."

They walked through the field, the herd of cattle shying away from them, and Kozz spotted a dead cow in the field near the barn. It looked to have been attacked by something only days ago. "That poor thing has been baking in the sun like a tomato," said Luciele, grabbing her nose. "Smells worse than walking behind these mules after they've eaten a belly full of skunkweed."

The barn had been painted recently and was in solid shape. Inside, hay littered the floor and Kozz found another dead cow in one of the stalls. It did not smell as bad as the other that had been baking in the warm sun and it looked like it had been alive not long ago. Luciele walked over to inspect the damage to see what could have killed the animal, but outside Caleb screamed and the both of them ran out the door before they could search for anything.

Red was in Kozz's hand as he rounded the corner of the barn and he found Caleb on the ground covering his eyes from the horrid sight in front of him. A woman stood in the shade between the barn and the house with a wood-chopping ax driven through her forehead, the ax pinning her dead body up against the barn wall. Streams of dried blood ran down both sides of her face and soaked into her white blouse. She was an older woman with gray hair, but not much more could be deciphered from the mess. Luciele picked up her son and moved him away from the scene. Kozz followed them to the front of the house. *That image will haunt the boy for the rest of his life*, thought Kozz.

"That woman looks like she's been there no longer than a day or so," said Luciele.

"She looks like grandma," cried Caleb.

Luciele held her son and tried her best to comfort him. "Do you think she was killed because she was one of the infected, Kozz? Or do you think one of the infected got her?"

"That's a brutal way for someone to kill another person,"

said Kozz, "but they could have done anything in self-defense. I think it was probably one of the demons that did it to her, though." Kozz lit up a stogie, his lighter held by the same hand as was Red. His heart condition had not gone away just because he had forgiven himself, but it had not been flaring up as bad as it once was. The smoke caressed his insides and made him feel better. "God help us all."

Kozz crept up to one of the house windows and looked inside. The house was cluttered, its drawers and cabinets were emptied all over the floor, but it looked empty of life and so Kozz had the others follow him as he went inside. Luciele and Caleb waited in the parlor while Kozz checked the other rooms. He told the others that all was clear. They all took a few moments to rest on the soft sofa before Kozz went into the restroom to shave his rough beard and Luciele tested the kitchen sink for running water. Clear, cold liquid poured out. She grabbed a few glasses from one of the cabinets and filled drinks for everyone from the faucet. Kozz started shaving while she and Caleb rummaged through the kitchen pantry for food.

Clink.

Luciele and Caleb both heard a noise from somewhere in the kitchen.

Clink.

Luciele moved towards the window. It sounded like

something small had hit the glass.

Clink.

"A pebble," said Luciele. She looked down to her son who looked back at her with a curious face. Then, at the same time, their eyes widened in sudden realization. Luciele leaned over the sink to look out the window when the front door ruptured inward and an old man burst across the threshold, his eyes glowing as white as his receding hair line. Plaid suspenders held up his tan pants, his shirt was half-tucked and all but one button was unclasped. He turned towards the kitchen and ran at the mother and son with a pitchfork held over his head in both hands.

Luciele had left her shotgun in the living room. She screamed for Kozz. The old man charged forward and threw his pitchfork at them like a harpoon. Luciele jumped aside to dodge the attack as Caleb ran low and behind the white-eyed man. The boy looked back to see that the man had stepped forward and grabbed his mother's wrist before she could escape. The man went to pick up his pitchfork with his other hand and Luciele kicked him in the face as he bent down. She ran past him to get her gun. The man ran after her.

KABLAM!

The sound of the blast shook the house as the man collapsed to the floor and screamed like a sewer rat that had been set aflame. His eyes beamed like spotlights and a moment later it was all over. Kozz stood in the restroom doorway with a half-shaved face, frothy razor in one hand and Red in the other, her barrel smoking. Caleb stood frozen with his hand on his laser pistol, and Luciele fell forward onto the sofa, heaving a sigh of relief.

"That is no fucking infection," she said matter-of-factly. Caleb transitioned from one state of shock to another after hearing his mother swear, surprised by her sudden choice of words. "You're right Kozz. This is something else. I can't believe my baby was like that." Kozz went to the bedroom where he grabbed a thick blanket to cover the body with.

"Why couldn't we save the man?" Caleb asked his mother. "Like Kozz saved me."

"We didn't have the chance, sweetie," she replied. "It was too dangerous. Now come here. I need your hug."

The group decided that they would not sleep in the house. The comfort of the beds and blankets was welcoming, but there were too many disturbing images around the home and they agreed that not one of them would have caught a wink of sleep that night with so much death surrounding them.

Kozz finished his shave and they all took baths to clean the woodland camping off their bodies. They washed their clothes and gathered extra food for the journey. In the barn they collected more feed for the mules and set out before dusk hit, hoping to get far enough away from the home to rid it from

Frostarc

their sight.

CHAPTER SEVEN

Secrets

Warmer days welcomed laughter and shared kindness, and the colder nights brought the group closer together as they huddled in their tent for warmth. They had grown close over their short time together, but the mystery of Kozz's past was like thick metal bars separating the mutual freedom of Luciele and Caleb from the imprisoned convict locked away in his lonely cell.

A cup of cocoa slid down Kozz's throat like warm silk as he watched the sun settle beyond the horizon, giving his sight the comfort of shade and letting the cool evening air place its first chilled grip on his exposed skin. Everyone shifted just a little closer to the fire as a chill set in, the three travelers were highlighted by the firelight against the darkening sky.

Since the run in at the farm it had been smooth traveling and high spirits for the tired trio. Their path took them away from homes and villages, avoiding any and all contact with lurking dangers. They slowed their pace to rest their aching feet and sore thighs, making the last few days feel more like a vacation than an arduous trek for survival. Luciele poked at a rehydrating can of mixed vegetables she was heating for her son as he sat with his elbows on his knees and his chin in his hands. Kozz put down his warm drink and stared into the flames as Luciele pulled out her son's food. Caleb sat next to his mother and ate his meal, falling asleep with his head on her lap before the stars replaced the sunset.

"Kozz, I've seen the way you look at Caleb," said Luciele as she ran her fingers through her son's unwashed hair.

"What do you mean, doll?"

"You have only known him for a few weeks now, but with every new day I can feel the warmth and love growing in your eyes. You care for him, don't you?"

"I wouldn't go saying all of that, but I care for the kid, sure. What are you getting at, Luce?"

"Don't call me 'Loose', and you are not being honest with yourself, or me for that matter."

"Sorry doll," he paused for a minute and ran over in his head what Luciele had just said, "about the name and the truth. The truth is I can't tell you the truth. There's things about me you can't know, no one can know. It's a complicated matter, Luciele."

"I know you've been hiding behind your secrets, but I have decided to trust you nevertheless. You have a past that you don't want to share, that's fine. You are here, now, helping us and leading us to wherever it is we are going, and since you are here with me and my boy I want to know why it is you find him so special. I want to know why you care for him so. What is it Kozz? Your care for my son does not go unappreciated, but I want to know why you are doing it Kozz, why you have such love for my son. I've heard only small mentions from you of your own son, and most of it was from that night you broke down and cried out to the world. Does Caleb remind you of Jake? Have you been using my boy as a stand in for your own son?"

Her words dug deep into Kozz's heart. She helped him understand that even though there were things he could not tell her or anyone else, there were parts of his life that he could share and had only chosen not to. His heart ached, but not in the same way as when it was over exerted. It ached in a way that it had been aching for years, dull and tucked away. He had chosen to keep all of his secrets to himself for years. It was time to let some go.

"Luciele, darling, I have something to share with you, something I've been keeping to myself for a long time."

"Go ahead, please." She put a pillow under Caleb's head and walked around the fire to sit next to Kozz. She placed one hand on his shoulder and the other on top of his hand. Her skin was cold, yet caring.

"If I look at Caleb the way you say I do, it's because he reminds me of my son." Tears filled Kozz's eyes. For ten years his emotions had hidden in his darkness, but Luciele and Caleb had unlocked the flood gates. Luciele rubbed a hand across his back. She made no move to speak and patiently waited for Kozz to continue. "His name was Jake. My beautiful wife Priscilla and I had a son twenty-three years ago, he died twelve years after that. He was our only child, and we loved him very much. There was somebody that was mad at me, somebody that wanted revenge. That somebody entered my home while I was away and killed Jake, murdered my son. Jake wasn't given the life he dreamed of, the life he was going to live. He wanted to be a pilot and a scientist for the Cooperation. He was smart and loving like his mother. He was strong and brave.

"Jake was also a quiet boy, like Caleb. He was a boy of few words, but the words he did speak were strong and important and interesting. Caleb reminds me of Jake in some ways, not all, but some. Caleb's interests and words and inner strength, his love reminds me of Jake. Caleb may not be as aggressive and physically strong as my son, but his courage, his heart is powerful and so was Jake's.

"Caleb is a great boy, and that's why I care for him. My eyes are warm for him because he makes my heart warm. He, no, both of you have given me something I have been without for more than ten years, love and personal strength. You have given me love. Caleb has given me love. A man cannot live without love and I felt close to dying not too long ago, not more than a month ago when I lived in my icy hell hole alone, staying away from love and warmth so that I could protect it and protect myself from losing it again."

There were a few seconds of silence as both of them wiped away their tears. "What are you trying to protect, Kozz? Who? Is it your wife, Priscilla? What happened to her? Does she need protection from the person who killed your son?" Kozz turned towards Luciele. She leaned back and her lips twitched, embarrassed about how forward she was with her questions. "I'm sorry Kozz, I—"

"I abandoned her." Kozz admitted as if pleading guilty to a jury. "I ran away to protect her, but now I have to find her and make sure she is safe from all this madness. It's still difficult to speak of it all. I don't wanna say anymore." Kozz returned his gaze to the flames.

"I'm so sorry about what happened to your son. He sounds like a wonderful boy." Luciele looked over to her sleeping child. "Caleb likes you, he told me so. I know you will keep him safe."

"Thanks. I've kept this all inside for too long."

"Thank you for telling me your story, and for putting your trust in me. I am sorry for trying to delve any further than you were willing to go."

"Think nothing of it, doll."

Caleb stirred awake from his sleep. Luciele stood up and walked over to her son and led him into the tent. Kozz stared into the flames until they dwindled into non-existence. When only the glowing coals remained Kozz followed the others into the tent to sleep.

In the morning they all awoke to a distant buzzing sound, one they were all familiar with. Caleb sat up, immediately followed by his mother and Kozz. "Do you hear that?" Caleb shouted in excitement. "It's an airship!" They emerged from the tent to see a small airship flying above, popping in and out of sight as the thin foliage of the treetops swayed in the dawn wind. The airship was a one-man personal carrier and flew past them without pause. Their fire had long been out and their campsite was well-hidden under a clump of young trees, but even if the person flying the ship had seen them, chances were they would not have stopped. Caleb chased after the ship for a bit, but he soon gave up and sulked back to the campsite.

Luciele assured her son that it was good to at least see someone flying a ship, that it meant there were others alive and unaffected by the disease, others who were doing what they could to survive, others who were on their way to Port Town, to the quarantine zone. "Unless those glow-in-the-dark freaks can fly our machines," said Kozz, "I'd say this is a good sign."

"They can't do that," said Caleb. "Can they, Kozz?"

"There's no reason to scare my child," said Luciele.

"I'm not scared, mom. Not really." Caleb was indeed scared, but he would never admit it in front of Kozz. "But do you think they can fly an airship?"

"Probably not," said Kozz. "I was just sayin' what popped off the top of my head. Those demons can be tricky, but there's no way they can be that smart."

The small ship flew eastward, towards the city. They followed the path of the now out of sight airship, hopes lifted slightly by the first sign of normal life they had seen in weeks. *Someone is up there*, they all thought in one fashion or another, *someone's survived outside of the quarantine zones just as long as we have. We aren't the last ones.*

By the end of the day they reached the top of a hill that served as the end to the forest. Ahead were open plains, farmland that was dotted with small towns, and not much in the way of cover from wandering eyes. They were going to have to brave the open.

The wind from the east was crisp and refreshing, laced with salt from blowing across the mass of water that stretched along the horizon. The Great River was not really a river at all, but a sea that spanned from one pole to the other on one side of the planet. The land ahead was separated by its miles-wide girth.

The ice was thick enough in the north and south where it was possible to walk across the sea, but nowhere in between was there a natural crossing. Only one bridge spanned the expanse at its thinnest section, and Kozz intended to use it.

CHAPTER EIGHT

Fray

Gunfire sounded the morning alarm. Distant snaps and crackles littered the east for several minutes until all was quiet again. The three travelers were going to run into others whether they wanted to or not. Kozz was first to gather his belongings and move onward. "It's a dangerous path we're about to take, but we need to get to that bridge. We're gonna have to go through that small town at the water's edge to get across the sea." He tightened the straps on the mules and led the animals downhill. Caleb and Luciele picked up their gear and followed after him.

"That town is Siletz," said Luciele. "It's where my parents used to live. Good place for seafood. Harold and I used to spend entire summers out on the sea before Caleb was born, back when we were young and cared diddly about any responsibilities."

"I never liked boats," said Kozz.

"Me neither," said Caleb.

"Well then," said Luciele, her voice as flat as an iron, "good thing there's a bridge."

They dropped into the middle of the valley and followed a road towards Siletz. More gunfire crackled in spurts throughout the day and Kozz chuckled every time he heard it.

"What's so funny?" asked Caleb.

"Laser guns, like the one you have," replied Kozz. "They sound like bug zappers."

Luciele chuckled despite her worry. "That's something my Harold would have said!" She found herself in a small fit of laughter and the next several times they heard gunfire she laughed along with Kozz. Caleb did not think it was funny, his laser pistol was not a joke. Kozz teased the boy, trying to get him to join in on the fun. Caleb forced a frown for as long as he could, but it cracked into a grin when Kozz imitated the laser blasts by buzzing his lips. "Bzzrrrrrpp....bzzrrrrrpp." Gunfire meant people were nearby, regular people, and the laughter helped relieve some of their stress.

The group stayed clear of the outlying homes that led the way to Siletz, but as they closed in on their destination the clustering streets became unavoidable and the gunfire grew louder. They were all well aware of their weapons and kept them ready to draw at a moment's notice.

Siletz was the most populated port on this side of The Great River, but it still was not large enough to be called a true city.

The buildings were taller than those in Edgetown and the streets were wider, but the town was empty and broken. They stepped around the shattered glass and forgotten belongings that lay scattered in the streets and kept their eyes on the silent buildings, afraid of what may be hiding inside. A salty wind funneled through the streets, howling through open windows and carrying a charred smell of burnt wood. They walked by a section of homes which were burned to the ground, coals still smoldering. The streets near the area were coated in black ash that swirled in the wind.

"Looks like a battle was fought here," said Luciele. She grabbed her son's hand and noticed that it was blackened from drawing figures in the ash. Gunfire clapped through the buildings and she squeezed Caleb's hand tight, pulling him to the side of a building to take cover.

tew-tew-tew ticka-ticka-ticka tew-tew-tew

"I don't think it's over yet, doll," said Kozz as he ducked low, pulling Luciele and Caleb down with him. The gunfire was close and echoed between the buildings. Shouts of men followed the blasts.

ticka-ticka-ticka tew-tew-tew

"Get 'em!"

"Ah!"

"We need to find whoever that is without surprising them," said Kozz. He crept alongside the building towards the direction of the gunfire and motioned for the others to stay where they were. He approached the corner of the block and peered down the street. Two men stood over the bodies of several others not more than a hundred yards down the road. One man had a black mustache large enough to be seen a mile away, the other had a wide-brimmed cowboy hat. It was almost like watching a cartoon. One of the men yelled something and Kozz saw a body dart towards them. Both men fired and the body fell.

tew-tew-tew

The men stood where they were and laughed with each other.

Kozz turned back to Luciele and Caleb. "Two men with guns. I think they were fighting off some demons. I'm gonna call out to them. Have your weapons ready just in case." Kozz turned back towards the street, seeing that the two men started walking in his direction. Kozz stood up, body mostly hidden behind the building. "Don't shoot!" he yelled from around the corner, "I'm not infected!"

"Who's that?" demanded one of the men. They ceased their jokes and both pointed their guns towards the voice. "Who'n the hell is that?"

"Name's Kozz," he shouted back. "I'm coming out." He moved halfway out from the building so that the men could see him.

"Show ya hands," commanded the one in the wide-brim hat. "You alone?" asked the one with the dark mustache, it was waxed and curled at the tips.

"I have a weapon for my protection," said Kozz as he showed both his hands, Red held upside down by the barrel in one. "There is a woman and a boy with me."

"You keep that antique where it is so we know ya won't be causin' us trouble," said the hat-wearing man. "Family man, eh?"

"Not my family," said Kozz. "Just friends."

"Tell them to come out," said the hat man.

"Not until you put down your weapons, hoss," said Kozz. The two men looked at each other and lowered their guns. Kozz lowered his hands and motioned for Caleb and Luciele to come out with him. They stood next to him with their guns holstered, but ready to draw.

"Looks like we've got some more survivors to join our crew," said the mustached man. "My name is Freddy, this other guy is Tim."

"Alright then," said Tim, "come with us and y'all have somewhere safe to sleep tonight. This town is overrun with those freaks."

"We haven't seen anything but you guys since we got to this town," said Luciele.

"Well miss, you were lucky," responded Freddy. "Our camp

has been attacked several times in the last few days. But we've got lots of guns. It's pretty safe."

"We're just looking to cross the bridge over The Great River," said Kozz.

"You ain't gettin' over that bridge," said Tim.

"Why not?" asked Caleb.

"Cause kid, they destroyed it." Tim spat on the ground. He looked pissed.

"Who destroyed it?" asked Luciele.

"Damn infected people blew it right up," said Freddy. "Crashed an airship into it. Can't cross it now. We tried."

"There's no way one of the infected could have done that." Luciele rolled her eyes. How dumb did these guys think she was? "Someone must have just crashed into it. Ran out of energy or something."

"Could be," said Freddy, "but I don't know. They're smart and they like to destroy."

"Evil sumbitches," said Tim.

"It can't be," said Luciele.

"I believe it," said Kozz. "I've fought enough of them already to know how evil and destructive they are, and how crafty they can be. They use tools and traps, and I've seen them destroy vehicles to prevent us from using them. I wouldn't put it past them to destroy important devices and infrastructure."

"I believe it too," said Caleb. "I think they did it. They know what they're doing."

Concern furrowed Luciele's brow. She bent down and hugged her son. He grabbed her tight as his face filled with worry and understanding. He shared a look with Kozz over his mother's shoulder, both knowing that something big was happening.

"Ok, enough chit chat," said Tim. "Let's get back to camp. We're near the base of the bridge. Y'all be able to see the damage for yaselves.

Kozz, Luciele, and Caleb followed Tim and Freddy through the streets. They walked downhill towards the water's edge where the breeze became brisk and the bridge came into view. The colossal structure had been built a decade ago and still displayed its pristine white color. Tall arches held suspension cables that seemed to stretch for miles and the midway support column rose into a peak high in the sky. Just beyond the midway support was a collapsed arch that floated in the air on suspension cables, and the bridge below it was missing in the depths of the sea. The remaining bridge structure was warped and twisted by the tense cables. From the shore the gap seemed small, but those who understood the bridge's immense size knew that the breach could have been a hundred feet across. Its length made it impossible to see the other end.

Dozens of ships and small boats along the shoreline had been burned to cinders or sunk, only the ropes that tied them to the docks had kept them from fully submerging or floating away with the current.

"No vessels left to carry us across the sea?" asked Kozz.

"Not a one," replied Tim.

There were more dead bodies along the docks than there were in town, and the number increased as they approached the camp. Corrugated metal was used to line the perimeter of the settlement, blocking off the areas between the buildings and the sea. Men with guns stood along the haphazard wall of debris and two of them greeted Tim and Freddy as they entered the camp. Other than the few men on guard, the camp was a ragtag bunch of beaten and desperate people. Cold. Starving. Sick. Weak. Kozz estimated about fifty people in all, maybe more, and most were scared out of their wits.

ticka-ticka-ticka

Shots rang out nearby. Kozz, Luciele, and Caleb ducked for cover, but got back up as burly laughter followed the shots, leading the way to hoots and hollers.

"Ha! Well howdy strangers," said a large-bellied man with a pair of dark sunglasses. He wore a bright red shirt that was tucked into black denim pants, separated by a belt with a large buckle on it that read "GAUCHO" in gold lettering. The whole outfit was bottomed off with a pair of black, sparkly boots. *What an asshole*, thought Kozz. "Sorry if I gave you beautiful people a little scare, I was just blasting away another one of those diseased freaks. Well, I thought I saw something anyway. The name's Daryll. The wonderful people here seem to have put me in charge of this place."

"Gettin' your jollies off, slick?" Kozz did not like the man. He learned way back in his childhood to be tough from the get-go with pricks and egomaniacs. "Or are you just firing that thing off like a lunatic? There are people here, learn some restraint." Luciele tensed up at Kozz's sudden remarks. She spat his name under her breath just loud enough for him to hear. Tim walked over next to Daryll.

"Hey champ," said Tim, "we ain't need the attitude ya bringin' to our little group here."

"Sorry," said Luciele, "we've just had a rough couple of weeks. My husband was killed and we have traveled all the way from Edgetown without any transportation other than our feet and these two mules. We're all just a little on edge. This big lug is Kozz, I'm Luciele, and this is my son Caleb."

"That's more like it, pretty." Luciele frowned at Daryll's comment. "We lucky survivors here would be glad to welcome the three of you into our little guild, if you can keep a cover on top of the big boy's steaming temper."

"The more you talk," said Kozz, "the more my blood boils."

"Hold on champ," said Tim, "now we're gonna be goin' out to the quarantine zone out in Port Town if ya want to be joinin' in with us. The mules and the guns y'all are carrying can be useful to us, and I'm sure the larger numbers we got can help ya get there if that's where y'all are headin'. But if ya have a problem with us, just put it away and keep it to yaself or go and head out on your own way."

"What he says is true my friend," said slick Daryll. "You may be large and want to be in charge, but Tim and I here have saved these folks from the horrors in the nearby towns and have made a plan to move out tomorrow morning. We welcome you into our survivors club, but it comes with peace agreements that must be made."

"We're going to Port Town as well." Luciele spoke before Kozz had the chance. "He will calm down, and I will make sure of it. Thank you for welcoming us, I'm sure we will prove to be helpful in this journey." Caleb hid behind his mother when she spoke, peeking around her to look at all the people.

"Very well my dear," said slick Daryll, "we are honored to have you aboard. Perhaps your friend will lighten up after a good night's rest. I hope to meet your handsome son tomorrow as well as the shy bug seems to have bitten him this evening."

Daryll and Tim wandered over to the perimeter and talked quietly to one another. Freddy guided Kozz and the others to an empty corner of the camp. "Well here you are miss, sir, Caleb. Don't worry about making yourselves too comfortable. We'll be moving on soon enough, I'm sure."

"We appreciate your hospitality, Freddy," said Luciele.

"Nothin' to it miss. My wife, she would give me quite the scolding if I wasn't to treat new guests proper and all."

"Oh, well I'd love to meet her."

"Well, um...sure, maybe. She's not well at the moment." Freddy looked down and kicked at the dirt. "Anywho, if you'll excuse me. I need to get some food cookin' for my son."

Luciele gave Kozz a stern talking to once Freddy walked away, saying how he was rude and gave off a bad first impression and now all three of them were going to have trouble fitting in with the group of survivors. She admitted that she did not care much for Daryll or Tim, but that it did not warrant the discourtesy Kozz had shown them.

Caleb lost focus on the grownup's bickering as he caught the glares of a few of the people in the camp. *Their faces are so sad*, he thought, *so pale and droopy and sad. Whenever I look at them they turn away like they're scared of us or something. I don't want them to be scared of me.* He followed his mother and Kozz over to where they were going to pitch their tent.

"Perhaps we should put our stuff to the side for the moment," said Luciele. "Let's go and introduce ourselves around the camp."

"Don't feel quite in the mood for a meet and greet," said Kozz. "You go ahead and take Caleb with you. I'll stay here and set us up for the night." Caleb did not want to go either, but his mother made him. Kozz lit up his last stogie and surveyed the camp from his perch, keeping an eye on Luciele and Caleb as they wandered off.

They first approached an elderly woman who sat all alone in a dark section of the camp near the water's edge. Behind her tent the small waves splashed on weathered rocks. Luciele introduced herself and her son, but could not make out a word the woman had said. She surely said her name, but her whispered mumbles were incomprehensible. Luciele tried to get the woman to speak more clearly, she wanted to make sure that the woman had been fed and well-cared for, but it was a struggle. Caleb slipped away from his mother's grip and went down to a small beach at the water's edge where he saw that some of the younger people had gathered on the sand and pebbles.

The dull roar of The Great River filled Caleb's ears. The bridge that crossed the sea was usually adorned with lights in the evening, but its broken form was nothing more than an eerie silhouette against the twilight backdrop. As he approached the beach, Caleb saw that the younger kids near the water were not so young after all. It seemed that other than a couple of babes in arms he was the youngest person in the camp. Most of the beach kids were older teenagers, but one was a little younger than the rest. Caleb walked over to a boy who was maybe fifteen with moppy red hair and a lime green shirt.

"Hi, my name is Caleb."

"Hi," said the kid. He looked at Caleb when he spoke but turned right back to a drawing he was making in the sand.

"What's your name?" asked Caleb.

"Samuel."

"What'cha doin' Samuel?"

"Nuttin. Just drawing."

"What's that?" asked Caleb as he sat down next to Samuel. "Is that a monster or an alien or something?"

"Suttin like that. I had a dream where my mom's brain was switched with this thing's brain and that's why she got infected and started acting all weird and scary."

"Oh," said Caleb with a long pause. "Did your mom get turned into one of the infected?"

"Yeah. My pop and I had to run away from her cus' she was trying to hurt us. She's still out there somewhere. Pop says maybe she'll get fixed soon and we can all be together again."

"You can get her back Samuel, I know you can. I..." Caleb considered his thoughts for a second before continuing. "I was infected for a little while and I was made normal again. My friend Kozz saved me. I was trying to hurt him and I didn't know what I was doing, and then I saw Kozz and I thought he was going to kill me but I came back to normal and have been fine ever since."

"Really?" said Samuel, finally breaking away from his

drawing. "You were really one of the infected people? And your friend saved you? Are you fibbing?"

"It's all true."

"Pinky swear?"

"Pinky swear." They locked their little fingers together and Samuel sprang up to his feet.

"I have to go tell my dad that we can save her!"

"But Samuel, wait!" Samuel ran off to find his father and Caleb's shouts went unheard, squelched by Samuel's excitement and the noise of the sea, or simply ignored. Caleb worried that what he had told Samuel might spread around, and he was afraid of what others might think of him after hearing it.

With Samuel out of the way, Caleb could fully see the drawing left in the sand. The creature looked powerful and as if it could come alive at any moment. The memory of his mind being pushed, bullied by some phantom force, caused Caleb's eyes to well up. His grandma, his dad, his friends— they were all gone. There had to be some way to stop it from causing more pain, whatever it was. Caleb kicked sand over the creature's face and ran back to find his mother.

Luciele was right where he had left her. When he returned she sighed in relief and used him as an excuse to get away from the old woman. "I couldn't hear a thing she was saying, but every time I tried to excuse myself away she grabbed my arm and reeled me back in like a big ol' fish she was trying to tire out. And I'll tell you what, I almost tuckered out and gave up. I was ready to plop down right next to her and listen to her little jibberings blabber on." They walked on to meet someone else, but Caleb looked back and saw that the elderly woman's mouth kept on muttering even after they had left.

They were met with sullen faces as they meandered through the camp and were ignored by those Luciele tried to start a conversation with. A young couple left the group at the shore and approached Luciele and Caleb.

"Hi there," said the petite girl with auburn hair, "my name is Kelly and this is my boyfriend, Richard. You both looked kinda lost and lonely so we thought we'd come on over and give ya a smile. There ain't too many happy faces around here."

"Not many talkers either," said Richard, a young man with blonde hair and a thin frame. "Welcome to the survivor's camp, full of the dreary and self-absorbed, the battered and broken, the pricks and—" He stopped and smiled at Kelly, seeing that she was giving him a level stare. "Anyway, nice to meet you both."

"Yes, well I'm Luciele and this is my son, Caleb. Say 'hi' Caleb."

"Hi."

"It's a pleasure to meet you two," said Luciele. "I'm glad there's someone around here who's willing to talk and isn't crazy. Poor old woman back there has a few too many badgers in her coop."

"We've been here a couple days and still haven't been able to get most people to open up," said Kelly, "that's why we've been hanging out with the teens and such. Even in the midst of all this chaos they still want to have fun."

"All the other folks are too sad or whacked out or mad," said Richard, "speaking of mad...." Richard nodded in the direction behind the group and everyone turned to see three men marching intently towards them. It was Freddy, Tim, and Daryll, all with their weapons drawn. Freddy held his weapon low and slowed as the men approached the group, but Daryll and Tim walked right up to Luciele with their eyes fixed on Caleb as he hid behind his mother.

"Show yourself, boy," said Daryll, "I've got a few questions to ask you."

"Hold on there slick," said Kozz as he pushed his way between Luciele and the men. "Why don't you take a couple steps back."

"Didn't know you were harboring an infected with yeh," said Daryll as he was forced to take a step back from Kozz's intimidating size.

"No one is infected, slick."

"We know about the boy," said Tim. "His own words. He tol' Freddy's kid that he was infected."

Caleb gripped his mother's dress tight and shrunk as small as he could behind her. She stood strong in front of her son and had Kozz move to her side.

"My son is a healthy young boy you nitwits. You leave him alone or I'll be jumping on you like a whitecat on a fluff rabbit."

"Your son is a threat to our community if he's carrying the disease," said Daryll. "Now, if he is indeed healthy and is just going around telling falsities then we don't have much of a problem. However, if he is sick, we will have to deal with him in a manner that will ensure the safety of our people. Freddy here told us what he said to little Sammy. I want to have a look at the boy and have him tell me the truth."

"I'm sorry ma'am," said Freddy, "I didn't mean for this."

"Shut up Freddy," said Tim as he whacked Freddy in the arm with the butt of his rifle. Freddy rubbed his bruised flesh and walked back to his designated section of the camp where his son, Samuel, waited for him.

"The boy isn't infected," said Kozz.

"Well what he told Freddy's kid," said Daryll, "was that he was and you..."

"He never was infected."

"I want to hear it from the kid."

"You've got my word, slick."

"I want the boy's word!"

"You leave the child alone or I'm gonna have to get nasty."

"I'd like to see you try."

"You're gonna regret those words."

"Enough!" shouted Luciele. Caleb moved away from his mother's guard and stepped forward. The point of Tim's gun lifted a nudge when the boy appeared, and Daryll's had taken a noticeable turn in Kozz's direction.

Richard and Kelly both moved to Caleb's side. Luciele put her hand on her son's shoulder, as did Kelly, but Caleb took another step forward and let their hands fall behind him. He thought about the heroes in his comics.

"Before you reach the clearing at the end of the path, go and blaze your own trails through the muck and grime of life."

"I was infected," muttered Caleb.

"What was that, boy?" asked Daryll. "I didn't hear yeh."

"Hush Caleb," warned Luciele.

"Caleb, don't!" Kozz huffed. The world turned into a blur. His chest ached and his mind raced through a thousand outcomes, all ending with Kozz unable to prevent Caleb's death. Past nightmares haunted him. He could not think. He could not move. He was going to fail again.

"Let the boy speak!" shouted Daryll. "Say what you need to say, boy. Tell us the truth."

"Do not be afraid to get a little dirt on your boots."

"I was infected!" Caleb's strong voice shocked his friends. It was the loudest Kozz had ever heard the boy speak, and it was a side of Caleb that even Luciele had never seen.

Tim raised his weapon and Kozz lurched forward to barricade Caleb with his own body. Daryll and Tim were stirred by the sudden movement and swung their weapons around in the excitement as everyone hollered at one another. Kozz's face was red hot. The commotion was a whirlwind in his head. From somewhere he heard Luciele comment that she could burn them a path through the sea with his forehead. He had to stay between Caleb and the men that were...between the boy and the...between Jake and.... All went to blackness.

CHAPTER NINE

The Caravan

A body wanders the desert. Many would see his smooth face and call him a boy, though all who have spoken with him would call him a man. Guthrow is dying.

Dark leather rests atop his head and shoulders, appearing to have seen more years than Guthrow himself. His hat's wide brim has several bullet-sized holes scattered throughout, and a section of the back has been sliced off. His coat at one point reached near his ankles, but the wears of battle and age have given it a ragged edge that now stretches just past the knee. Dark jeans resemble an old black dog with gray whiskers and sores, and his shirt looks like a dirty washcloth that has been rolled in the sand for hours on end.

At first glimpse you would notice the adolescent features of a pubescent boy, smooth skin that is only broken by the few facial hairs of a young man, the stubble accentuating a prominent jaw line with rough precision. A closer look reveals the hard years that have given age to the young face. That spring one would associate with youthful skin is fading, giving way to gravity. The oils that make young men shine are all but lost in Guthrow. Small cracks grow in the corners of his eyes and lips, and his fingers have lost their grip. His striking eyes put fear in the hearts of wicked men, staring them down with the pale yellow of a sun in its final days.

And beside him is his crow. The sun does not reflect a sleek shine off of what is left of the black bird's feathers as one would expect, instead it returns the sun's rays with a dusky gray glow. One look at the bird and a person would hesitate to go near the sickly looking thing. The bald spots are expanding, and a colorless plague is spreading from its beak into its eyes. Guthrow's faithful companion hops alongside its master, leaving little cross marks in the orange desert sands.

"Times are tough my small friend," says Guthrow to the hopping bird as it gives an attentive look to its master. "This is going to be our final assault." The crow tries to caw in response, but all that comes out is a dry hack. Water has been scarce in this latest venture of theirs, a portent to the duo's eventual demise.

Behind them lies a city in ruin, and ahead in the distance is Loh'khal, desert palace of the last Demon King. The craggy architecture looks like a small hill on the far horizon, but Guthrow knows of its immensity. The mountain's face is forever obscured by shadow, and its belly reaches to unknown and fathomless dark depths. The King surely rests at the top where she can ruminate over her dark kingdom and worldly destruction.

Ages have passed as man and demon have waged their wars against each other, both striving for dominion over the soils of the planet. There was a time when the era of men was almost at an end, but their strong hearts and brave souls galvanized in their final hour. The demons poisoned the seas and burned the forests, almost eliminating all life on the planet. After centuries of struggle, the lives of men and animal are once again beginning to bloom. The world of man is being rebuilt, and the forests are sprouting anew. The darkness has been fought back to the deepest corners of the world where men rarely venture. It has now come to this, our weary warrior marches into the blighted lands of the last Demon King, bent on eradicating the final nightmarish plague and putting an end to humanity's horrific bane.

The torrid sea of sand sings its silent song of swelter and emboldens the air above it to dance around Guthrow and across the vast horizon. The slight wind is a breath of fire that lifts Guthrow's coat like a cape and robs his skinny figure of its remaining moisture. His blind companion hops across the scorching desert fast enough to avoid most of the direct heat, but it must take leave every so often to rest atop its master's hat. Together they share a few sips of their remaining water.

Night is the best time for travel and for nourishment. A small puddle of an oasis appears in the distance. "This is the last stop for us, friend," Guthrow says to the crow as they approach the water's edge. "Any liquid past this point will be poison to you and I." Guthrow fills up his pouch with water that is sharp on the tongue, then he snags a couple of small lizards and a flat-eared fox for what will be his last meal.

The food is hard to swallow, and harder to keep down—even the sickly crow can only eat a few small bugs. The taste of the meat is not bad, but Guthrow's body is older than it appears, and he is a dying man. Only his friend, the little crow by his side, knows how pale he has become below the deep tan of his skin. Guthrow's tawny eyes were pallid even in his younger days, but now most of the yellow has washed out and they have turned a creamy, flaxen white, mirroring the ailing eyes of his blind friend.

Dawn is approaching and the duo decide to get up and put a few more hours of sand behind them before they rest during the high heat of midday.

The next few days of travel grow increasingly more difficult. The shadowy mountain in the distance moves ever closer, and so with it grows a weight in the air and the swathe of blighted ground expands. The heavier air is thick with malice, and the darkened, cracked soil is almost painful to the touch. Figures appear along the wanderers' path, faint shadows and ghosts of the past that disappear when Guthrow and his crow come near. Unseen beasts torture the night with their sordid cries that extinguish the courage of weaker men.

"Stay close to me friend, we're not safe anymore." Guthrow always looks at the crow's eyes when he speaks to it, and the crow has always looked back. Now that the infection from its beak has taken over its eyes, it can only direct its attention to its master's voice. "There are phantoms about. The demon we're after knows we're coming, and she's afraid. She'll send all of her evil creations after you, because she knows I cannot defeat her without your help."

At this moment Guthrow drops to a knee and opens one of the small cloth pouches tied to his belt. From the pouch he pulls out a pinch of sparkling white powder and sprinkles it on the head and back of his little friend. The crow is aware of what its master is doing as they have been in situations like this many times before. After a few moments the crow glows with a very faint white light. Again they walk, but now the crow leaves behind ashen white footsteps that slowly swell across the landscape behind them and cover the dark, blighted ground with a dull white that glitters in the moonlight. "This will give your body some protection," Guthrow says with more hope than fact, "and it will prevent the phantoms from following our path and creeping up on us from behind."

A normal man would have a hard time noticing it, but

Guthrow has been subject to increasing pain the last few nights and his body is becoming weak. The weathered wayfarer knows that he cannot possibly go against the entirety of the demon kingdom, and so he is going to have to find his way to the King without entering the heart of her domain.

It is no more than a day's walk to the mountain, now. The closer they move to the brooding, craggy cliff, the cooler the air becomes. The flat, sandy surface is being replaced by small, gritty rocks upon an incline that leads to the mountain's base. Small structures dot the landscape, marked in some foul language that humans have never been able to decipher. Large stones lie in the distance, and soon the dusty brown of the desert will meld into the dull blacks and grays of the mountainside.

The crow has been resting atop his master's hat far more than usual this day. A deep, gurgling hack frequents its old body. Guthrow lifts the crow from his head and holds it in his arms like a mother would a newborn. "You must survive this one last day my old friend. Soon we will have the chance to rid this planet of its dark disease. A thousand or more years we have traveled together, and it has all come down to this. If we can kill the last Demon King, we will never have to suffer their wretched kind again." With that, the crow forces out an almost clear "caw" and drops to its feet with a few weak flaps, falling gently to the ground.

Night approaches. It is no longer safe.

Ghastly howls and enigmatic gargles come forth from the shadowy mountain. The climb has become more steep. Guthrow and his crow have reached the base. On the soles of his feet, Guthrow can feel the pulse of the darkness and wicked magic that lie within the hidden kingdom. Black smoke seethes out of cracks in the rocky surface, lingering along the ground.

The lesser demons appear once more, but now they are aggressive. The dark figures resemble human silhouettes made of liquid charcoal and they float across the landscape like impressionist paintings in motion. Guthrow finds himself surrounded by their shadow and knows that he must protect the crow and himself. He reaches into a jar stationed at his right hip. From the jar Guthrow grabs a handful of lotion, then with his other hand he grabs a pinch of the white, sparkling powder from a pouch and mixes the two together. He spreads the increasingly glowing paste on his hands, then lifts them and holds out his palms towards the hostile figures. Strong yellow beams emit from his palms like spotlights powered by the sun. Guthrow slowly motions his hands around his body and across the nearby terrain, dissolving the demons which fall prey to the light and warding off the quicker and more powerful foes. "These light tricks will keep us safe for now," says Guthrow, "but the higher our road becomes the more dangerous it is going to be."

The magic light helps the duo make it to dawn, but this side of the mountain will never see direct sunlight. The peak curls over the desert facing edge and casts a dark shadow over the only scaleable side of the mountain. The shadows hide in the shade, present but not as daring as they are at night. There is no true path to follow; the wispy figures need no footpath. The crow hops from rock to rock, opening its wings for the larger leaps. It sometimes trips and needs help in finding its footing again. Guthrow moves with an ardent haste, but minds each step on the rock surface; his boots have thinned over the years and a twisted ankle would mean his doom when night falls.

A quiet pain has been lying dormant in Guthrow's forehead since leaving the oasis, but once he reached the base of the mountain it has intensified and has become an agonizing distraction. The weakness that has crept into his body can only mean that his time is near. The crow fares no better, as the infection that plagues its face has nearly covered its entire head and taken many feathers with it. Both share a ghastly white complexion and utter exhaustion, physically and mentally. There will be no tomorrow for these wanderers, one way or another. Guthrow knows this and plans for the final assault.

Guthrow adjusts his belt and the sacks tied around it. From his back he brings forward a large pouch, full of cream-colored marbles that will explode with lights and colors upon impact with the hard ground. In a moment of rest the duo finish off the remaining nourishment and dispose of the containers. Before dusk settles Guthrow sheds himself of his coat and hat. He pulls out a few jars and the sparkling white powder, mixing together a concoction that is similar to the previous night's spotlights. He empties the jars and throws them down the cliffside. Little white powder remains. The thin man spreads out the ivory cream mixture on a flat rock and uses his hands to smear the cream along the outside of his tattered coat and the top of his hat, creating a shiny glaze. "Tonight is the night, my friend," Guthrow says to the crow as he applies the last of the mixture to the brim of his hat. "You know this. Our world will be at peace once again if we finish this undertaking. The evil spawn of mankind will be exterminated and our human and animal worlds will thrive once again. I'll give you everything I have, friend, but there is not much left of me to give. My exhaustion is severe, as is my pain. I will do all I can to get you to this last Demon King so that you can do your duty. I only hope that your blindness and inability to fly will not hinder your power. May those we fight for be in our hearts this night."

Guthrow grabs his gear and equips himself. The sky grows dim. Guthrow's coat and hat shine white against the dark backdrop of the fading day. On the edge of darkness stands a man whose outside is brighter than the now fading sun, but underneath that holy shell is the dark contrast of a dying man staring at the peak of the mountain where his life will surely end.

Night strikes with a fury. The moment the sun falls behind the horizon the ghouls and demons of the mountain ooze out of the caves and cracks in droves. The black blurs their movements create conceal their true numbers, but Guthrow knows that the entire kingdom will be after him and his crow tonight. "Come to me you desperate wretches," Guthrow shouts to the wicked masses, "your time is at an end."

The mountain looks as if it has erupted with rivers and waves of black lava all streaming towards Guthrow and his crow. "Take cover my friend." The crow hops into his hands. He places his companion in a large pocket pouch on the inside of his coat, "your time is soon, but not yet."

Black bolts that pulse with energy fly through the air towards the white warrior. The glow of his clothing attracts and absorbs the ranged attacks. With his enemies still at a distance, Guthrow opens up the pouch containing the cream colored marbles and launches them into the darkness with lightning speed. Bright, smokey explosions litter the steep and rocky landscape. Clusters of demons are blown out of existence, and cream-colored smoke lingers in the air, forcing the rivers and waves of evil to flow through tight passageways.

The flow grows nearer, and more dark bolts rain from the

night sky, blocking out the twinkles of starlight that had only just become visible. Guthrow knows that if even one of these demons makes its way to him and lands a successful attack it will all be over, he has to do all he can to hold them off.

The crow peeks through the opening of Guthrow's coat. It cannot see the events taking place, but it has the ability to sense demons when they are near. The crow can perceive the horde that is surrounding them and is familiar with the feeling. There are differences this time, though. Extinction is on the table today. The desperation and utter drive to survive is empowering the demons with fear and courage. The crow also knows how weak Guthrow has become, knows that he will not be able to keep up his pace for long. The crow shivers, feeling that the last Demon King has left the safety of her mountain peak and is making her way towards the freckles of light that wage war on her kingdom.

From somewhere along his belt Guthrow grabs for another pouch that contains what appears to be dull shards of a broken mirror. He throws them into the air and they explode into a shimmering mist of electricity and light. The mist encircles Guthrow, blocking off the remaining paths between himself and the demons. Small flashes of energy strike the first few demons who dare near the electric mist, warning the rest to stay back. From this position Guthrow launches an all out attack against the dark masses. More explosions and magical light potions cover the landscape, engulfing the mountainside in a hellish blaze of white fire and ivory-colored smoke that burns through the forests of demonic creatures in its wake.

Guthrow nearly exhausts all of his supplies by the time the electric mist begins to fade. The weakness and pain in his body is escalating, his aching head will soon become too debilitating to ignore any longer. Growing holes in the electric mist allow increasing numbers of shadowborn through the defenses. It means close quarters now, and Guthrow has to do everything he can to protect his friend.

Numberless black bolts continue to rain from the skies, absorbed by the glimmering white coating on Guhtrow's clothes. The crow makes itself secure in the deep pocket in which it hides, knowing Guthrow will have to defend them both in the small arena that he has created.

Guthrow runs forward and twirls his body with greater agility than most healthy men would be able to muster. The shining white coat cuts its way through several dark masses and extinguishes their existence. The holes in the mist grow and more demons make their way into the circle. Guthrow tumbles through the air like a gymnast and spins across the ground with the speed and fury of a sunfire ballerina. Any dark being that grazes Guthrow's coat turns into a small pile of ash that becomes indiscernible from the dull gray dirt which it falls to.

Soon the wall of electric mist fades to nothing and Guthrow finds himself completely surrounded. The blur of white spins through the blackness like a figure skater with a spotlight in the darkness. Guthrow begins to slow and decides to take his hat off and use it as a weapon. This leaves his head open to the black bolts in the sky, but he has no other option. Still Guthrow twirls through the masses, but now the spin of his coat is aided by the brim of his hat which acts like a razor cutting through the thin bodies of the demons.

He blazes a path towards higher ground where he hopes to find something on the landscape to aid him. He makes his way upward to the remaining patches of cream-colored smoke to ward off the enemy attacks. The crow against his breast begins to squawk and squeak, and Guthrow understands that this is out of fear. What Guthrow does not know is that the crow senses that the Demon King is near and is about to strike.

The phantoms disperse, opening a path to the King. Guthrow has barely enough energy left to keep the darkness at bay. His white glow begins to fade. The Demon King stands with her arms outstretched, balls of black energy swirling and magnifying in her open hands. Her face is complete darkness, but Guthrow feels her death stare. She is about to launch an attack on her weakened foe.

"Now," says Guthrow to the bird at his chest, "go my friend. The time has come." The crow chirps in an unusual fashion as

Guthrow opens his coat and holds his friend in his hands. The Demon King roars evil as she claps the balls of darkness together and hurls them at Guthrow. In front of him he holds the crow. The swirling ball of darkness flies towards the duo and slams into the crow. The massive ball explodes with white light upon impact, flinging bits of light like shrapnel through the crowds of lesser demons. From the explosion emerges a pure white bird. The crow spreads its wings, lifting straight up into the sky and out of its master's hands without a flap.

The crow rises further into the sky and the lesser demons try to hide from the light that it emits. The Demon King slithers forward towards Guthrow and hurls more black energy at the weakened soldier of light. The crow drops lower and intercepts her attacks, deflecting them away from its master. The Demon King halts her charge and the angelic crow beams forward in a streak of white light that pierces the heart of the wretched soul. The Demon King bloats to an incredible size and holds for a mere moment before rapidly imploding in on herself. An atomic explosion of white encapsulates the entirety of the mountain like a snow globe. The light disperses just as the sun emerges over the horizon.

The rocky cliff is silent and empty except for a lanky body that crawls across its surface. Guthrow pulls himself to the spot where his friend collided with the last Demon King. On the ground next to a rock he finds a small, black body that is barely breathing. He reaches forward and lifts the soft body of feathers. The crow looks young again. Its body is covered in oily feathers that shine in the sunlight and its infection has fully retreated. Its black-pearl eyes are no longer cloudy, and it can see its master once again. In the reflection of the bird's eyes Guthrow can see that he, too, looks young again. His features are smooth and his yellow eyes blaze.

The end of every battle they fought had given them the strength to carry on to the next. The crusades soon became countless and the years passed by like seconds in a day. Time had caught up with them, and both man and bird knew that this holy rejuvenation would help them no longer.

With the last Demon King gone, they have fulfilled their duty. Complete exhaustion has taken over the two warriors, and they are ready for their long-awaited sleep. They rest with each other on the cliff side as the sun crosses the sky, satisfied that their world can finally be at peace. As night falls they close their eyes, never to open them again.

Kozz opened his eyes and woke with a searing headache. *Where's Caleb?* Kozz pushed his pain aside and turned to put his feet on the floor. He found Caleb sitting on a cot next to his own, reading another one of his comic books, this one with a crow on the cover.

"Kozz, you're awake!" Caleb put down his book and picked up a glass of water, handing it to Kozz. "Here. You have a fever or something."

It was true, maybe. Kozz's head felt hot but his body was shivering and soaked with sweat. He took the glass and drank most of it in one gulp. Luciele came over from somewhere in the camp and quickened her pace once she saw Kozz up and sitting in his cot.

"You stay right there and rest, mister!" She walked over to Kozz and pushed him back down into his camp bed. "You dropped like a dead horse last night, we thought we lost you." She bent down and fiddled with a bag next to Kozz's cot. "Take your heart pills. I had to force them down your throat last night and I'll be damned if I let you forget to take them again."

"I didn't forget to take them, Luciele."

"Then I don't know what happened with you, but I'll swim across the damn sea before I let you go a day without taking them. You turned all red and passed out on us. All night long you went through hot and cold flashes, moaning like a son of a gun."

"Sometimes I go through fits like this. Go through 'em when I'm angry or scared or thinking too much about the past. It's nothing to worry about, doll."

"Nothing to worry about? I was up all night taking care to

make sure you didn't die on us. I was pretty damn worried, and so was Caleb. And stop calling me doll!"

"Sorry, Luciele." Kozz reached for a cigar in his bag, but pulled back when he remembered that he had smoked the last one. "What happened last night anyways? I was sure Caleb was gonna be in trouble with Slick and the others, and I failed to protect him. I failed again. I'm so sorry."

"You didn't fail anyone, Kozz," said Luciele. "We're alright."

"Yeah," Caleb cut in. "I told them that I was infected once, but then you fell to the ground and started shaking. They thought you was gonna turn into one of the infected. They wanted to shoot you before you could attack us, but me and mom and Richard and Kelly all stood between you and them."

"Who are those two kids anyway?" asked Kozz.

"New friends," replied Luciele.

"Yeah," continued Caleb. "They're nice and believed us when mom told everyone about your heart problems. Mom showed everyone your medication and Daryll and Tim left you alone and turned back to me. But I told them straight up that I'm not infected anymore and I'm not gonna hurt nobody. I was brave, like Guthrow." Caleb shook his comic book. "Then mom and the others told Daryll and Tim that they needed to care for you and there was no time for arguing with a kid. Then they left us to take care of you and they haven't come to talk with us since."

"So in a way," said Luciele with a smirk, "you did protect Caleb again. You distracted them enough to quell the situation."

"I still feel like shit," said Kozz. "I should've been standing there with you." There was a pause where Kozz closed his eyes and sorted his thoughts. "Who's Guthrow?"

"Um..." Caleb's cheeks turned red. "Just a hero in one of my comics. This one, see? He was scared and hurt, but he still saved the world and stuff."

"Well good for him," said Kozz. He let out a deep sigh. "Lord, I could use a fat cigar right now."

"I haven't seen anyone around here smoking anything but little cigarettes," said Luciele. "I could ask someone for one if you want."

Kozz waved off the foolish suggestion.

"Be picky then. You need to rest up some more anyway. The camp is heading out in a few hours. You're in no shape to make the trek south. We'll have to saddle you up or something."

"I'll be fine." Kozz put his arm over his eyes and started snoring a moment later.

Luciele let Kozz sleep for a few hours. When Daryll, Tim, and Freddy began to round everyone up, Luciele decided it was time to get Kozz all set up to leave Siletz. She had piled most of their gear onto one of the mules and saddled the other for Kozz. He protested, but as soon as he stood up, tremors of pain ravaged his body. Kozz had to use Luciele as a crutch to stay on his feet, and she could not hold up his weight for long. He was forced to cede his pride and mount his ride.

Luciele and Caleb carried as much as they could to lighten the load on the mules. Daryll set off first and the others followed.

The members of the camp left one by one. Everyone moved at a slow pace with respect to the elderly and injured. Freddy left with his son when the camp was about half-empty, then Tim took the lead and pushed on everyone who remained to get moving before they were left behind. Richard and Kelly stopped by to check on Kozz before they left, but he was not in much of a mood to chat. Kozz was polite, but embarrassed to meet them while he was in such a fragile state. The young couple moved out and soon after them Luciele, Caleb, and Kozz followed. Tim, purposefully last to leave, helped rally and guide the stragglers.

Southward they traveled along the river's edge. They passed though the fenced entrance of the camp and left the empty town of Siletz behind. Tim was the only other member of the camp with a mule for transport. He crept up on the others from behind.

"Ya look sicker n' a dog, buddy," said Tim.

"I'm not your buddy, guy," said Kozz. "And I'm fine. Just

tired from last night."

"Was sure ya were gonna turn into one a them muties. Was ready to shoot ya if."

"There was no 'if' about it," said Luciele. "You know about his heart condition."

"Well now I do, girlie, but I didn't then." He pulled in closer to the others. "Look, it was only fer protectin' myself n' the others. I didn't want anybody to get hurt."

"It's not worth trying to lie to us," said Luciele. "You've been harassing us ever since we showed up at your camp."

"No, no. I've only been trying to protect everyone and myself. We're all on edge with this armageddon happening. I know Daryll has been tough on ya guys specifically and I don't like some of the things he does, but he's a good leader and has kept us all alive. We're all juss tryin' to survive here."

"Something's not right about that guy," said Kozz. "He's been itchin' me in the wrong spots ever since I laid my eyes on him."

"He can be eccentric," said Tim. "Sometimes gets on my nerves but I just put the anger somewhere else n' think about how it's all just gonna work out in the end."

"At least that's a positive way to go about it," said Caleb.

"Yeah," said Tim. "If he keeps acting the way he does he'll get his eventually." Tim tipped his hat to the others and backed away, taking his position at the tail-end of the caravan.

They were on a week-long journey to Blackwater. The town was named after the nearby lake. The water had been tinted black since before people inhabited the world over two centuries ago. Large coal deposits surrounded the lake and kept the water completely lifeless. The coal had been eroded by ice and other rocks into pebbles and fine sand that outlaid the area of the lake, forming blackened beaches. The town itself was prosperous and used the lake as a tourist attraction. It was a famous spot on Frostarc to find a warm drink in one of its numerous pour houses.

The front end of the band of travelers would stop during the day to allow the others to catch up. The going was slow and Kozz did not think they had a chance of getting to Blackwater in a week. Night soon came and campfires stretched down the riverside, all powered by wood ripped from abandoned homes and shops. Clear skies led to a bright night as the moons reflected in large, undulating beams across the water's surface.

Excitement flared early in the evening as shots rang out down at the front of the line. Kozz wanted to check on what it was, but Luciele convinced him to stay with her and Caleb. The front of the line was a mile or so away, but word eventually spread down that a young woman's eyes started glowing and she attacked a mother and her baby. Daryll swiftly took her down.

The night was silent as everyone in the camp pondered the

journey ahead. No one knew what the facts were about this disaster, or how far it had spread. All forms of global and interplanetary communication had ceased near when everyone could remember first hearing about the infected and their attacks. Not a person in the camp had any more of clue than the other.

Kozz found himself staring at the stars, thinking of his wife and son. His thoughts were disrupted when Richard and Kelly approached the campfire.

"Well hey there Kozz," said Kelly. "Are you feeling better now? You looked a mess earlier. We've not yet formally met. I'm Kelly, and this is my boyfriend Richard."

"Howdy," said Richard.

"The pleasure's mine," said Kozz. "You two could have put yourselves in a rough spot standing with Caleb and Luciele yesterday. I'm glad you did."

"Those bastards were picking on a little kid," said Richard. "I would've ripped their nutsacks off if they touched him."

"Sounds like something I would've said twenty years ago." Kozz laughed at the comment. "Don't let that mouth get you into too much trouble. It took me a long time to learn to hold my tongue."

"And you're still not very good at it," chimed in Luciele. She gave Kozz a wink.

"Don't worry about me," said Richard as he turned to Kelly.

He wrapped her in his arms, turning her sidelong glare into a bright smile. "I've got Kell here to keep me in check when I go too far."

Luciele pulled out a blanket and laid it out for the young couple to sit on. She made sure they were comfortable, and when she decided they were she bent down next to Richard and gripped his shoulders.

"Now Richard," said Luciele in a firm, but kind tone. "Any more talk about ripping off nutsacks or any other graphic language around my son and I'm going to have to have a word with your beautiful girlfriend. Caleb's seen and heard more in these last weeks then I ever would have wanted him to experience in his lifetime, and I don't need any more of it than there already is."

Caleb burst with laughter from the other side of the fire. He was usually on the receiving end of such a lecture. Luciele turned towards her son, and his laughter ceased. She turned back to the young man she still held in her grip.

"Yes ma'am," said Richard, flashing an "ok" sign with his hand.

Luciele squeezed a little tighter and Kelly leaned over to Richard, beaming a stare that he knew all too well. "You're not going to like what happens if Kelly and I have to get together and have a little talk about you," said Luciele. She smiled wide and turned Richard's head so he looked straight into his girlfriend's eyes.

Richard looked back and forth between the two thunderstorms on either side of him, both whirlwinds of fury that could tear into him at any moment. He submitted the only response he thought might dissipate the surging electricity which surrounded him. "I understand." And with that, the impending storms disappeared as if they had never existed. Both women remained where they were for a moment, their smiling faces as soft and radiant as ever. Luciele stood up and patted Richard on the back before walking over to her son. He looked over to Kelly who leaned back to her previous posture and tilted her head, shrugging her shoulders and displaying a cute smile and sparkling eyes that showed none of the intensity they had held only a moment earlier.

Kozz watched the entire event unfold. Richard turned towards him with a look on his face that asked 'What the hell just happened?'

"You've still got a lot to learn," answered Kozz. He gave Richard a smile that said he had been there before.

The rest of the night Kelly and Luciele were as sweet as they ever were. They shared stories with each other while Kozz taught Caleb the importance of properly cleaning his pistol, following up on the shooting lessons from before. Richard sat quietly until the night was through.

Everyone was up and off early in the morning. Tim rode up

and down the line of campsites to get the old and slow ready to go at daybreak so that they would not impede an early start on the day's travel. Kozz still felt weak from his attack the other night, but he refused to ride alone any longer. He put forward the effort to walk alongside the others.

Richard and Kelly rose and left with Luciele, Caleb, and Kozz. The entire day was a slow walk, but that gave everyone plenty of time to talk. Kelly shared that her and Richard were both originally from the city of Quartz, but had moved out to the shoreline of The Great River less than a year ago to start a life of their own together. Richard was making a living on the sea as a charter fisherman's deckhand while Kelly collected research on the mostly undocumented marine life of the western sea shores, relaying the information to the dean at her former university.

Current events left their futures uncertain and they had not been able to contact their families since the calamity started. Right now, all they both wanted was to make it back to Quartz and find their loved ones. They were worried about their families back in the city and had not been able to learn a single thing about the infestation or how far it had spread.

As they told their story, Luciele saw the young couple's strong personalities crack and falter. They spoke of their own loved ones separately, as they had never gotten the chance to know each other's family over the years. Kelly came from an introverted household that did not socialize with many others, preferring to live life in comfortable solitude in the suburbs of the city. Richard loved his family, but he considered them to be a bit crazy and over the top with their emotions and actions. They were outspoken activists who found themselves in and out of jail on a regular basis, and the couple of times he did try to bring Kelly over to meet them they were screaming at each other or somebody else, altogether too busy with their own affairs to bother much with his. They first grew to take pleasure in each other for the escape they created from their former lives, but that affection blossomed over time into a love that bound them together and sparked their plans to move out on their own.

Though the group did their best to entertain each other, the days passed slowly under the warm sun. The small masses of people that formed the caravan remained huddled in their packs and rarely spoke to anyone else. The gentle splashes of rolling waves remained constant like a metronome.

CHAPTER TEN

A Plan

The caravan arrived at Blackwater and camp was set at the edge of town behind an old bank. Daryll motioned to Freddy who then dragged an empty crate to the center of the camp where Daryll used it as a soapbox and stood with his thumbs tucked under his belt, waiting for the nervous masses to quiet and gather around. His face remained stern until there was complete silence, then he looked down at the upturned faces and a smile slid across his lips. His eyes wandered across the crowd, and Kozz thought his sight rested on Caleb for a moment longer than the rest.

"We each have our own story about how we first came across the infection," said Daryll. "I'd like to share my own. I was asleep in the house I shared with my father until I was jolted awake by the screams that blew through my open bedroom window. I thought it was just teenagers being the way they are. My eyelids were heavy and so I just tried to ignore the sounds from outside, but they didn't stop. I covered my head with my pilla' and tried to muffle the noise, but it only got louder. I just couldn't get back to sleep.

"I hear my pops moving 'round the house, thinking he was also up because of the screaming. More voices added to the fray so I thought I would git up and turn on the telepod in the living room to drown out the cries. I put some clothes on and opened the door, and as soon as I entered the hallway I heard quick movin' footsteps. Before I knew it I was hit hard in the gut and I dropped to the floor.

"My pops started kicking me. He kicked hard, even harder then when he used to come home from the taverns after ordering a few too many drinks. I hollered for him to stop. I asked him why, what did I do. Then I looked up to his face and saw that his eyeballs were lit up like old, dusty light bulbs and I knew something was wrong. His face was twisted like I'd never seen it before and I knew right then that he wasn't going to stop. The old man may have been able to deal some tough blows, but I knew I was stronger than him. I reached for his kicking leg and tripped him up, twisting his ankle and bringing him to the ground. The screaming outside intensified and I heard people run by the window. A woman yelled for help as she ran by my home and I heard her keep screaming as she continued down the street.

"Something bad was happening, that was for damn sure. I knew that he wasn't the only one like this. I jumped on top of my father and tried to hold him down, but he was somehow stronger than he ever could possibly be and pushed me off like I was a little child. He jumped up and ran into the living room. I went to stand up, but he was back before I was able to recover. He hunkered low to the ground and pounced on me like a wild animal. My pops slashed at me with something in his hand, but it was too dark for me to make out what it was. All I could see were his eyes. Their glow was fierce, and in them all I could detect was pure determination. There was no bloodlust, no anger, no fear, no love. Whatever my father had become was simply attempting to end my life, as if it were its job to do so. This monster that used to be my father had no passion in what it was doing, but I held on to a strong passion to survive. That was when I no longer saw that man as my father. I felt the desire to beat him, to end him simply because he didn't have as strong of a desire to end me.

"Outside the night terrors grew nearer and more numerous. Many people were running around screaming their heads off while others were fighting the same fight I was.

"I fought back against the monster, dodging its attacks. The sharp thing in its hand slit my skin in several places. Pops stabbed at my gut and that's when I planted a knee in his sternum. He momentarily fell back and I used that opportunity to scuttle back into my room and shut the door. Someone else was now fighting for his life in the street right outside my window, but I had to ignore his battle to focus on my own. My pistol was in the drawer of my nightstand. The monster slammed through the bedroom door and I leaped onto the bed, reaching for the gun. The glowing eyes found me as I grabbed the pistol. I swung my arm around and fired as many shots as I could before the energy charge overheated.

"I dropped the pistol and looked over the edge of the bed. On his back and looking up at me was my father, my pops. The glow in his eyes disappeared. He let out a quiet moan and then he was gone, forever. His hand opened and the moonlight that shone through the window revealed his weapon of choice, a belt buckle with big letters that poked out over its smooth edges. 'GAUCHO' it said, my father's lifelong nickname."

Daryll paused and stared at his feet for quite a while. The somber crowd held its silence in respect to Daryll's father and for their own stories. Everyone in the camp shared some recent suffering. Even Kozz felt sorry for the man, but it did not much change his opinion of Daryll's character. Luciele welled up in tears over Daryll's story, finding many similarities with her own tale. She bent down to hug Caleb and the both of them shared a moment that only they could, remembering their beloved Harold.

Daryll lifted his face and gazed upon the crowd, his expression strong and committed. He spoke again with a calm determination in his voice, sharing that he was now determined to help save everyone he could from the infection, to defeat the complacent evil that was trying to destroy them. He said that ardor and passion would defeat the creatures that attacked without enthusiasm, that attacked as if it were just something they were required to do. He laid out his plan.

Daryll wanted to camp at their current location for two nights. Tonight they would rest from the travel and tomorrow a team would be selected to go to the surplus market warehouse. The team would retrieve supplies the camp needed to make the journey south across the iced-over sea and then northeastward to Port Town. That night the camp would prepare for travel and the following day they would set off. Many of the people nodded in agreement with the plan.

Daryll stepped down from the soapbox with his thumbs still tucked under his belt and his head hanging low. Tim and Freddy worked on separating the people into their assigned task groups. Kozz joined a small group of men designated to go out into the town and find debris to use as barriers for the campsite. His team included Richard and Freddy, and several other men who were not fit to carry the weapons they held. Kozz took the lead of the group that Freddy was supposed to run and had the other men remain far behind as "guards" for the trip. Freddy held no reservations in seceding the group to Kozz as he was unsure if he would be able to run it properly anyway.

Luciele and Caleb were to help pitch tents for the campground. Daryll's story had touched Luciele, and she felt that the tents could wait until after she spoke with the man. She grabbed Caleb's hand and pulled him forward as she made her way to Daryll. He was sitting by himself on a flat rock at the water's edge.

"I'm sorry about your father, Daryll."

Daryll's gaze was transfixed in the dense fog that hung above the sea just off shore. For a moment he said nothing. Then, as if it took him all that time to actually hear the words, he blinked and turned towards Luciele. "Thank you," he said. His eyes fell from her to Caleb. "How's that boy of yours doing?"

"He is well. Listen, Daryll—"

"What was your name again, sweetie?"

"Luciele. Don't call me sweetie. Anyway, I—"

"Luciele. And your boy is Caleb, right?"

"Yes, but listen to me for a second you oaf!" Luciele sighed, taking a moment to calm herself. She waited to see if Daryll was going to keep jabbering, but he did not. "I just wanted to let you know that your story really hit me like a brick to the face. I almost broke down in front of everyone. I understand what you went through, and what you are going through now. I lost my husband to this infection, Caleb's father."

Daryll was about to say something, but Luciele gave him a

look to let him know she was not finished and he kept quiet.

"And it was by my hands that he passed. I had to shoot him in self-defense, just like you did with your father."

The man turned his sight back to the sea. "That is sad indeed, Luciele. I'm sorry for your loss as well."

"I just wanted to let you know that we're not so different. My son and I have been through just as much as you have in these last few weeks. Caleb is a good boy and would never purposely harm another. Ever since it came out that he was once infected, you and Tim and everyone else have been treating us like criminals and have been staring at my son in menacing ways. He's just a boy, Daryll. He's not going to do you any harm."

"I just want to make sure these people are protected. I don't want to hurt the boy."

"His name is Caleb."

"Caleb. I don't want to hurt Caleb. I just don't like thinking there's a threat right here in the middle of the camp. You all just walked up to us one day without any uh us knowin' who you were and that big fella started giving me a hard time and then we find out that your boy, Caleb, was infected. I didn't want to pick a fight with anyone, but you all started causing a bunch uh ruckus when we were finally getting organized around here and Tim and I decided we had to lay it out straight that we weren't goin' to put up with any trouble. All I want is the people's safety."

"When you put it like that it does seem like we brought it all with us. Truth is though that Caleb isn't infected anymore, and that's because Kozz saved him. Kozz may be a big lug who likes to push his weight around, but it sounds like the two of you share the same values. He has only been trying to protect Caleb and myself. I never even met the man before all of this started, but I know that he'd put his life in danger just to keep us from harm without a second thought. All he's doing is trying to protect, just like you are."

"We may be sharin' the same values, but we definitely don't see eye-to-eye. At least now I get why he's been so pushy." Daryll put his hat back on and turned fully towards Luciele and Caleb. "Now, you say Caleb is perfectly fine? You truly believe your boy doesn't have an ounce of infection in him anymore?"

"Kozz got it out of him a couple of months ago and he hasn't shown even the slightest sign of it since. He's perfectly healthy as far as I'm concerned and I'm not afraid that he'll turn ever again."

"Then maybe I'll have to ease up on him some." Daryll looked back down at her son. "I'm sorry Caleb. Maybe I shouldn't have been so tough on you."

"It's ok," muttered Caleb. He remained a step behind his mother.

"Well I hope to get to know you some more, Daryll," said Luciele. "I suppose I better get back to the camp though and help the others set up their tents. There are an awful lot of elderly and ill people in this camp that need the help. Do you think they'll all be able to make the trip?"

"I hope so," said Daryll. "That's why we've got to get to that surplus warehouse so we can stock up on everything we can to make the journey as comfortable as possible for them. The walk here was almost too much for most, and we took it pretty damn slow too. Our group of survivors are the ones who were left behind when everyone else ran off."

Luciele turned around and took her son back to their tent. She saw Kozz watching her from the other end of the camp. He turned away as he saw her leave Daryll's company and joined his group of men who were to head into town.

Kozz, Freddy, and Richard went forward as Kozz ordered the rest of the men to remain fifty paces behind them. He did not want to worry about having to save a dimwitted man or a jittery trigger finger shooting him in the back. They slid past the side of the large bank building that served as an edge of the camp and Kozz pulled Red from her holster. He took the lead while Freddy and Richard covered his flanks. Kozz moved with tactical precision, sweeping all areas expeditiously and completely before moving forward.

A block away from the bank was a small quad. Various

shops lined the streets all around, apartments occupying the stories above ground level. Kozz hunched at one of the corners of the grassy quad and looked around the area and into every broken window. He ducked low and ran forward to one of the trees, Richard and Freddy followed, then Kozz turned around to look into the windows behind him. He took his time, studying every darkened room and possible hiding space before pulling his shoulders back and standing tall. Freddy and Richard stayed on edge until Kozz put Red back in her holster, but even then they still held their guns up and ready.

"S'all clear boys," said Kozz. "Ain't nothing to worry about around here."

"How do you know?" asked Freddy.

"Experience," said Kozz as if it were as simple as that.

"Hope you don't mind if I insist on keeping my guard up," said Freddy. "I'm scared shitless."

"Not at all," said Kozz. "No reason to be scared though. There ain't anything around, not in this quad at least. Not a sign of anyone being here in days. All the windows are dark and quiet."

"Alright," said Freddy. He tried to stand tall and confident like Kozz, but his eyes darted every which way and gave away his ruse. "Let's see if we can find a hardware store or something then."

"Sounds like a plan," said Kozz, "but I don't think we need

to go that far. All we have to do is pop some of these doors off their hinges and find some bookshelves or other furniture to bring back. Heck, we're only a block away. We can find everything we need right here."

Kozz led them over to a restaurant with a red and white checkered pattern painted across its windows. Outside the door hung a wooden sign that read "The Checkered Omelet". Kozz opened the unlocked door and was greeted by a rancid smell that burned like acid inside of his nose. He put one hand on Red and used his other arm to cover his face from the stench. The dining area appeared untouched as if it were waiting for the evening customers to arrive. Square tables with checkered tablecloths were adorned with salt and pepper shakers and wilted centerpieces. A lattice-style wall at the back of the dining room held hundreds of varieties of wine and was decorated with fake vines that crawled along the wooden lattice. Richard entered next and cursed the offensive smell. Freddy followed last and was overcome by the odor. He started belching and had to run back outside, signaling to the others that he would wait for them out there.

The horrendous smell was stronger near the kitchen door. Both Kozz and Richard heard the buzzing sound of flies coming from the next room. Kozz pushed through the swinging door and expected to find decaying bodies scattered on the floor, but was relieved when all he found was hunks of rotten meats and produce left behind on counter tops and in cooking pots. Flies and maggots abounded. Kozz left them to their foul meals and exited the kitchen. He motioned for Richard to follow him out the front door to escape the smell so that they could talk.

"Well I think all these tables and chairs are a good place to start for our barrier," said Kozz.

"What was that smell?" asked Freddy. He was as white as a ghost and his eyes were watery. "Were there dead people in there?"

"Nah man," said Richard, "just a bunch of meat the chefs left behind."

"Oh, thank goodness," said Freddy. "First thing I thought of when that smell hit me was decaying corpses and I almost hurled."

"Calm down, Nancy." Kozz went to grab a cigar from his pocket, but his pocket was still empty. Lord knows he could have used a cigar to clear his lungs right then. "Let's grab some of that furniture and bring it back. We'll get some other able-bodied gents to help us out."

They walked back to the others who were standing guard and Kozz directed them to start grabbing furniture, then he turned his attention towards Freddy.

"Since we've got a moment here alone, Freddy, why don't you tell me why you follow those two knuckleheads around?"

"Who? Daryll and Tim?"

"Yeah, those are the two knuckleheads I'm talking about."

"Well, I dunno," said Freddy. "They just kinda put their hands on the wheel I guess. They're good at giving orders and at keeping us safe."

"I've seen them boss you around, Fred. They give you all the crap work to do. Seems to me they go ahead and run things the way they want without giving any of you other people a say in the matter."

"Well that's the way it goes sometimes, isn't it?" Freddy hung his head low. "I lost my wife and had nowhere to go until I found them and the camp. I couldn't take care of Samuel all by myself. They took me in and I just kinda do what they say 'cause I'm grateful for their help."

"They don't seem very helpful to me," said Kozz, "at least not to anyone but themselves. I think they just like to hide in the numbers. As soon as me and Luciele and Caleb showed up they started harassing us. Did you see the way they hunted down Caleb? I thought they were gonna shoot the poor kid. I know you're the one who told them what Caleb told Samuel, but I don't hold anything against you because you didn't go after my son."

"He's your son?" asked Freddy. "I thought"

"No. Caleb, no. He's not my son. A slight mix up of words. But they went after him. They were ready to kill him. I can't say that they're protective at all after seeing that. I can't side with them. I think my little group is gonna have to separate from the camp soon. This isn't a safe place for us to be."

"Well that's too bad," said Freddy. "Things may not be perfect here in our community, but Samuel and I feel safer here than we would out there all on our own. I wish y'all the best wherever you wind up bein'."

They hauled their load back to camp and rounded up a few more men to join in on the collection. Kelly volunteered her help and was scoffed at by the older fellows, but Kozz and Richard welcomed her to join along. The group spent the next several hours carrying loads of furniture back towards the camp. Most of the collection was from the restaurant, but later in the day men started to come back with doors that were broken off their hinges, sheets of painted plywood, and large furniture from neighboring buildings within the quad. A hefty amount of debris was piled at the edge of camp, and throughout the day more and more of the men left the supply train to begin constructing barriers, sandwiching the camp between the large bank building at the end of the nearest street and the water's edge.

All work ceased when night fell. An exhausted air rested on the backs of everybody in the camp that night, thick and tiring. Men and women had worked throughout the day to fully prepare themselves for the night ahead. The barriers around the camp had been set, and everybody had a place to sleep.

At their campsite, Luciele explained to Kozz the conversation she had with Daryll. She told Kozz of the passion Daryll had for protecting these people and how he apologized for treating Caleb the way he did, but Kozz shrugged it off and said that he still did not trust the man. "Something is wrong with them," said Kozz, "both of them. Something about Daryll and Tim just isn't right. They're trying to play with you."

"He was right when he said we were unfairly causing him trouble," said Luciele. "He was scared for his people because you started acting all tough as nails and then they found out that Caleb had the infection. He was right to be scared. Now I'm not saying he took the best actions along the way and is innocent of causing unneeded trouble himself, but he just wanted his people to be safe."

"That's it right there, Luciele," said Kozz. "What's with the 'his people' thing? That's exactly what I don't like. I know I started showing my muscles from the moment we met these people, but it's the way him and his lackey Tim have been treating everyone in the camp like children, or...or subjects to their god damn almighty throne that I don't like. They've been tryin' to corral us into their little peasant parade and the reason why they think we're trouble is because we won't let them. I won't let them make us their slaves just so we can hide behind their thin veil of protection. We're not any more safe here than we would be out on our own. We'd be miles closer to Port Town by now too."

"What," said Luciele, "do you want us to leave?"

"Yes, I do." Kozz lowered his voice. During the intensity of their conversation his voice had increased in volume and began to rumble. "I think we should take what we need after we raid the surplus store tomorrow and head out on our own way."

Luciele stared at Kozz for a moment and rubbed her son's back as he sat next to her near their fire, the child's head bobbing in and out of consciousness. "Alright," she said. "If you want to leave tomorrow, we will."

"Just like that?" he asked, expecting more of an argument.

"Just like that," she said. "Ever since you first came across my son you have spent every ounce of yourself to protect him. You may be bull-headed and rude sometimes like a trash-raiding whitecat, but you have treated my son and I with love and respect since the moment I met you. I owe you my trust if nothing else and will leave this collection of people if you think it is best. I still believe that there is more to these people than you give them credit for, but if you say we should leave then I will agree with you."

"Thank you, Luciele." Kozz nodded to himself and rubbed his chin. "Tomorrow then, after the raid. We'll take only what we need and move out on our own."

Luciele nodded. She wrapped a red blanket around Caleb and stood him up, then walked him over to their tent where they both disappeared for the rest of the night. Richard and Kelly were also sitting at the fire, resting quietly during the conversation between Kozz and Luciele.

"I feel sad for Daryll and Freddy," said Kelly. "They both seem like sweet guys that have been through more than some of us these last few weeks. Poor Freddy just likes all the work he gets, if just to take his mind off of things. Daryll, on the other hand, has taken a great passion in seeing everyone here through to safety. They're both good-hearted men who are just lost.

"I think Daryll has taken on a much larger responsibility than he expected and is afraid of leading all of these people. His fear is causing him to make mistakes and bad judgments, like going after Caleb, but I don't think he intends to be mean."

Kozz looked at Kelly as she spoke, but she thought he seemed to be focusing his attention somewhere behind her. He stared without blinking as he considered her words. Kelly thought he may have fallen asleep with his eyes open as his blank stare continued long after she had stopped speaking, but then Kozz shifted his focus back on to her and spoke.

"What about Tim?" he asked.

"I don't know," said Kelly. "He doesn't talk all that much. I don't know what his story is. He hasn't really ever done anything good or bad though. He just kind of does whatever Daryll tells him to do."

"I talked to him for awhile, once," said Richard. "He told me he just recently traveled to Frostarc from Erde for an extended business trip and hasn't heard anything about what is happening back at his home. That's the most I really got out of him though. He doesn't seem like that bad of a guy. Can be sort of bossy and sometimes yells at people and takes things out of context, but who isn't a dick once in awhile?"

"They both irritate me," said Kozz. "The way they look at people, the way they talk to people. The way they raised their guns at Caleb. Maybe they have sad stories and say they have good values, but the way they go about holding to those values is shit. I'll bury them if they ever touch the boy, if they ever even look at him the wrong way again."

Richard fried some sausages over the fire for himself and Kelly, then they bid Kozz a good night and took their meal into their tent. Kozz sat alone by the fire for hours, lost in his thoughts. He had to get his friends out of this town before something bad happened.

CHAPTER ELEVEN

Shots Fired

In the morning Daryll had Tim round up everyone and split the camp into two groups. In one group stood Kozz, Freddy, Daryll, Richard, and a handful of other men. In the other group was Luciele, Caleb, Kelly, and the rest of the camp. The group full of men were the selected individuals to travel to the surplus warehouse, chosen for their strength and assessed ability to adequately use weapons in case they encountered infected people on their trip. They were ten in all. Tim was chosen to remain behind with the others to help maintain an organized camp and defend it in case infected beings attacked their stronghold.

Luciele attested to her skills. "You've gone and made a big mistake assuming I'll be of no use on your little excursion. I've darn near had a gun by my side my entire life and I'll bet a prairie over a tea kettle that I can take down a target quicker than any of you."

Daryll held up his hands in defense. "T'aint that we didn't

think you couldn't—"

"T'aint this and t'aint that." Luciele cocked her shotgun. "I'll be heading out with the rest of you."

"Ah hell!" Tim hiccuped a laugh and slapped his knee. "Let her go, Daryll. Put her to use."

Luciele asked Kelly if she would watch over Caleb while they went into town to gather supplies, and she agreed.

"I don't want you to go, Mom." Caleb pulled at her dress.

"There's no need to worry." Luciele bent down and picked up her son. "We won't see hardly a speck of trouble, but I need to go and make sure Kozz doesn't get himself hurt out there. And Kelly will be here to make sure you're alright. You like Kelly, don't you?"

"Yeah, but I'm scared."

"Me too, baby. I'll only be gone for a little bit. We need to get more food and clothing and such to survive the trip."

"I know...."

He will be just fine, thought Luciele. *It should only take a few hours for us to get to the surplus warehouse, load up, and haul the load back.*

Daryll ordered everyone to go back to their campsites and cook up hearty breakfasts so that they would have plenty of energy for the day ahead. He told the surplus team to meet at the back of the bank building in one hour.

"Do you feel safe going with Daryll into the town?" asked

Caleb while looking up at Kozz as they walked back to their campsite.

Kozz was inclined to answer no, but he looked over to Luciele who glanced back at him and he decided that it would be best not to worry the boy. "I feel safe," he said. "Your mother and I will be just fine."

"I don't really feel safe with Tim," said Caleb. "He's creepy. At least Daryll has emotions, I don't know if Tim has any."

It then struck Kozz that Caleb was going to be left alone without himself or Luciele for protection. His gut dropped, but he did not know what to do. He could not leave the surplus team. They were going to need his strength to carry the load and his fighting skills if they ran into trouble, but he also knew that there would be no way of convincing Luciele to stay behind. She obviously trusted Kelly to take care of her son in her absence and Kozz knew that it was not his place to argue the decision.

Kozz bent down beside Caleb and whispered to the boy. "You still got your pistol and my knife, right?" Caleb nodded. "Keep them where you can grab them quick if you need to, and remember our target practice." Kozz stood up and saw the curious look on Luciele's face.

"What did you tell my son?"

"Just reminding him how to defend himself." The sternness in his voice was foreboding, purposefully. "Just in case something were to happen while we were both gone."

A chill wind blew from the southwest. Fog had rolled in over night and was being held inland by the breeze. The water vapor was thin enough to see the nearby area, but anything more than a quarter-mile away faded into a gray blur. The heavier gusts of wind were salty and damp as they slapped across the men and women of the camp. Condensation had built up on the tents and many people were drying their belongings near the morning fires. The sun was nothing more than a dull wash of pale light in the distance.

The group returned to camp and Kozz grilled up a fat fluff rabbit Luciele had caught the previous night in one of the snares she had set away from the camp. Even after she had skinned the mammoth rodent it still was plump enough to feed all five people at their fire. Caleb helped Luciele unpack some dried vegetables which they soaked in water and wrapped in foil to cook over the flames.

After breakfast Daryll walked over to the bank building and the other men in the crew grudgingly joined him. Richard gave a passionate farewell kiss to his girlfriend. Kozz and Luciele both took turns hugging Caleb and giving him directions on what to do while they were gone. Kelly made sure to hug them both goodbye before they left. She wished them all good luck as Kozz, Luciele, and Richard walked away to join their group.

Kozz and Luciele unhitched the mules on their way to the

bank building as the animals would be needed to help haul back as much from the surplus warehouse as was possible. They were the last to arrive to the meeting, and when they did Daryll went over some basic instructions.

"Alright everyone. Make sure to stay near and not get separated from the herd unless I say otherwise. It'll be too easy to get lost in this large town if yeh don't know it n' go off wandering around. Fred says the streets can get a little twisty and confusing. Tim here will pass out guns to those of yeh who don't have yer own. We may run into some infected on the way. Best be prepared."

"Don't have much more than some small laser pistols," said Tim as he handed them out. "Goin' to have to make due until y'all return with better stuff from the warehouse."

"I've never fired a gun before," said Richard as Tim placed one in his hand.

Tim turned and shot a blast at a nearby building. "Point and shoot," he said. "That's all there is." A black mark smoked on the brick wall. Satisfied that everyone had a gun, Tim walked back to the camp with the remaining weapons he held.

"Now from what I understand," said Daryll, "is that we do have a few expert marksmen on our team, myself included. If we run into trouble, and we probably will, leave it to us to handle it. That's me, Freddy, and Kozz." Daryll scanned the team and jolted when he saw the hard look on the lone female face. "And Luciele! The rest of you should only have to use yer weapons in an emergency when you need to defend yerself. There are so many of us because we need to carry back lots of supplies, and venturing into town like this is too dangerous to be making multiple trips."

As Daryll spoke Kozz watched Tim return to the camp and walk over to Caleb and Kelly. Kozz was ready to run back and bash Tim's face in if he bothered either of them, but Tim only handed Kelly a pistol and then he moved on. Kozz's focus shifted when Luciele gave him a light slap on the face. "Come on you big lug," she said, "we're moving out." Kozz turned to see the others walking around the building and down the street, led by Daryll and Freddy.

The streets were quiet and mist swirled around their feet as they marched into town. Freddy had once lived in Blackwater and knew the streets better than anyone else in the group, and so he took the lead in guiding everyone towards the warehouse. They passed the quad where they had gathered materials from the previous day. Several of the shops, including The Checkered Omelet, were now ransacked and torn apart. The rest of the buildings appeared just as they had the other day, still and empty.

The roads beyond the quad was littered with trash and debris. Papers bounced across the pavement, propelled by the wind. Household items were smashed in the streets, many appliances, pictures, and knick-knacks having been tossed out of windows and forgotten. The damage became more apparent as the group noticed blast marks and bullet holes around the buildings. Small fires still smoldered in places where homes once were, and dismantled vehicles lined the roadways.

Then they came across the bodies. Some were in crashed cars, some were gathered near houses, but most were just sprawled in the streets. Bones were visible, and it was obvious that most of the bodies had been where they were for at least a few weeks. Limbs were gnawed at by rodents and insects crawled across the pavement from one feast to another, unaffected by the cold morning weather. At one intersection the body count was startling. Swarms of bugs ran in rivers around the deceased and flew in clouds between the members of the crew, the buzzing so loud it was almost painful.

A few of the men became squeamish and were frightened, proclaiming that they should all just return to the camp and leave the place immediately. Daryll knew that running was not an option, so he and Freddy pushed the frightened men to the front of the pack and hurried them forward through the chaos. A few people dropped to their knees after passing the intersection and vomited in the streets. Others let out their breaths, having to hold off their breathing to avoid the putrid smells that engulfed the street behind them. Richard did not look too well himself and Luciele tried to calm his nerves.

Freddy ran over to the side of the road and into someone's front yard where he heaved behind a fence.

Daryll and Kozz went around to everyone, giving words of encouragement and trying to lift morale. After a few minutes they brought all the men back to their feet and gathered the group together. Many of them wanted to turn back, but Daryll again warned them that they would not survive the trip ahead without getting more supplies. Kozz asked them to be brave for their friends and loved ones back at the camp, those relying on the warehouse team to return with what was needed for everyone to move forward.

The group pushed onward and left the dreadful buzzing behind them. The number of dead bodies decreased the further they distanced themselves from that particular intersection. Daryll took the lead with Freddy and they marched forward, trying to inspire the others behind them. Kozz remained in the back and helped push ahead anyone who was having second thoughts. Many of the men had never seen death before, and the scene they had just walked through had shocked the strength right out of them. The stronger members of the team worked together to reignite the courage in the hearts of the terrified men. It took effort, but soon everyone was marching forward of their own will, until a terrible scream stopped the entire crew in their tracks.

Caleb was showing Kelly how to use the pistol that Tim had given her when a distant scream from somewhere in the town caught the attention of the camp. It echoed through the streets like an eagle's call in an empty canyon.

"Oh no!" one woman yelled.

"What was that?" demanded a man.

Everyone ceased what they were doing and listened, looking towards the town. There was nothing else to be heard, but that single scream was enough to instill fear in the members of the camp. Some people started to panic, some went to hide, some wanted to run into town to help the surplus team. Tim hollered orders and visited with the panicked to gain control over the situation and calm the people. "No one is going anywhere," he said to everyone in earshot. "We've made a plan and we're stickin' to it. It was just one scream, coulda been anything."

"He's right," said Kelly as she looked at Caleb. "Just one scream. Maybe someone just got spooked."

Caleb lowered his eyes to the pistol in his hand. "Didn't sound like someone got spooked. Sounded like someone who got hurt real bad." *But we've gotta be strong*, thought Caleb, *like Guthrow was. He didn't give up because he was scared. He didn't give up because he was hurt, and he helped his crow friend when it needed him.* Caleb looked up at Kelly and saw that tears filled her eyes. It was time for Caleb to be there for his friend. "Didn't sound like anybody we know, though."

"No," she said not only to him, but also to herself. "No, it didn't."

Caleb pulled her hand away from her watery eyes and held it tight. "They're gonna come back. We'll be seeing them again in no time." Kelly looked at Caleb and smiled with her wet cheeks.

Samuel ran over to Tim, but the man was preoccupied with calming down everyone else in the camp and ignored the boy. After seeing that he could not get Tim's attention, he looked over to Caleb and Kelly and ran to them.

"I'm scared you guys," he said.

"Don't worry Samuel," said Kelly. "I think they're fine. And it didn't sound like your pa."

Samuel calmed down after hearing her words. He sat down next to them and ripped out handfuls of grass from the ground. They all sat in their own personal tribulations for a while until Samuel spoke. "I'm sorry for telling on you, Caleb."

"It's ok," said Caleb. "I didn't know everyone would think it was such a big deal. I mean, I'm fine now."

"My pa still doesn't want me to play with you," said Samuel. "He's afraid that you might hurt me."

"I'm not gonna hurt you."

"That's what I told him, but he doesn't believe me."

"This is way more than you guys should have to handle," said Kelly. "You're just kids. You shouldn't have to worry about crazy stuff like this. You're both acting very mature about it." As she finished what she was saying Kelly realized that their situation was also way more than she should ever have to handle. She played with the clam shell pendant that hung around her neck and thought about Richard and her family.

The scream was deep and painful. Every person in the surplus team focused their attention down the street to where the sound had come from. A heavyset man loped out of an office building a block away, then he tumbled forward and tripped down the short flight of stairs that led to the street. Most of the group ran forward to aid the man. He was moaning in pain when they arrived. The back of his shirt was drenched in blood, and fluids pooled on the ground beneath him.

"Run," he cried out, barely able to turn his face off of the pavement towards the others. "They found us." He spit up blood and continued to cry as snot and tears and sweat poured from his face. Luciele and Richard bent down to the man's side wanting to do something for him, but his wounds were too much. "Their eyes..." said the man, weak and guttural. "They killed us...us all." He cried into the growing puddle for a moment longer before going silent forever.

One of the men from the group turned around and ran back down the street towards the camp. Daryll and a few others yelled after him, telling him that they had to stick together, but he just kept running. The man ran into the distant fog and disappeared from sight. Most everyone else in the team backed away from the building and stared into the windows, knowing something was in there that would attack them if given the chance. They decided to not venture into the building to look for the monsters or whoever else may be inside. The team was not looking for a fight. They wanted to make their way to the surplus supplies while avoiding any contact with the infected, if they could. The purpose of this excursion was survival, not revenge, and they had to move forward.

"Bastards," said Kozz to no one in particular. "Damn demons are tearing our world apart." He grumbled under his breath, seething at the thought of whatever was happening to humanity. He wanted to destroy whatever was causing it. It pissed him off, but it was damn exciting.

Fear propelled the group forward, and even Kozz found himself looking over his shoulder to make sure they were not being followed. The group, which had been spread wide when it first entered town, was now packed together like a can of sardines. No one wanted to be the odd man out if something was to attack.

But Kozz did not like crowds. He stopped in his tracks and let the others slide by him. Luciele and Richard noticed he had fallen behind the group and they stepped back to join him.

"What's the matter, Kozz?" asked Luciele.

"I felt stifled," he said.

"Being close to some of those guys is tough," said Richard. "Some of them smell like ass."

"Couldn't have put it better myself," said Kozz. "Too paralyzing being stuck in a crowd like that anyway. I could hardly turn around to see behind us. They're all scared and walkin' too fast, I couldn't scan the area quick enough at that pace."

"You really do look everywhere, don't you?" asked Luciele.

"Everywhere, darlin'." Luciele thought about reprimanding Kozz again for calling her a condescending name, but she did not feel offended by it anymore. She completely trusted Kozz, a man she had met not long ago, and she was comfortable with him calling her by that name. *That's just how he talks after all,* she thought.

Luciele watched his face as they walked. Kozz's expression was stoic and he did not appear to be looking around, did not appear to be observing his surroundings and scanning for danger. He appeared to be looking straight forward, aloof and uninterested. The rest of the men were turning their heads, craning their necks and jumping at every odd sound, but Kozz never wasted the energy. He was truly focused. After watching him intently for a few moments, she saw his eyes flicker ever so slightly. She saw his pupils change, growing and shrinking in rapid succession as he altered his focus on object after object. His senses were trained to drown out the noises of the world and listen for the dangerous subtleties that hid in the silence.

Kozz's eyes turned towards Luciele. She jerked her head backward, realizing she had stared for too long. Kozz huffed and cracked a smile as Luciele turned red in the cheeks.

Freddy stopped at an intersection and spoke with Daryll, then they changed direction and turned down a wide avenue. The rural housing was replaced by large apartment complexes and office buildings. Nearly every window was smashed, the sides of the streets glittering as the foggy mists left water droplets on the fallen shards of glass. They walked down the avenue, their feet crunching the debris with every step.

Kozz felt a heavy dose of adrenaline pump into his system as he walked down the avenue. A number of small signs told him that something had changed when the group turned down the street, though he would not have been able to say what they were if anyone had asked. The odd feeling had caused his senses to heighten and his prudence to increase. Luciele commented on his change in posture, the way he was now stalking down the street, but he ignored her to maintain his focus on his surroundings. Kozz was about to tell the others to slow down and take more caution, but the blast of a rifle shot interrupted his thoughts before he could speak and he watched Freddy fall to the ground.

Kelly took Caleb and Samuel down to the water's edge. She tried to coax others into joining, but they all chose to hide inside their tents instead. The boys skipped rocks and Kelly taught them about the variety of shellfish in the shallow waters of The Great River to pass the time and help take their minds away from any unsettling thoughts. The bang of a bullet ricocheted through the streets and emptied out over the campground. A few people panicked at the sound, but most were in control of their emotions this time around. Just like the previous scream that had come from inside the town, there was only one shot that rang out. The surplus team had guns, and they might have to use them. That meant they were still out there, and they were still alright.

Samuel started to weep again, but Caleb and Kelly comforted him and he soon relaxed. Everyone was stressed, and if people started to have mental breakdowns it would only compound the problem. Caleb asked the others if they wanted to hear a story. Kelly and Samuel both thought it would be a good idea. Caleb ran back over to his campsite and opened up his backpack. He pulled out one of his comics and ran back to the shore. They all sat down on the pebble beach and Caleb read aloud from his book.

A push.

A push and I'm falling. From where I stood a moment ago I could see the city in all of its glory as the twilight reflected glowing reds and oranges off of the glass buildings, enlivening the skyline with dancing flames. Now I'm falling. All of that beauty and end-of-the-work-day satisfaction has disappeared. The warm lights have been replaced by the blackness of the street and the scum and dirt all around it.

I'm falling. It's taking so long. I catch my image on the reflective tower as my bloated body tumbles through the air. My hat is gone and the thin hair on my head reaches upward, upward in desperation at the ledge I left behind. The shock in my aging, round face is punctuated by the excessive white in my gaping eyes. I don't scream.

Sounds are different now. The noise of the city has muffled

and louder than it all I hear the voices of my loved ones. My teenage son Curtis tells me that he'll be a professional sports player someday, my beautiful wife Shelby hums that song she wrote for me when we married, and a couple of my close buddies laugh with me like we were back sharing stories at the pub. And the wind, the wind is loud.

The people below are getting closer, a few have become onlookers and one of the cabbies is rubbernecking to see what they're pointing at. The streets are brimming with men and women who are stuck in rush-hour traffic and just want to be home. There's nothing they can do, they only watch. I must look like a chubby, spiraling silhouette against the fiery sky. I should be down there with them, I should be going home.

Will I feel the pain? Of course, I'm feeling it now. My body is out of its element and doesn't know what to do. My muscles, my organs ache in anticipation of the cement below. I don't know what to do. I ask God for forgiveness, in case that whole thing has been true all along. I wish I could call my family and tell them I love them just one more time, just one more time.

Nearer and nearer they come to me, and larger do their numbers grow. There are plenty of people watching me now. I'm sure one of them is taking pictures or video and this'll be all over the news by the end of the day. What am I worrying about that for? Never mind it.

The ground is close now, but I see the metal outcroppings

that decorate the perimeter of the building at the 25th floor. Should I even try to grab them? I won't be able to hang on. I might just wind up impaling myself or bashing my head. Doesn't matter, it's my only chance. It probably only takes me a split-second to fall far enough, but it feels like there is enough time to consider all of the possible approaches. I stretch out my arms and grip with my hands.

I'm not moving. My whole world goes haywire and my body is pumped full of adrenaline and pain and laughter in its confusion. My body was braced for impact with the solid ground and when I stopped moving it thought I had been pulverized into a pile of goop.

But I'm hanging from this wonderful decoration, this beautiful ornament. Thank God for the architect who made this aesthetic decision. My right hand is at my side, my left is up in the air. I'm not holding on to anything. My left arm is wedged between two not quite smooth, not quite sharp pieces of black metal. I can see that the arm is dislocated from my shoulder and has been shredded to ribbons. I'm dangling twenty-five stories up from nothing but my elbow joint and a few scraps of ligaments or tendons or whatever they are that haven't ripped yet.

Something feels wrong. Not pain, not yet. I can just feel my injuries. The blood trickles down my side at first, then it begins to flow. My white shirt and tan pants turn a dark red. I feel a similar sensation on my leg. My left thigh, just above the knee, is bleeding and broken. I didn't even know that my leg had hit anything, but it must have slowed me down enough so that my arm didn't sever completely.

The pain, now I feel it. The sensation hits me like a kick in the nuts. All reservations of preserving my manliness are gone. I scream, and I scream loud. If you couldn't hear me from a mile away, even over the noise of city traffic, then you weren't listening. Dangling from bits of my body I never thought I would see, my blood pours like a waterfall off of my brown shoe to the ground below and I'm screaming like a goddamn banshee.

My body turns away from the street and towards the glass of the building that I hang from, that I scream from. I'm right up against the building now and can see inside. There are office desks and machines everywhere, and about two dozen people who just stare. A couple of them cover their faces and run away from the horrid view that is me. I see these people through my reflection, and seeing what they see isn't pretty. My eyes are even wider than before, and now I'm screaming, staring at the people inside who just watch. They see a fucking maniac before they see a man in dire straits.

I scream loud and kick the glass because it feels right. I'm not even thinking about how all this movement might cause the rest of my arm to give way, I only kick and scream. A young man inside gets the right idea and picks up a chair, swinging it at the glass. He gives it a couple of good swipes before the chair breaks. Someone hands him a fire extinguisher and one smack with that does the job. The kid puts a little too much effort into it and nearly falls out of the hole he has made, dropping the fire extinguisher to the ground below. No one is standing on the pavement directly below and the metal can lands on top of an empty vehicle, its alarm adding to the maddening din of the city.

They pull the young man back and a couple of older guys begin clearing away the glass, making the hole big enough for a man my size to fit through cleanly. I'm still screaming, but I don't think my voice is as loud anymore, it's hard to tell. Inside they realize that they won't be able to easily pull me inside with my arm the way it is, so they reach out and tie a couple of cords and wires around my torso and good leg. One of them, a balding man in an expensive suit, tries to make a tourniquet around my bleeding left thigh.

The dying screams turn to cries and a couple of tears squeak out, though I think most of my moisture has escaped with the blood. My mind starts to fade in and out. A wave of warmth and blackness washes over my head a couple of times. The pain pulses and dulls until a sharp, white feeling hits my forehead and I'm out.

I wake up in a white room with a bright white light. My

eyes adjust themselves and try to focus for a solid minute. I'm all by myself. I try to feel around my body to make sure I'm actually here, but most of me is held down and cast up. I'm here alright.

A few minutes pass and a nurse walks by. She peeks in and expresses shock and joy to see that I'm awake. She must be new to the profession. She runs off to get the doctor. The doctor tells me all the medical stuff, how they had to cut off my arm to get me down and that they're doing everything they can to save my leg. I tell her that they can cut off whatever they want as long as I'm still here with my wife and kid.

I've been out for four days. She says that my wife and son have been here every day and are out right now getting dinner, but they'll be back soon to catch me up on the rest.

I rest.

I wake up to warm hands on my face. Shelby. I open my eyes and she smiles. I hear Curtis jump from his seat and he gives my remaining hand a strong squeeze. I'm still here.

Kozz saw the spark of the rifle a split-second before he heard the blast. He initially thought someone had fired it from inside one of the buildings, but now he saw the tripwire Freddy had walked through and found that the rifle was perched inside one of the smashed windows, hooked up to a device that was connected to the wire.

Freddy's face was splattered with specks of blood that had exploded out of his shoulder when the bullet bounced off of his collarbone. It was not a life-threatening injury, but it rendered his left arm useless and he wailed out in pain when he tried to lift it. At first everyone thought Freddy's life had come to an end. The man had dropped like a rock when the loud gunshot shocked the group, but it had been more due to Freddy tripping over the wire rather than being taken down by the bullet.

Freddy was lucky to escape with his life. If he had not tripped forward the bullet could have hit him in the neck or head as it likely was intended. When the group realized that Freddy was going to survive they discussed exactly who would have set up such a trap.

"Prolly somebody set 'er up to kill them diseased freaks," said one of the men.

"Coulda been someone trying to defend themselves," said Richard. "It'd be smart to set traps. The infected people probably don't have enough going on in their heads to look for traps before they walk into one."

"I think someone set it up to catch us," said Daryll as he bandaged up Freddy's shoulder. "That wire would've been tripped long ago by one of the infected. Someone must have set 'er up recently. Today, maybe. Must've known we were comin' this way."

"No way!" shouted one of the men.

"Couldn't have been," said Freddy, wincing as Daryll tightened the medical wrap. "Who would attack us?"

"Could be someone else is holding out at the surplus store," said Luciele. "Maybe they want to keep others out."

"They did it," yelled Kozz from down the street. He ripped the rifle off of its contraption from inside the window.

"They who?" asked several people.

"The demons," replied Kozz. "The damn infected. They set this trap for us. They knew we were coming, just like Daryll said."

"Not a chance," said Richard. "They're not smart enough."

"Yes," said Kozz, "they are. Luciele and I saw one try and set a trap for us back at an old farm we came across on the way to Siletz. Old man made a distraction at one end of the building and then attacked from another." Everyone turned to Luciele, and she nodded in agreement. "They know we're going to that surplus store. They haven't attacked us yet, and I think it's because they're trying to set us up. That rifle blast was a warning shot, and they know we're closing in on our destination. They don't expect us to be prepared for their attack. We need to outsmart them." Kozz pumped the rifle and held it across his body. "We need to prepare for battle."

The faces of the group looked back and forth at each other, trying to make sense of the reality and gravity of the situation.

"How do yeh know that they're planning to ambush us, Kozz?" asked Daryll. From the tone of his voice Kozz could tell that the man believed his words.

"It's in my blood," said Kozz. "My life has been one war after another. I've hunted men and learned how to read them from the trails of violence they leave behind. I can smell the bloodshed that lies ahead, I can feel the heat of conflict that surrounds us. There is a big gunfight in store for us."

Daryll considered Kozz, then he nodded to himself. "Alright everybody, you all heard the man. There'll be no turning back now, so prepare yerselves for a fight. We'll move slower. Keep yer eyes peeled for anything out of the ordinary. If yeh see something, anything where it shouldn't be, let the rest of us know right away."

Daryll took Freddy by his good arm and led him forward. The rest of the group followed, some toughened by the knowledge of what waited ahead, some more timid. Luciele swapped her shotgun for Freddy's rifle.

"It keeps bringing me back to when I shot my husband," said Luciele. "I'd rather be rid of it."

"Th-thanks ma'am," said Freddy, stammering through the pain.

"I'll help you reload it if you ever need to. Still hard to aim it with one arm, but better than this long rifle." Luciele looked over her new weapon. She liked the feel of the rifle. It had good balance and weight, and there were no upsetting memories tied to it.

Freddy was able to hold the shotgun in firing position with one hand comfortably. He managed to prop the butt of the gun against his hip so that his good hand could grip the gun and pull the slide back and cock it. *At least he'll be good for one shot*, thought Luciele.

Thick patches of fog formed in the streets as it clustered together to fight off the morning sunlight. Tension was high as nobody knew what would be waiting inside the fog or the clearing beyond. The lack of any commotion in a town that size was frightening for some, and down-right odd for everyone else.

The sensation of hearing her own footsteps echo in the streets as she walked by broken buildings, destroyed vehicles, and the occasional dead body sent chills up Luciele's spine. She was thinking about her son and began to worry about her decision to leave him behind. She trusted Kelly to look out for him, but what if something happened at the camp while she was away? What if something happened to her out in town and she was never able to see Caleb again, leaving him all alone, fatherless and motherless. Moments earlier she had been as unyielding as a rock, ready to risk the danger to get the supplies everyone needed, but now she found herself at wits end and on the verge of a nervous breakdown. Her thoughts grew wild about what waited ahead and what might be heading for her son at the camp. Luciele fought to calm herself before she made a scene in front of all of the men, and it was then that she realized the truth in what Kozz had said. Something had changed, and she had not realized that she felt it as he did until now.

Trepidation had not consumed her after she saw the mass of dead bodies strewn across the intersection, nor did she feel it after witnessing that man run out of the office building and die in the street at her feet. It was the trap that was set. *They're trying to catch us off guard*, she thought, *they're trying to trick us. The infected are smart, maybe smarter than us, and it wasn't only the tripwire trap they set, it's the fight ahead that they're leading us in to. A gunfight Kozz had said. He put the pieces together before anyone else had. The group hadn't been attacked by anything in town yet. The infected are waiting for us to get to the surplus store. They know where we are heading and they are probably gathered at the warehouse to launch a full out attack. And if they know about our group and where we are going, Luciele pondered, then that means—"*

"They are going to attack the camp," shouted Luciele. "They know we left them nearly defenseless!"

Caleb put away his comic book just as Tim approached.

"What've you kiddies been up to?" asked Tim.

"Nothing, sir," said Samuel.

"Caleb was just reading us a story," said Kelly. "We're trying to pass the time."

"You not talkin', boy?" said Tim, kicking a puff of dirt at Caleb. "Ya're not gettin' sick again, are ya? We don't need you turnin' infected again." He made sure Caleb could see the rifle strapped to his back and the pistol in his holster. "If trouble pops up, I'm the one in charge of seein' that it's taken care of."

"Leave Caleb alone," demanded Kelly. She stood up, her thin frame as tall as Tim's stout body. She walked over to him and stood on her toes, forcing her face close to his and staring down at him from above. "He's just a boy and he's done nothing wrong and I will not let you bully him you immature little weasel. Now get on out of here and leave us alone."

Tim stood solid as Kelly yelled in his face. He grinned the whole way through and patiently waited for her to be done. "Alright miss," he said with the smile still on his face, "I'll leave ya children alone for now. Just checkin' in to make sure everything was under control. Y'all have a good time now. Keep readin' ya stories."

Kelly did not move until Tim was far enough away that she felt comfortable enough to sit back down in a huff. "Now I know what Kozz was saying."

"Thanks for scaring him off, Kelly," said Caleb. "But what was it Kozz said?"

"Oh nothing," she replied, "just about how he thinks Tim and Daryll are trouble. I didn't really see it until now. I know they were freaked out when they first heard about what happened to you, but I didn't think they were holding any hostilities after finding out you were just as healthy and not infected as they are."

Caleb was about to speak, but behind Kelly he saw a man appear from beyond the bank building and start running towards the camp. Caleb stood up. Kelly and Samuel turned to follow his gaze and together they rose to their feet as well. The man held a gun in his hand, raised it towards the camp, and fired.

Kelly grabbed Caleb's arm and pulled him to cover. The man with the gun ran towards them. Caleb tripped over a rock and fell.

"Mom," he cried to himself. "Come back."

"Well we better get a move on and get what we need so we

can head back as soon as possible," said Daryll. He told Freddy to stay back in the crowd, then he volunteered himself to lead the group forward and warned the others to keep an eye out for any further traps.

"We're already walking right into one," Kozz mumbled.

The crew traveled down the center of the ominous roadway. Daryll took the lead on his own, but right behind him was Freddy and the other men, and lagging in the back were Kozz, Luciele, and Richard with the mules. The separate groups lost sight of each other as they pushed through thick patches of fog where they saw each other drop in and out of visibility. A soft breeze pushed the dense clusters of fog through the streets, adding an eerie presence to the ghost town.

After some time Richard learned to avoid noticing the dead that littered the town, but the occasional glimpse still sent shivers up his spine and produced a sinking feeling in his gut. He was supposed to help look for traps set along the way, but could not make himself turn his head to peer into the windows of the lifeless homes and down the alleyways where bodies were sure to lie. He tried to walk silently, but the footsteps of his companions echoed against the buildings and he felt like they were as conspicuous as a holiday parade marching down the streets, warning whatever was waiting for them of their imminent arrival. Trash tumbled in the breeze, Richard's nerves causing him to jump at the sight of it. Broken windows creaked in the breeze and more small shards of glass fell every now and then, crashing to the ground like cannon fire in the muteness of the air.

Bursts of sunlight penetrated the morning mists, burning spotlights through the water vapor. Richard turned his head and met Luciele's eyes, eyes which were full of tears of motherly concern. They shared a comforting moment with each other in that look, saying more than they dared to speak. They both knew that they should not have separated from their loved ones, but it was too late to turn back now.

"We're nearly there," said Freddy, his voice aching with the pain he was feeling in his shoulder, "should be just left down the next road."

Daryll stopped and turned to face the group. "There's a sea of rigged explosives in our way," said Daryll. Dozens of small piles were scattered about on the road ahead. "We'll have to find another way around."

"No we won't," said Kozz. "We can just shoot them from here and blow 'em up without risk."

"They'll know we're here if we do that," said Daryll. "Don't be a fool. We can just walk around the block and approach the surplus warehouse from another direction."

"They already know we're here, slick. Blowing up their shit won't warn them of nothing. And if they've got this road blocked, I'm pretty damn sure they'll have the others ways in blocked as well. I told you they were smart."

"We can't waste time arguing about this," said Daryll. "What you propose is stupid. The sensible thing to do is turn around and find a different route. They can't have every way trapped, at least not as well as this. Now let's go and try another street."

"What we can't waste our time doing," said Kozz, "is walking around like idiots for another couple of hours. We need to get back to that camp A-sap because I have a feeling that they're gonna be needing our help." Red had slipped out of hiding and risen to face level, her barrel staring down the road towards Darryl. "Now you best get out of the way, I'm in a hurry."

Darryl stood in shock. Freddy and the other men parted to hide away from the path of any bullet that would be fired. Luciele was unsure whether to try to stop Kozz or not, but remembered that she had told him that he had her complete trust. Richard found himself confused and moved forward to stop Kozz, but was held back by Luciele's hand. Darryl reached for his rifle, and Kozz fired.

KABLAM!

Daryll lurched forward as an explosive blast lifted him off his feet. He fell to the ground with his rifle in his hands as the burst of flame behind him was quickly consumed by smoke.

Fragments from the explosion flew in all directions. Daryll cursed as he lifted himself to his feet, but several more explosions were triggered by the flying fragments and he was knocked down again by the concussive blasts. It looked as if a barrage of mortar fire erupted in the road. Flashes of white flame burst from the pavement like lightning strikes, and black smoke billowed into the sky. Each explosion sent a booming quake that rocked the ground underneath everyone's feet. All stood unsteady in the disorienting shock waves, all except for Kozz who stood tall like a sea captain on his ship with a lifetime spent learning the motions of the undulating ocean waves.

The explosions ended and Daryll rose to his feet once again. Behind him was a war zone. Nearby buildings on either side of the road had taken damage from the blasts, their rubble falling into the newly formed craters in the street. Smoke lifted from the burnt tar and was taken away with the wind.

"You fucking moron," shouted Daryll. He reached for his rifle again and aimed it at Kozz. "You might've killed me! You might've killed us all!" Kozz stood where he was, unmoved. Daryll shook with anger, but he looked at the faces of everyone around Kozz and saw fear and disapproval in their eyes. He lowered his weapon with a raging sigh. Daryll was in visible turmoil, everyone able to see him fighting his own emotions. He pushed his rage aside and put his weapon away. "I suppose the way is clear now. Yeh all prepare yerselves. If they're waiting for us, they know we're here now. I suggest Kozz lead the way from here on out, just in case any of those explosives weren't triggered by his idiocy."

"I agree," said Kozz. He walked to the head of the pack, and stepped right past Daryll. "Let's move. We're in a hurry."

Luciele and Richard were the first to follow and they hustled to catch up with their friend. Everyone else came after, Daryll and Freddy taking their places behind all the others. Kozz marched onward through the smoldering street and made it through without trouble. An older man behind him tripped over a crumbling pile of tar and sprained his ankle, but Daryll acted as a crutch and helped the man get through the uneven throughway.

Kozz found Red in his hand once again as the warehouse came into view, her satin finish sparkling in the sunlight. Bold letters reading "SURPLUS" hung outward from the building over the sidewalk. The street seemed as lifeless as all of the others, and Kozz did not see any traps laid in their way.

They walked toward the building, everyone else falling further behind Kozz as he approached the warehouse. The surplus shop itself was only two stories tall, but it was wide and stretched quite a way behind the taller apartment buildings which surrounded it. A chain-link fence with barbed wire separated the yellow-brick building from the street, but the gate was broken and had been tossed out into the road. Across the street from the warehouse were more apartment buildings, and at street level was a pub that took on the look of an old time saloon, equipped with rustic lettering on the unbroken windows, weathered columns that ran across the front deck, and a pair of double-arched swinging doors which looked as if a man with stirrups and a ten-gallon hat could walk right through them at any second.

Kozz scouted for signs of trouble in the windows of the apartments and down in the alleys between the buildings, but he could not find anything. Still, he knew that something would be waiting for them inside the warehouse. He stopped in front of the chain-link fence and turned to the others as they caught up to him. "Get your weapons ready, people. We're gonna have to fight before we can get to those supplies."

"Go on ahead Kozz," said Daryll. "Knock on the door, they're waiting for yeh."

"Hush yourself," said Luciele. "Act like a man or I'll start whooping your behind like the child you're behaving as. This is serious and you better take it so."

"I'm scared," said Freddy. "I don't know if I can go in there after all I've seen."

"I'm scared too," said Richard. "But we have to do it. I have to do it for Kelly, you have to for your son. We all have to for everyone at the camp, or we won't be surviving the days ahead.

You can do it, man."

"Alright Kozz," said Daryll. "You and me. We'll go in first. I'll open the door and you take the first look inside."

"Sounds as good as any plan I can come up with. Let's move quick, there's multiple storms brewin' and I don't want any of us to get caught in the rain."

Daryll walked through the crowd and made his way to Kozz. Together they moved towards the front of the building. Kozz placed his ear on the door. "There's something in there alright." Daryll moved to the side of the doorway and Kozz stood straight in the entrance way. He nodded to Daryll. Everyone else stood scattered in the street behind them as Daryll turned the doorknob and pulled open the door. Inside Kozz could only see darkness, and all he heard was quiet. He took a step forward and a dozen pair of eyes lit up in the blackness. "Shit." Red reacted as soon as she saw the glow.

KABLAM!

One pair of eyes was gone in an instant, but the rest retaliated. Inside the floating eyes fired their weapons and Kozz dove to the ground behind the brick wall. Laser shots beamed out of the open doorway and burned holes in the brick. "Run," yelled Kozz and was repeated by Daryll. Everyone in the street ran into the saloon and down the alleys on either side of it. Richard grabbed the reins of the mules and led them down the wider of the alleys. Daryll ran with the others and Kozz kicked the door shut before getting back on his feet and turning down the side of the warehouse. Holes burned through the door, the laser fire melting the metal. Daryll found cover down one of the alleys as the door burst open and out ran several of the infected with guns drawn.

Tim fired his rifle and took out the lone gunman with one well-aimed shot while panicked people ran towards the shoreline. Kelly and Caleb had grabbed for their guns, but the excitement was over before they could do anything with them. Samuel had run inside a tent and hid.

"I ain't never seen one a 'em use a gun before," said Tim. "Couldn't a been an infected. Musta just been a maniac."

"His eyes were glowing," Kelly huffed as she lifted Caleb from the ground. She rushed over towards Tim with Caleb trailing right behind her. "I saw them," she said, "we both did."

"Nonsense," said Tim. "It can't be. Ya kiddies must be seeing things. Scaring yaselves with ya stories."

"He was one of the infected," said Caleb as if it were just a matter of fact. "Doesn't matter what you think, Tim. They're smart, just like Kozz said. We've got to be careful."

Tim snarled at the way Caleb spoke to him. "Doesn't matter what ya say, boy. What's done is done. The man is dead and we don't need to be worrying about what he was or wasn't." Tim looked down at Caleb. "Where'd you get that pistol, boy?"

Caleb took a step back and put the gun back in the holster he had under his shirt. "It's mine and that's all you need to know."

Tim was about to reach forward to grab it, but decided against it. "Then that's all I need to know. Keep it safe." He walked back towards camp to put things back in order.

Caleb wanted to go and see the body of the man Tim had shot. Kelly tried to convince him otherwise, but he needed to make sure the man was not still alive. They walked over to the bank and found the young man's body covered in blood from a hole in his chest. Caleb thought he saw the man's eyes flicker as they approached, but the body did not move again.

"I only wanted to see if we could help him," said Caleb. "That's all I want. I just want to save these people like Kozz saved me. I know it's possible. Why can't we just bring them back to normal? Why do we have to kill them all?"

Kelly did not think Caleb was directing his questions specifically at her, but she felt that he needed an answer. "Because sometimes it's hard. Sometimes it's too dangerous to try to save someone. If Tim hadn't shot this man he might have run amok in the camp and killed some of us. It's just not possible to save everyone."

Tears rolled down Caleb's red cheeks. "No. It is possible.

Just because it's hard doesn't mean we shouldn't try. If my mom tried harder, maybe my dad would still be here."

Kelly felt the power of Caleb's emotions and knew he only wanted to do what was right. She looked at the young man lying dead on the pavement and saw Richard's face, but it was only a flash of her fear taking over. It was not him. Kelly knew that if Richard turned into one of the infected she would want to do whatever was possible to bring him back, and then she realized that Caleb felt that way about everyone. "Why should anyone suffer this fate over another?" she asked herself.

They moved away from the dead man. Kelly took the time to rest on the bed of grass and warm herself in the brightening sun. She was falling asleep, thinking of her family back in Quartz, when a far-off explosion ripped her out of her dream. She sat up and saw Caleb standing nearby, looking into the town. She felt rumbles underneath her as more explosions shook the ground. Black smoke lifted into the air, rising above the few low patches of fog that still hung in the streets. She heard shouting and cries coming from the camp and turned to see everyone running around in panic again.

Tim hustled to calm the crowd once more and Kelly went over to help. She wanted to alleviate as much stress from the others as she could, but found it impossible to do so as she suffered through her own terrors. After some time she gave up on her efforts and looked back towards Caleb. The conflicted child was staring into the city.

She walked back towards where Caleb stood near the last patches of dissipating fog and she thought she saw something running in the street.

"Caleb," she said.

"I know, I saw them too."

"Them?" she asked, "more than one?"

"Yeah."

"We need to go," said Kelly as she grabbed Caleb's hand and started back towards camp. He resisted. "Caleb," she shouted, "let's go! I promised your mom I would watch out for you." He let her lead him away, but looked over his shoulder as he ran.

"We can try to help them," he whispered to himself.

They ran back to camp and Kelly warned the others of what they saw. Tim immediately called his defense team forward and ordered everyone else to hide in their tents. Samuel ran over to join Kelly and Caleb, but Tim shouted at him to go back in his tent and he did as commanded. Tim told Kelly and Caleb to run away as well, but there was no convincing either of them. Tim's defense team gathered and Kelly knew that they were going to need her help. Besides Tim, his team consisted mostly of elderly and injured men who were not fit to make the journey to the surplus warehouse. She did not have much experience using a weapon, but these men were going to need whatever help they could get in the fight. Caleb refused to leave the defense front as well, determined to find a way to save however many infected people he could.

Gunfire crackled from somewhere in the city, the distant sounds bouncing down the concrete and metal ravines of the city streets. Kelly grabbed Caleb's hand. She squeezed hard and was hurting the boy's boney fingers, but he did not care. They heard more than one shot this time. Dozens. Hundreds. Out there somewhere a big fight had started, and for Caleb and Kelly another was about to begin.

Tim split his team into two groups and had them hunker down behind the two strongholds the camp had built along their outer wall. The strongholds were nothing more than larger and denser piles of chairs and tables, but they were going to have to work. Shots were fired from outside the camp. Several infected people with glowing eyes peeked around both sides of the bank building, using the walls for protection.

ticka-ticka-ticka

Laser weapons fired into the camp. Blackened marks were left on the makeshift blockades as the weapons rained down fire upon the campsite. Tim was the first to return fire. His initial shots missed their targets and tore away at the stone structure of the bank building. Other men fired back as well, but the frequency of their shots was low and they had poor aim. Kelly crawled to the side of the blockade and laid flat on her stomach. She stuck her gun through a hole in the wall and fired blindly at her assailants.

ticka-ticka-ticka tew-tew-tew ticka-ticka-ticka

A couple of the infected had fallen, though no one knew or cared who had the lucky shots. Caleb refused to shoot back, and no one took the time to push him into it. He sat and wondered if those that had fallen were still alive.

The wall of furniture held against the first round of blasts, but the laser shots would soon take their toll and begin to penetrate the defenses. A few infected appeared on the roof of the building and fired down at the camp below. The defense team moved closer to their barriers to avoid the attack from above, but the rest of the camp was vulnerable. Shots were fired into the campground. One blast blew through a tent and the two twin sisters ran out screaming. Shots continued to fire and one of the women was taken down. The other sister stopped running and turned back to her fallen twin, dropping to her knees and wailing over her lifeless sibling. Laser fire speckled the landscape in black burn marks. The woman mourned despite the danger, and others evacuated their tents to run for the protection of the rocks down at the shoreline. The elderly and sick moved slowly, and Caleb watched as many of them fell, one by one.

What about them? Caleb asked himself. *What about saving them? That's what Tim and Kelly are doing, why aren't you?* Caleb wrapped his arms around his knees and pulled them into his chest. He rocked back and forth as the loud gunfire, shouting men, and crying women all mixed together in his mind and made him dizzy. He felt sick from it all. *You want to help the infected so bad, but why aren't you helping everyone else?* He saw Samuel run out of his tent as several blasts ripped through it. The boy ran towards the sea but tripped and hit his knee on a rock. Caleb watched as Samuel laid on the ground, rolling in pain. He tried to get up, but he could not put weight on his hurt leg. He started to crawl towards the water, crying for his father. *I have to help him.*

Caleb stood up and ran for Samuel. Kelly turned around and screamed for him to come back, but he ignored her. Tim saw Caleb run to Samuel and ordered the other men to focus their fire on the rooftop. The defense team blasted away at the infected above. One was hit square in the head and fell forward over the ledge it was perched behind, landing on the hard ground below with a loud crack that was heard over the gunfire. It screamed a deathly wail as light beamed from its eyes. The others on the rooftop were forced to take cover as Caleb made his way to Samuel and did his best to lift his friend off the ground. Samuel cried in pain and his knee had already swollen to the size of a grapefruit. Caleb acted as a crutch for Samuel and dropped him off where the others had taken cover, then he ran back into the camp.

More infected appeared on the roof, all women. They blasted away at the defense team that was huddled in the barricades below. The walls of furniture were smoking heavily from all the laser fire and were beginning to crumble. One of the women on the roof saw Caleb darting across the camp and took aim at him. Caleb ran in and out of tents, searching for anyone who had not made it to the safety of the rocks. The woman on the roof kept shooting with her pistol, but Caleb was too far away to make an accurate shot as he ran to the twin who was crying over her fallen sister. He tried to pull her up from her kneeling position, but she would not budge. Laser blasts landed near Caleb as he tried to get the living twin to run to the shore.

Should I try to shoot back? I won't be able hit anything. The woman next to him screamed as a shot tore through her arm. *Doesn't matter, it's my only chance.* Caleb pulled out his pistol and aimed it square at the woman on the roof. He fired his gun and she fell on top of one of her murderous friends. Light beamed from her eyes as she was shoved over the rooftop ledge and bounced off of a stone outcropping. *That push was all I needed.* Caleb was amazed that he had landed a perfect shot from such a distance, but then he saw Kelly aiming at the roof. She turned towards Caleb and he heard her yell "I got her! Run Caleb, I got her!" So he was not an expert marksman, but he had still decided at that moment that killing the infected person was necessary to save a human life. He felt his heart mature in that decision and he decided it was right.

Caleb snapped the woman out of her sorrowful paralysis and she stood up of her own volition, running over to the rocks without needing Caleb's guide. When he was sure there was no one left in the tents Caleb ran back to the outer wall and crawled to the barricade where Kelly was. He pulled out his pistol and started firing alongside her. Tim ordered everyone to keep blasting away at the infected while he ran over to grab furniture from other sections of the wall to throw on their barricades.

Wooden piles were completely burned through by laser blasts, forcing people to move to less fortified locations. The corners of the Blackwater Bank were torn away by gunfire, but very few of the infected had been taken down. The camp found itself in a losing battle and needed to figure out a plan before their defenses fully collapsed.

Infected men and women ran out of the entrance to the warehouse and spread out across the street, taking cover behind destroyed cars and in the doorways of neighboring buildings. Two hid in the warehouse doorway, and another two fired from second-story windows. None of the infected took notice of Kozz as he moved along the side of the warehouse, instead they focused all of their attention and firepower on the saloon across the street. Kozz took advantage of his situation and decided to find a way into the surplus store and sneak up on anything waiting inside.

The mules were scaring themselves into a frenzy and Richard was having trouble controlling them. He led them to the back of the saloon where the sounds of the gunfire blasts were not as deafening and tied the animals to some pipes that stuck out of the ground. Luciele remained at the front of the alley and pulled out her rifle. She lowered herself to the ground and hid from her prey as if she were in a hunting blind. In the other alley Freddy and Daryll hugged the saloon wall to avoid the heavy fire which targeted them. Daryll was the last of the team to find a place to hide, and many of the infected saw where he had run to. Inside the saloon most of the men cowered, but a couple crouched near the entrance and fired back.

Kozz hustled down the side of the warehouse and found a locked back door. He kicked the door handle and it flew off. The door glided open with ease. He could not see a thing inside other than where the front entrance was. Bodies moved about in the dim light at the front of the store, but everything near his location was pitch dark. The noise of gunfire inside the building was like a thousand feet stomping inside a gymnasium. When the infected fired from inside the building the flash of the shots flickered light throughout the warehouse and gave Kozz brief moments to study his surroundings. *Doesn't look like any demons are left in here other than the ones up front, the ones trying to kill my friends.*

Luciele took her time and followed her prey as it moved behind a destroyed vehicle. Her rifle swayed as the infected man did. He moved from one car to another, almost methodically. Luciele took in a deep breath and held it. The infected man hid behind a vehicle, stood to fire, hid again, and then ran down the road to another vehicle. Luciele pulled the trigger, and the bang from her gunshot squelched all other gunfire in that moment.

BAM!

The man's head received a new hole right between his eyes and he collapsed to the ground. His body twitched and strained as the light burst from his orifices and he screamed a guttural cry of anguish and defeat. Richard ran back down the alley and almost tripped over Luciele, not expecting to find her where she was. He saw the dozen or more faces with glowing eyes firing weapons in his general direction and whipped out the gun Tim had given him. In the second-story window of the warehouse was a woman firing a semi-automatic laser rifle at the saloon. Her body jerked with each shot fired and she waved the weapon around like a lunatic. Richard raised his blaster and fired unskillfully at the woman, not even hitting the building he was aiming at. The woman took notice of his attempts and directed her fire at Richard and Luciele. They both jumped against the saloon wall as a torrent of laser fire blistered the opposite side of the alley.

An infected woman ran from her cover at the warehouse entrance and made her way to a vehicle just outside one of the alleys. Freddy watched the woman run across the street and could not believe his eyes.

"Emelia," he whispered.

"What was that?" asked Daryll.

"Emelia!" Freddy shouted her name and ran towards the infected woman. Daryll tried to grab Freddy by the collar, but he missed and lurched back as laser fire singed the back of his hand. Freddy's injured arm fell out of its sling as he ran, but he took no notice. "Emelia!" he shouted again. "My Emelia! It's me! It's Freddy! Your Freddy!" He screamed in pain as laser fire tore several shots into his right leg, but he limped onward and around the vehicle where the infected woman waited for him.

"Oh no," said Luciele. She watched Freddy emerge from the other side of the building and heard his heartbreaking cries.

"He's going to get himself killed!" said Richard.

"My Emelia!" cried Freddy as he approached the infected woman. "Samuel and I were so scared, so alone without you.

Wait 'til he finds out that you're back!"

The woman's glowing, solemn eyes rested on Freddy. She watched him without emotion, her body stiff and her face as blank as a board. Freddy rounded the side of the vehicle and raised his arms to wrap around her. She watched his hands rise and then she raised hers to attack, jolting forward with her fingers wrapped tightly around his thin neck.

Foomph!

The infected woman, Freddy's former Emelia, let go her death grip and dropped to the ground like a sack of potatoes. Her eyes blazed with white fire, and she screamed in such a way that it brought Freddy to his knees. Daryll's rifle blast had taken out the back half of her skull and destroyed the creature she had become. Freddy kneeled over his wife's fallen body and put his good arm under her, pulling her to his chest. He held her up with the one arm and cried into her remaining ear.

Crossfire whipped across the street, and Daryll knew he had to get Freddy to safety. He leaped behind the vehicle during a momentary break in fire and raced towards his companion. In the middle of the street Freddy held his Emelia close to his heart and was hit in his side by a blast. Daryll tried to pull Freddy away, but he shrugged off the man who had shot his wife and remained where he was. Another blast hit Freddy in the chest and he still did not move. The infected in the buildings nearby took notice of the men in the street and focused their fire. Daryll made one last effort to pull Freddy away before running from the onslaught of blasts that targeted their location. Freddy was hit several more times in his back and chest before a shot blasted into the back of his skull and he collapsed over Emelia's fallen body.

Inside the warehouse Kozz skulked towards the front of the building. The total darkness made for easy cover, but it forced him to take his time walking around the pallets of materials and piles of supplies that had been ransacked and thrown all about the floor. Only once did he trip over what could have been a heavy sack or a fallen body, not taking the time to find out which one it was. He counted the number of infected he perceived to be in the building. Seven from what he could see, but he felt like there had to be more. Three were up on the grating at the second floor windows, and four were taking turns at the doorway in the front entrance. Firing Red would give away his location, and Caleb still had his knife. Kozz had to find something else in the warehouse to use as a weapon.

There was a hunting supply section in the warehouse, but Kozz knew that all of the weapons would be magnetically locked, and without knowing the proper codes to unlock the weapons it would take him a long time to make use of them. The darkness made it difficult for him to know where he was going, but he opted to find the sporting goods section.

Locating the correct area of the store was easier than

expected. Kozz knew he found the sporting section when he stumbled over the various sport balls that were scattered up and down one of the aisles. Most of the expensive equipment was locked, but on the next aisle Kozz found a sledgeaxe like the kind he and other H2O farmers used to chop away at large blocks of ice. It was encased in a plastic mold that prevented it from being used until after purchase, but Kozz slammed the blunt edge of the sledgeaxe into the concrete floor and shattered the molding. The noise it made was loud, but the nearby gunfire echoing against the walls drowned it out. *This bitch is heavy, but those damn demons won't see me coming.*

A pair of floating eyes appeared around a shelf of goods. *Maybe smashing the sledgeaxe on the floor like a mallet on a gong wasn't the brightest idea,* thought Kozz, *but it doesn't look like those damn demons see well in the dark either.* The pair of floating eyes moved slowly, turning back and forth to examine the area and squinting to focus better in the darkness. Kozz heard the infected person step on a piece of the broken plastic molding. As the infected eyes looked down to see what it was, Kozz lifted the sledgeaxe behind his back and raised it above his head, aiming for the black emptiness right behind the creature's eyes. The sledgeaxe fell and Kozz forced it down with all his strength, his hand sliding down the wooden handle as the metal raced towards the floor. He felt no resistance until the axe bounced up off the concrete floor. The eyes beamed as the creature's head rolled down the aisle. A small voice gurgled as if trying to scream and then the eyes went dark forever.

Kozz stepped away from his kill, feeling liquid pool around his feet as he stepped. He hoped that none of the other demons saw the light show that had rolled across the floor, but part of him did not care if they did. Kozz's blood was pumping, and it felt good. The demon's dead head rolled to a stop as it hit an end-cap display of fine cigars. Kozz pocketed a box in his bag for safe keeping.

Outside, Daryll ran back into the alley he had been taking cover in earlier. He went to the rear of the building and leaned against the saloon wall, letting his body sink down into a sitting position. Of all the people he was trying to lead to safety, he could not even protect the person he had taken under his wing. Daryll shook off his sorrow and got to his feet. *Freddy was foolish anyway,* thought Daryll. *He knew well enough that his wife was gone. That monster she had become tricked him and killed him. There were no worries of bringing people back from their infected state until Kozz and his friends showed up. Now everyone thinks they can save their lost loved ones. Well there was no saving Freddy's wife Emelia, there was no saving my father, and no saving anyone else. We've got to save ourselves. I've got to help everyone else in this camp before they lose their lives like poor Freddy.*

Daryll moved to the entrance of the alley and tried to find a good position to launch an offensive attack, but the stream of opposing laser fire did not give him much to work with. He decided to search for somewhere else to attack from and backed down the alley again, finding the rear entrance to the saloon. The door was locked, so he punched through one of the small diamond-shaped windows next to the handle and unlocked it from the inside. On the coat rack he found an old, dusty cowboy hat. He grabbed it and tried it on. It was a perfect fit.

Luciele held her position in the other alley and continued to snipe off the infected one at a time while Richard provided cover fire. Luciele was not a very fast shot, but she had precision. Richard had taken down one of the infected and so had Daryll, and with Luciele's three that meant they had eliminated about a quarter of their attackers. She had not seen the men inside the saloon hit anything and rarely saw them so much as fire back. Luciele wondered where Kozz had been this entire time, but she trusted that he was in the least amount of danger of them all and probably had a plan in mind.

Kozz crept down the aisles and was a little disheartened to find that none of the other demons were alarmed by the bright lights of their fallen comrade. He was looking for trouble and marched up the grated staircase that led to the catwalk where a couple of the demons were using the upper walkways to shoot from the second-story windows. Kozz pulled himself up the railing with one hand and held the sledgeaxe low to the ground with his other. Stealth came naturally after living a life such as his, but the darkness and noise made the effort unnecessary.

Kozz slithered up to a hefty man whose head was hanging out a window as he fired down at the street below. Kozz lifted the heavy hunk of metal and swung it sidearm, slamming the blade with all of its momentum into the man's back, splitting his spine in two. The man's body spasmed and launched itself out of the window with the sledgeaxe still in its back. *Damn,* thought Kozz, *I was just starting to have fun with that.* Another pair of glowing eyes on the catwalk surprised Kozz and ran towards him, but Red slid out as soon as Kozz lost his axe and she fired a canon blast that shook the walls of the warehouse.

KABLAM!

The flash of explosive gunpowder lit up the building like a firework. At a window further down the catwalk the woman firing the automatic rifle turned towards Kozz and pulled her weapon away from the window. Red swung over to the infected woman, but before Kozz could pull the trigger he heard the distinct *BAM!* of Luciele's rifle and saw the woman's head explode like a water balloon full of bloody chunks.

Through the window Kozz witnessed a scene straight out of

one of Caleb's stories. The swinging saloon doors burst open and several men hustled out, all armed with rifles and pistols that blasted away at the infected varmints across the way. Last of all to emerge from the bullet-laden saloon was Daryll in his ten-gallon hat, shiny boots, and bold GAUCHO belt buckle. The men took cover using the columns on the deck of the saloon. The columns blistered away as fire rained down upon them, but the men launched an offensive and ravaged the enemy's defenses. Daryll dropped to a knee just outside the swinging doors and fired his rifle at the enemy lines. Luciele and Richard held their position and continued to fire, enlivened by the sudden support.

Kozz saw several of the demons run back inside of the warehouse for cover at the sudden onslaught. He fired through the steel grating he was standing on, the bullets bursting through the metal frame and ripping through the bodies of the demons below. Blood spilled in pools, and soon the street once again was silent. When all the shooting had finally ceased, Kozz exited the building and joined the others as everyone gathered in the street. They formed a circle around Freddy, the only one of their group who had fallen in the fight.

"Poor soul," said one man.

"Poor fool," Daryll corrected. "Was a good man, even if a stupid one. Who's goin' to take care of yer boy now, Fred?"

"He was kind," said Luciele. "A good father, too. We should

take his body back to camp and hold a proper burial."

"Sure," said Daryll. "His boy will need it."

"Let's get a move on," commanded Kozz. "There's shooting coming from the camp."

"Oh no." Luciele put a hand over her heart. "We have to hurry."

Richard ran back to the rear of the saloon and unhitched the mules. They were shaken, but hidden enough from all the carnage and were not overly frightened. Everyone heard the crackle of distant gunfire coming from the camp-side of town, and they knew they had to be quick. Inside the warehouse Kozz found a bulk pack of everlights to help the group see in the darkness. He cracked some open and threw them about the warehouse, creating small patches of light in the aisles. Luciele grabbed the remainder of the pack from him and handed out one everlight to every person so they could guide themselves through the store and find what they were searching for. Daryll laid out a list of items that the entire camp needed, everything from food to heavy coats to medical supplies. He ordered everyone to search out specific items from the list and bring back what they found and pile it near the front entrance. Kozz and Luciele were in charge of strapping the supplies securely on top of the mules. Daryll announced that anyone could bring back anything they felt like their loved ones would need for the journey so long as they could carry it on their back.

Faint sounds of gunfire continued to pop in the distance.

"We need to go now, Kozz," said Luciele. Her nerves made her voice shake. "The camp can't hold out for long, they need our help!"

"They really do," said Kozz. "Let's run off, you and me. These guys have enough guns to protect themselves, and enough muscle to carry back a heavy load of supplies. They've only got kids and geezers defending the camp."

"My little b-b-boy," stuttered Luciele, "I can't stay here knowing he's being shot at. We need to g-g-go now."

"I'll tell Daryll and the others," said Kozz. He jogged from the mules over to Daryll who was standing over the growing pile of supplies resting outside the warehouse entrance. "Luciele and I are gonna make a run for the camp."

Daryll spit out a piece of grass he had pulled from a patch beside the warehouse and had been chewing on. "We need you both here to help carry back supplies." Kozz went to speak, but Daryll continued on before he had the chance. "I hear the gunfire. If they're still shootin' that means they're still livin'. They can hold, Tim's a great shooter and has seen combat before."

"Tim's only one man," said Kozz, "the rest are next to useless. We took the best gunners with us and left them with barely anything to protect themselves with.

"If we don't carry back enough supplies none of us'll be

surviving the trip we have to make. If we all run back we're bound to get separated and could get picked off one by one. Some of these guys can't even run. It's too dangerous! I'm in charge here and I command you to keep packing them mules. This is what's best for everyone!"

"My boy is going to die if we don't help them soon," said Luciele. She stomped over and shouted louder than Daryll, forcing him to stop and listen. "Kozz and I will go ourselves. You'll have to find someone else to pack those mules. If we don't leave now it might be too late, if it isn't already."

"I want to go too," demanded Richard as he exited the building. "Kelly's in danger, and every gunshot I hear rips into my heart. I have to make sure she's ok."

"I can't be having everyone leave on me like this," shouted Daryll. "There's goin' to be no one to carry back the supplies we need, so what was the point of comin' out here if we're all just gonna go back and die anyway?"

"He's right," said Kozz. Everyone looked at him, shocked by his agreement. Even Daryll looked surprised. "You should stay here, Richard. Luciele and I know how to shoot, and you're not much good in a gunfight. I'll make sure Kelly is just fine for when you return with the others. They need you here more then we will." Richard wanted to protest, but he kept silent and nodded. "Luciele and I are going. We'll see the rest of you there later on."

Kozz opened his box of fine cigars and pulled one out, sliding it under his nose as he took in its earthly perfumes. He put the one cigar in his jacket pocket and placed the remainder of box in the growing pile of supplies, making a mental note to look for it later.

"Pack those mules heavy," said Luciele. "They can take it. You boys will be fine." Kozz and Luciele backed away and ran down the road. Luciele took one last glance at Freddy as they ran past his body, and the cool steel of Harold's shotgun, her husband's death, caught her eye. She never wanted to see it again.

They both took long strides and hustled as fast as they could. Luciele's hunting dress gave enough room for her gait, and Kozz's large body had no trouble in keeping up. All of the traveling they had done had built up their endurance and they were both able to run for long stretches without a break. They knew that they needed to hurry and so put in every ounce of energy they had.

Only a handful of warriors remained at the front lines. Many had fallen back to the protection of the rocks along the shore, but Caleb, Kelly, Tim, and a few others burrowed into their fortifications and volleyed their attacks whenever the opportunity rose. They had taken down some of the infected, but the opposing torrent of gunfire only seemed to grow stronger. As time went on they found themselves having fewer chances to fire back. How many infected they were facing was unknown, and their defenses were collapsing around them. They crawled as deep as they could under their barricades, but time was not on their side.

The infected attackers had become more bold, moving towards the barricades and entering through the weakened portions, launching their barrage from various angles. The daring infected which attempted to hurdle over the wall of furniture were easy to pick off, but more were trying in rapid succession and soon the camp would be overrun. Caleb had moments where he felt a pain in his heart for not trying to help bring the infected back to sanity, but he knew now that it was impossible to help them all.

The defenders were outmatched. Some infected started to run straight for the beach and Tim took down as many as he could. As time ticked by the pockets of safety shrank as the walls burned away. Soon the last defenders were crammed together in a tight bubble of protection, but that too was being blasted apart.

Several infected broke through the barricade at once and those remaining on the front line scrambled to take them down. One man was hit in the shoulder and fell to the ground in pain. Tim quickly took down two of the infected, but then his weapon jammed. Caleb fired his pistol and hit another square in the chest. The blast knocked the infected man backwards, but he recovered and fired back at Caleb and the others. Caleb closed his eyes and fired blindly, and when he opened his eyes again the man was thrashing on the ground as the white glow in his eyes beamed towards the sky.

KABLAM!

BAM!

Caleb recognized the canon crash of Kozz's gun. More infected broke through the barricade, but they quickly turned and fired back into town. Tim took another man's pistol and fired at the infected while they were distracted. Caleb and Kelly crawled out of their cubby holes and saw that the infected were all firing at the bank rooftop where Kozz and Luciele were peppering the infected with bullets. They hunkered low and held the barrels of their guns along the roof's ledge like guards in a watch tower, firing repeatedly at the glowing eyes below.

The camp's defenders erupted from their hiding spots and fired everything they had at the remaining infected on the street in front of them. There was nowhere to run and the residual twenty or thirty infected fell like flies in a poison mist.

When not a glowing eyeball remained Luciele hustled down the roof's fire escape. She ran to her son and dropped her rifle to the ground, picking up Caleb and squeezing him as hard as she could. Kozz sat down on the roof ledge and took in slow breaths. He loved the excitement of it all, it made him feel young again, but the extended running and adrenaline-fueled fighting required his heart to pump excessively at an accelerated pace. The ache in his chest reminded him of his age and brought him back to reality. His pills were keeping him alive, but they could not do enough to stop the pain. Once his heart reached its breaking point every pump felt like a punch to his insides. He let the pain run its course as he watched mother and son bask in each other's presence in the heart-warming scene below. He pulled the cigar from his jacket pocket and lit it up. The stogie tasted moist and mossy, different than his usual brand, but it still relieved the fire in his chest. The smoke swirled in his lungs as it flowed with his breath, and it let him rest.

A couple of hours passed before the remainder of the surplus team arrived at the camp. It may have taken them longer to gather supplies without Luciele and Kozz around to help, but no one would have arrived in time to save the camp had Kozz and Luciele not split off when they did. The mules were fully packed with bags piled high and hanging off every side. They also dragged a makeshift sled that several of the men helped push from behind. The sled was stacked with crates of munitions and packaged foods of all sorts. All of the men walked in with as much as they could carry on their backs and looked completely exhausted. They were lucky enough to have no trouble on the return trip, other than having to walk through the eerie, corpse-filled streets once again. Richard stayed with a couple of the older men who lagged behind the main group. He was one of the last to return and when he and Kelly saw each other they ran into each other's arms.

Most of the people on the shore did not come out of hiding until the surplus team arrived with its bundle of supplies. Samuel ran from the rocks and searched for his father. He looked all around for him, asking the others where he was. The men of the surplus team were all speechless and could not give Samuel the answer he needed to hear. He asked one after another until Luciele heard the boy's questions. She grabbed his shaking hands and knelt down beside him. Luciele spoke softly and told Samuel that his father had passed on, his death in sacrifice to the protection of all the people in the camp and to protect his son. Luciele mentioned nothing about his mother Emelia and instead left the boy to remember his parents as the loving mother and father that they were.

Samuel started crying as soon as Luciele began to speak, but his wails turned into cries of denial. Luciele held him close, trying to calm the boy, but he refused to believe that his father was gone. Daryll walked over and told Samuel that it was true. Samuel was silent as Daryll spoke. His sobs sank deep inside until all that could be seen was the pain on his face. Kelly came over to help Luciele comfort the boy, but he was as emotionless as a stone and had gone mute.

It was decided that every able-bodied person would help dig graves for the fallen members of the group. Nearly a quarter of the camp had been killed in the fight. Freddy's body would be buried at dusk, a funeral held for him and all others lost in battle. A grassy knoll south of camp on the sea's edge was the chosen location. Daryll assumed there would be more lost than his fool of a friend Fred, and so he had made sure to grab some shovels from the warehouse.

With much of the day still ahead most of the camp members found that all they wanted to do was sleep after such a harrowing morning. Tim and Daryll did their best to round up enough diggers for the graves, but many were too frightened to leave their tents at the camp, Samuel included. He sat at the opening of his and his father's tent, staring out into the town of Blackwater. Luciele tried to coax the boy into joining their group around their campfire, but he ignored her.

Kelly told Kozz and Luciele about the odd way Tim had been acting towards Caleb before the fighting started, how he had threatened and bullied the young boy. Kozz and Luciele looked at each other, both regretting their decision to leave Caleb alone with Tim around.

"That's it then," said Kozz. "We're gonna have to leave this camp behind and go out on our own." Luciele nodded as Kozz spoke. "Daryll and Tim may be trying to save the lives of all these people, but damn them for threatening a child and pushing us around like we've been nothing but trouble."

"What do you plan to do then?" asked Richard.

"We'll head out tomorrow before the rest of them do," said Kozz, "and we'll only take what we need. Shouldn't be any trouble staying ahead of the rest of the pack."

"And you are both welcome to join us," added Luciele. "We'd love to have you along. You've become good friends."

"Yeah," said Caleb. "I'll miss you guys if you don't come with us. You have to!"

Richard and Kelly both considered each other's facial expressions. "We'll have to talk about it," said Kelly. "Thank you though, we'll definitely consider it."

"Yeah," said Richard. "It's a tough decision. We have to make sure we do what we think is best for us as far as surviving the long trip to Port Town and then finding a way to Quartz. Let us sleep on it."

"Sure," said Luciele. "Take your time and let us know your decision in the morning."

The burials were solemn and exhausting. Afterwards large portions of food were handed out in celebration of the bounty that was gathered from the surplus warehouse. Everyone used the opportunity to fuel their bodies for the journey ahead where food would be rationed and they would all be pushed to their physical limits. Luciele tried once more to get Samuel to join their camp and share a meal, but he was content to sit where he was and stare into town. Daryll walked over later in the evening and put a plate of food in front of the boy. After Daryll had left Luciele watched as Samuel took the plate and went into his tent. She did not see him again for the rest of the night and she went to sleep wondering if the boy was going to be alright.

Kozz woke before sunrise and started packing his belongings. When the sun peaked over the horizon he grabbed one of Luciele's and one of Caleb's toes and shook them gently until they both woke up. Luciele looked rather perplexed, but Caleb woke up giggling. Kozz smiled and left the tent, letting them get up at their own pace. They all had their belongings wrapped up and put away as everyone else in the camp began to rise.

Richard and Kelly walked over from their tent, wrapped in blankets to keep warm in the cool morning, and sat down with the others. They both offered to cook up breakfast and fried up a heaping pile of grits and opened several packages of peppered bacon.

"We've decided that we would like to go with you if the offer still stands," said Kelly after everyone was finished with their meal. "We thought that it might be more wise to travel in the larger group with all the others, but you all are our only friends in the camp and we've both come to dislike Tim and Daryll. We don't trust them like we do you."

"The offer still stands," said Luciele with a smile. "Welcome aboard."

"Yay!" yelled Caleb. He ran over to Kelly and gave her a big hug. Then he jumped up on the rock they were sitting on and hugged Richard as well.

"Glad you'll be coming along," said Kozz. "We'll be heading out fairly soon, so you might wanna start packing. I'm gonna head over to where all the supplies are being held and grab some for ourselves."

Richard and Kelly did as requested and started packing their gear right away. Luciele and Caleb followed Kozz over to the pile of supplies. They hauled their near-empty bags over and started filling them up with food, medical gear, and other miscellaneous supplies. Caleb's coat was badly torn from yesterday's fighting and so Luciele grabbed him a new puffy blue jacket from the pile of clothing.

The supplies were right near Daryll's tent and he came over to see what was going on.

"Grabbing stuff already?" he asked. "I thought our plan was to hand this all out in an orderly fashion this morning before we left." Tim came over to stand by Daryll's side.

"We're heading out on our own, slick," spat Kozz. "We

think it's better for us to get away from you and your little buddy Tim. This way we can stop interfering with your plans, and you can stop harassing our little Caleb."

"Is that so," said Daryll. "Well this pile of supplies our camp gathered from the surplus store was intended to be used for this camp, not to share with other travelers."

"Ya sayin' ya tryin' to steal our food and medicine, partner?" said Tim.

"We're only taking what we need," said Luciele. "We've put in our fair share of work and deserve our fair share of the reward. We need this to make it over the ice fields to the south."

Others from the camp gathered around the scene, interested in what the commotion was.

"Looks like yer takin' a wee bit more than you three are goin' to need," said Daryll.

"Richard and Kelly have decided to come with us," said Luciele. "We're grabbing what they need as well." She raised her voice as she turned to the gathering crowd. "Any of the rest of you are welcome to come with us. We aren't putting up with Tim and Daryll's oppressive leadership any longer." None of the people in the crowd took interest. As she scanned the faces they turned away from meeting her eyes, then she spotted Samuel and walked over to him. "Would you like to come with us Samuel? Caleb could sure use someone to play with. I know you miss your mom and dad, but we can be there for you now. We can help you if you want our help." Samuel pushed Luciele away and ran over to Daryll's side, hiding behind his legs.

"Looks like y'all've got a small group there," said Tim. "No one else wants to join yas."

"That's fine with me," said Kozz. He went to grab more packages of dried meat, but Daryll moved to block him. "Look, slick. You're either gonna get out of my way or I'll have to force you out of my way."

"Yer not taking the supplies these people are goin' to need to survive," said Daryll.

"What's fair is fair," said Luciele. "We'll take what we need, but you can have my mules. Your group is going to have a lot more to carry than we will, and some of these people can't hold much on their backs. You take both the mules and let us take what we need and we'll be on our way. You'll never have to bother with us again."

Daryll turned from Kozz's glare and looked at Luciele. Tim tried to speak but Daryll quieted him, wanting to ponder his thoughts. "Ah'right," he agreed. "Take what you need and be on yer way." Daryll grabbed the reins of the mules and walked away towards his tent. He hitched them and turned back towards Luciele, Caleb, and Kozz. The "GAUCHO" took off his hat and held it against his chest. "Have a safe trip. I regret our differences and wish you no harm." He turned away and walked into his tent.

"I'll make sure they don't take too much," Tim yelled over to Daryll. He looked back at Kozz and held his hand over his new rifle. "Hurry up now. Grab what yas need and get lost. Take that infected kid as far away from us as ya can."

Kozz grimaced and wanted to pound Tim's face in, but Luciele put a calming hand on his shoulder and eased his tension. They filled their bags to the brim. The weight of their backpacks would be grueling to carry, but Richard and Kelly walked over with a sled they fashioned out of their tent cover. They were able to throw some of their supplies in the fabric sled and pull it smoothly across the ground. Kozz found the box of fine cigars he had set aside for himself and it was the last thing he grabbed.

All packed up and ready to go, the five of them walked through the crowded camp and looked at the faces of those they were leaving behind. As the small parade left the town of Blackwater Luciele turned back to see Daryll standing outside his tent with Samuel standing close at his side. The child had made his choice. She shed a tear for the boy and did not turn back again.

CHAPTER TWELVE

Glacier Crossing

It wasn't as bad this last time, thought Kozz, *my heart didn't hurt as much. It feels like the weight of a boulder has been lifted off my chest and I can breath again. Luciele and Caleb are the medicine I should have been prescribed a decade ago. Even those kids Richard and Kelly have helped to ease my tension.*

I feel strong again, alive again. My heart beats as strong as a lion's. I let my mistakes cripple me, and my son's death destroy me. All these lonely years spent on this ice block have been tough, but in the midst of all the chaos and otherworldly carnage I find myself feeling more at ease than I have in a long time. Battle has been my life, and it has returned. Family has been my reason for life, and in my friends I have found a family. I must find her, my dear Priscilla. I should have never left.

"I'm so sorry, Caleb," Luciele cried into her son's shoulder. She still did not forgive herself. "I'm sorry I left you behind, I thought it would be more safe in the camp."

"It's ok mom," said Caleb. He gave his mother a strong squeeze. "I'm still here. That's all that matters. Kelly took care of me and everything turned out alright in the end. None of us got hurt. It's impossible for you to be with me a hundred percent of the time."

Luciele released her son and nodded. No, she could not be with him all the time, and that was the problem. She once shared that responsibility with her husband, Harold, but he was now gone. Even when Caleb was away from his mother and father he was cared for by his grandmother, Harold's mother, but she was gone as well. Luciele was now all alone in caring for Caleb, and sometimes the weight of the responsibility felt as if it would crush her. On the surface she tried her best to be strong for him, but inside she worried that she was not a good enough parent to watch over Caleb all on her own, especially in the middle of the crazy world they were now in. She longed for her fallen husband and wept in silence as the group marched south towards the icy wilderness.

They spent the nights in abandoned homes until they had traveled far beyond the outskirts of Blackwater. The campfires of the men and women they left behind flickered along the northward horizon, but after a few days of walking they could no longer be seen. The shores of The Great River were covered in mounds of slush which melted away during the blue skies of the day. The further south they traveled, the larger the slush mounds became, and the longer they remained throughout the day.

The frozen landscape in the south was different than the near lifeless ice fields in the north that Kozz had been accustomed to, especially near the sea. Southern ice pines dotted the landscape like dandelions in a see of white alyssum. Their bare stems extended high into the air where pliable branches spread wide with their hair-thin needles, covering the wide areas underneath them like large canopies. Their light and rubbery attributes allowed the snow to slip off their branches, creating a crater-like formation of built up snow around their perimeters.

Sheets of ice stretched across the sea's surface, but it was not thick enough for crossing. The group needed to reach the solid glacial ice farther south that would allow them passage across the vast sea. The cold shallow waters were alive with fish of many varieties. Small abandoned docks and marinas lined the water's edge. An expansive flock of gulls swam in the waters and nested on the shore, feeding on the wealth of fish and hatching their young during the warmest season of the year.

Kozz and Richard did not want to bother the wildlife, but Kelly was absolutely obsessed with every little critter she found. At one point she sneaked her way close to the nesting gulls to catch a better look at the freshly hatched nestlings and found herself bombarded by the aggressive adults. She ran away screaming and found refuge in Richard's arms. The angered gulls continued their assault and everyone was forced to run a short ways before the birds stopped attacking.

The southern glacial wall was more striking than they had expected, none having seen it before. The thin ice that stretched across the sea had grown thicker during their journey, but the glacial wall was a staggering blockade of ice that stood twenty feet above their heads and appeared to rise taller like a mountain beyond its face. Not one in the group knew how far east or west it extended, but it at least spanned the width of The Great River and would serve as their passage over the sea.

"Shit," said Richard, "how the hell are we going to get up that?"

"There," said Caleb, pointing to a dip in the glacial ice near the edge of the frozen sea. "We might be able to climb that part."

"There is water pouring out of that dip," said Luciele. "It's a stream of ice melt."

"The river ice is thinner near there," said Kelly. "What if one of us fell in?"

"There might be another way," said Richard.

"There isn't," said Kozz. "Look around. There isn't another

break in the ice as far as I can see, and we didn't pack any climbing equipment. That stream is our only choice."

The wall of ice was the beginning of the southern ice cap. On this side of the world it was broken by the warm habitable valleys, but the ice wholly consumed the other uninhabited half of the planet where the south and north ice caps met without interference.

Kozz made the decision to scale the obstacle, and everyone else followed. The stream fell into the sea from a couple of feet above the water's surface, dropping a small waterfall into the icy water. They had to walk a short way on the sea ice to get to the dip in the glacial wall. The sea ice near the shore was strong enough to hold each person's weight, but the closer they walked to the waterfall the thinner the ice became. Kozz took the lead, and everyone spread out from each other to reduce the strain on the frozen water. They clung to the glacial wall where the ice was at its thickest.

Kozz reached a point where he could see cracks in the ice a few feet away from himself and knew he could move no further. He could not make it over to the lowest point in the ravine without falling into the ice-cold water. The waterfall was still several feet away, but the erosion had been slow and the v-shaped valley was wide with a gentle slope. They were going to have to scale the wall where they were. Kozz reached above his head and could just barely feel the lip of the eroded wall. He felt for something to grip, but there was nothing more than snow and smooth ice. He asked for Richard to pull out his hammer and tent spikes which were thick and specifically designed for the ice that they knew they would be traveling over.

"We really should have thought to grab some climbing gear from that pile of supplies," said Luciele.

"No kidding," replied Kozz. "Dumb mistake on our part."

Kozz raised his frigid hands and hammered a spike into the ice. His first attempt ripped off a chunk of the glacier that fell to his feet and slid off the ice and into the sea. He tried again, his shifting weight causing the cracks below himself to grow longer, and planted a spike deep into the glacier. He stood on his toes and slammed the sharp back end of the hammer into the wall, then he pulled himself up with both arms, his weight sinking the hammer into the ice and bending the tent spike. His feet clamored for something to aid his arms and he found nothing until Luciele walked over and grabbed his feet, pushing him up onto the icy slick surface. Kozz held to his hammer and spike until he gained enough traction on the slippery slope to hold himself. He found several small crevices which gave his feet some friction to hold on to.

Luciele lifted Caleb and Kozz pulled the boy up on top of the sloped wall. Next came Luciele, and then Kelly, and finally Richard. They all managed their way onto the glacial ice and slid down to the bottom of the v-shaped erosion of the stream. The stream was small and not much of a hassle to avoid, but crawling up the other side of the slope was going to be tough.

"What about all the others?" asked Caleb. "How are they gonna get up here? I don't think they are all gonna be able to climb this thing." His concerned eyes met the exhaustion and sorrow in the eyes of his friends. "What are they gonna do if they can't make it?"

Everyone looked at each other, not knowing what answer to give the child.

Kozz asked Caleb for his knife and Caleb gave it to him. He turned around and crawled back up the ice to where they had all climbed the face. He pulled out another tent spike and used it to help himself climb up a little further, then he pounded the spike into the ice and pulled out a rope from his sack. He hung the rope down to the sea ice below to measure it and cut it off at that length, then he tied the rope to the spike and put the rest back in his pack before sliding down to the others.

"That will help them," said Kozz. "It's the best we can do. They should have some sort of climbing gear that can help them out, too."

Caleb nodded. "Thank you," he said to Kozz. *It is the best we can do,* Caleb thought, *and they're just gonna have to do the best they can with it.*

Richard handed out spikes to the group. Everyone held one

for each hand, except Kozz who gripped the hammer in one. They used the spikes to pull themselves up the slick incline. Fatigue set in as some parts of the slope were slippery and difficult to surmount. Kozz took the lead and used his hammer to tear little divots in the ice where the others could stick their feet in to give their arms a rest. Every two steps forward came with one step back, but they each conquered the arduous climb and heaved for breath when they reached the top of the glacier. To one side they could see the iced over waters of The Great River stretch into the horizon, and on the other side the glacier grew in mass and appeared to have troughs and crests like ocean waves. Kozz slammed another spike into the ice and let down another rope into the eroded valley for those behind them to use. Caleb smiled at this as the group moved away from the edge of the glacier and set up camp on top of the block of ice.

The wind kicked hard throughout the night. Caleb woke up before the sun and had to excuse himself to take care of nature's business. The cold air and blistering winds made it painful to be outside the barrier of his tent. The night sky above him was filled with billions of stars, all vibrant in the clear black sky. Caleb looked out towards the sea and saw that the fog had taken over the lower landscape. In that fog, though, Caleb thought he saw a small light flicker, something brightening up the fog in the far distance. The wind howled with a fury and blew cold flecks of snow at Caleb's back, pushing him in the direction of the faint light. "Come back to bed," his mother yelled over the wind. *I hope they make it,* thought Caleb. He turned around and went back into his tent for the night.

The following days were war against exhaustion and frost bite. Everyone consumed more food than they were accustomed to, using the energy to heat their bodies and move their feet forward one step at a time. It felt as if for days they were slowly making their way uphill, trudging through drifts of snow, their feet aching from stepping on the hard, uneven ice. *If there was anywhere we would be safe from the demons it would be here on top of this glacier*, thought Kozz, *but we would never be able to survive long enough to wait it all out.*

Days passed before they were traveling on a noticeable down slope. A blizzard of stinging snow pelted them from every direction, the wind whipping the frost around in cyclones. Only after a long journey downhill did the wind let up, allowing the snow to drift lightly to the ground and land in loosely packed fluff. Before they knew it they were walking on the earth again, the snow drifts blurring the line between the glacier and the permafrost they were now standing on. They never saw where they had left The Great River behind, but it was now far out of their sights.

Plowing through the piles of snow, they pushed onward

with their eyes glazed over. The energy had been zapped from their bodies by what felt like an eternity of frigid travel. They turned northward after leaving the glacier behind and eventually found an abandoned home where they spent a couple of nights resting and recovering from their journey.

CHAPTER THIRTEEN

Heartache

Kozz barreled down the corridor, explosions blasting away the structural integrity of the building behind him. Armored men and women blocked his passage to the entrance of the Narnkazi Complex. They fired their weapons, unleashing a flurry of plasma which disintegrated the walls around him. Kozz's glossy black armor reflected the fire of the explosions he left in his wake and absorbed the gunfire that he was unwilling to dodge.

The coilgun cannon fused to the armor on his left arm whined as it powered up and pulsed with firepower, shredding the enemy's defenses with high-velocity expansion bullets. The two power-armored guards who remained were taken down with two swift blasts from Red's smoking barrel. Kozz charged through the steel door with his bulbous armor and dove off to the side as an inferno of flames roared through the complex entrance as if it was an industrial furnace.

The quad within the complex filled with Narnkazi warriors.

Kozz reached into his explosives compartment and pulled out a handful of pulse grenades, throwing them in every direction. The grand room filled with smoke and bolts of electric light. He seized the opportunity to run down a large hallway which led to the location of his primary objective, his orders being to eradicate the Narnkazi Regime and eliminate the Narnkazi Prime Dictator. Kozz tossed proximity mines around the entrance of the hall as he ran through it. Narnkazi warriors chased after him and triggered the explosives, collapsing the steel and stone structure and closing off the hallway. Kozz slowed his pace and marched towards the unguarded elaborate wooden doors in his path.

He opened the doors and found rows and rows of pews filled with people and at the opposite end of the room was the Narnkazi Prime Dictator reading from a document at a lectern. The audience turned towards Kozz and looked at him with fear in their eyes. A woman stood up within the crowd, it was Kozz's wife Priscilla. "No Kozz. Don't! Please!" She did not make any sense, and why was she here listening to the preachings of the leader of this bloodthirsty anti-Cooperation regime? No matter, he would take her away after completing his duties. The Prime Dictator remained where he was, staring at Kozz from behind his podium. Red found her mark. "No!" screeched Priscilla. Red fired and filled the room with her blast. The bullet screamed down the center aisle and punctured the chest of the dictator, destroying the heart of the man.

Somehow the dictator still stood. He stumbled down into the aisle with his hands over the gaping hole in his chest and walked towards Kozz. The dictator fell at Kozz's feet. He rolled on to his back and stared up at Kozz with his dead eyes. Jake's dead eyes.

Kozz awoke with a cavalcade of emotions parading through his head. Though he had released many of his personal demons, his memories still haunted him. The dreams would not go away.

CHAPTER FOURTEEN

Port Town

Looming in the distance were the darkened suburbs of Port Town. From the rocky outcrop on the hill where they stood, the group could see the sprawling cityscape that was before them. A grid of streets was hidden under the swath of buildings. The city's size, complexity, and density was unlike any other place on Frostarc.

But the city was wrong, stripped of its liveliness. Port Town was the metropolis of Frostarc, a bustling city that could stand strong against any of the major cities in the Cooperation. Even Quartz, the only other large city on the icy planet, could not compare to Port Town in size. The skyscrapers in the heart of Port Town looked like empty silhouettes, shadowing the silent city below and serving as a ghostly monument to what the city once had been.

But on second look, those skyscrapers were not completely dark, and a focused ear revealed that the streets were not silent. Port Town may have been wounded, but it was still alive.

People roamed the streets, looking worried and frightened. Airships hovered over the city, circling the skyscrapers like curious flies. It was awfully dark for a city, but it still emitted enough heat and light for Kozz and the others to feel its energy from where they stood.

Is it safe? thought Kozz. *Are our people in control, or did those demons take over? They know how to play tricks, and learned how to use our weapons. I wouldn't be surprised if they figured out how to fly our ships and run our cities.*

We have to go in. Luciele and Caleb need to reach the quarantine zone. Richard and Kelly need to get to Quartz to find their families. I need to get to Erde and find my wife, my Priscilla. There is nowhere else for any of us to go, and there are no other options other than getting to the heart of that city.

No use trying to sneak through a city of that size, we're just gonna have to march right on through and fight our way past the danger. I might not be able to protect everyone all of the time, but every one of these people following me is my responsibility. I offered them help to where they need to go, and took them under my guard. I must get them to the quarantine zone, I must protect them through to the end of this journey.

The outskirts of the suburbs were as spread out as any small town on the other side of The Great River. The fenced yards decreased in size as they moved closer to the city, and the buildings became increasingly taller and thinner to accommodate more living space as the claustrophobic air of the city settled in. Faces appeared in windows and peaked around corners, but their eyes did not glow. Luciele, Kelly, and Richard tried to reach out to some of these people, but they ran or hid as soon as they knew they were noticed. Some figures followed the group through the streets from a distance. The creepy stalkers crept closer, but Kozz pulled out Red and let her beaming scarlet surface swing at his side. The potential thieves and miscreants backed off for the time being.

"I don't like this," said Caleb. "These people don't look nice."

"Just stay close to us and you'll be alright, baby," said Luciele. "Those people are nothing more than rats. They'll try to take from you what they can, but they'll run as soon as we show them we're not scared of them." Luciele turned to Kozz. "What do you think is going on?"

"The city's in chaos. There's no order left out here."

"Then where are the police?" asked Kelly, "or the military?"

"I betcha they're all just on lunch break or something," said

Richard. Luciele and Kelly both gave him a flat stare while Caleb chuckled and Kozz let a smile lift one of the corners of his mouth. "What? I'm just trying to lighten the mood."

"They don't have the manpower to keep watch way out here in the suburbs," said Kozz. "All hell broke loose in this city. It looks like a war was waged here, just like in every other godforsaken town we've passed through. They probably lost a lot of good soldiers to the demonic sickness that's taking over and had to fall back to the center of the city. I bet the Cooperation's forces are holding their ground in downtown where the quarantine zone is, that or they jumped ship and left this world behind." That last comment dropped everyone into a somber mood, leaving even Richard unable to strike back with a witty joke to ease the tension. What if there was no escape from this madness?

They searched for vehicles to borrow or tools they could use, but everywhere had been ransacked long before they arrived.

Richard spotted their first infected city-person as it chased a man and woman down the street ahead. The woman found a sharpened wooden rod on the street and turned to stab the demon in the throat. It cried a wet scream as light jetted from its eyes. The woman turned and ran after the man who had left her behind.

The daytime was dark with a dreary atmosphere and tall

buildings blocked out the sun, but as night fell it became a different and more dangerous story. The stragglers who roamed the streets during the day were gone, and larger groups funneled out of hidden alleys. Kozz knew that these were the gangs that had taken over the undefended streets. Anyone caught out at night without a large group of others to protect them was in trouble. Up ahead was a group of twenty or more, all dressed in dark clothing to hide their numbers in the blackness of the night. Kozz kicked open the next door he saw to his left and hurried the others to get inside.

Kozz led them into a tight hallway with a carpeted staircase which led up to a closed wooden door on the second level of the building. Kozz held Red close to his chest, ready to defend the doorway as the gang approached, but the bandits in black never arrived. Kozz looked out of the broken door and saw that the immediate streets were empty. He sighed in relief, but with a modicum of disappointment.

They needed to find somewhere to spend the night, and this building appeared to be as good as any other. Luciele was at the top of the flight of stairs with Caleb and tested to see if she could open the door. It was locked. She knocked on the door and shouted into the wood, searching for an answer on the other side. She heard nothing and knocked again. Luciele pressed her ear to the doorway and heard a low mumbling coming from the other side, something she recognized but could not place. "Hello," she shouted, but again found no answer.

Kozz was wide enough that he touched shoulder to shoulder on either side of the hallway and had to turn sideways to slide past the others to make his way to the top of the staircase. "Thank the lord I don't have too much of a gut anymore after all of this walking," he said as he pardoned himself past Kelly. He pushed his shoulder into the door to test it's strength, and did so once again with more force for certainty. Everyone moved a step or two down to make room as Kozz backed up. He was snug against the walls and flexed his arm muscles to gain more traction as he raised his foot to kick in the door.

Click.

"Shit," Kozz shouted, "everyone down!"

Boomph!

Splinters flew like shrapnel in the air as a hole the size of a basketball blasted through the door and the slanted ceiling above them. Kozz and the others all fell down the staircase, piling on top of one another with Kozz's heavy mass weighing down on everyone else.

The door was pushed open from inside and in the doorway stood a short old man with long gray hair which melded into his long gray beard. He pointed the barrel of his electron pulse gun at the pile of bodies at the base of the stairs, his bold brow casting a shadow over his eyes. Kozz held on to Red all the while and had her pointed at the crest of the staircase during his entire fall, holding her there as the old man showed his presence.

"Don't shoot!" shouted Caleb from somewhere in the pile. His voice was muffled by the bodies of his friends. "Please, don't shoot!"

The old man turned his head as if pointing a good ear to the source of the sound. "That a kid?"

Kozz did not know if Caleb was yelling to him or the old man, but he was glad the child spoke up when he did. "Yeah. A young boy. Also his mother, two young lovers, and me. We're not here to hurt you."

The old man stood with his mouth open, staring at Kozz as if slowly understanding the words he said one by one. He closed his mouth and nodded to himself. "Mhmm, mhm, mhm. Why'd you en try en break down my door for then, hmm?"

"Because you didn't answer the door," said Luciele as she popped up and out of the pile.

"Ah mhm," said the old man. He lowered his weapon and raised a large smile that stretched from ear to ear, his wrinkled skin extending it from one puff of hair to the other. "Afraid! I was en thinking you were thieving me!" He licked his lips and stared at them all, lost somewhere in his thoughts. Kozz put

Red down and was about to speak, but the man burst forth with what he figured he wanted to say. "Come on in then. Must be looking for a bed then. Too dangerous en cold out there for the kids en the gals. Come on in then."

He turned and walked back into his home without a concern. They worked themselves out of their pile and walked up the stairs, sharing looks of confusion. Caleb's chest hurt from the weight of the others falling on top of him, but it was not overwhelming. It seemed that his fractured rib was healing well.

"What a crackpot," said Richard.

They entered the man's small home. Lights were on in every room with thick curtains stapled to the walls to block any of it from escaping out into the streets. Water was just starting to boil on an old electric stove top, and a decade old Rebel Moon documentary was playing on the man's telepod.

"You have electricity, and television?" asked Kelly. "Do you have a way to communicate with anyone? Has the Presider or anyone said anything on the telepod?"

"No no," said the old man. "Dear no. No communication works en no broadcasts on the telepod. I have my generator en my film player en that's everything. Always stocked up heavy on canned goods en now it's finally come in handy. You try en get broadcasts and it's just that same message they've been playing for weeks en weeks about the quarantine zone. Had some news at first awhile back en that went down as quick as the rest of the communication."

"Did the news say anything about what is going on?" asked Luciele.

"Nope nope. Nobody know nothing en they just say get to the quarantine zones." The man sat in an old reclining chair and rested his weapon on the table at his side. His pockmarked, bulbous nose was a bright red. "Please sit sit. Not so much room but at least it's warmer en out there."

"Have you been by yourself this whole time then?" asked Luciele.

"Yup, pretty much, pretty much. Don't go outside. Military checked on me twice, gave me a little fresh food and water but that's all I've seen."

"Wait," said Kozz, "the military has been by? When did you last see them?"

"Mmm.... A week ago maybe. They just stop by en see if I need help."

"Why haven't they taken you to the quarantine zone?" asked Kozz.

"Because I don't want to go. This is my home en I'ma staying right here come hell or high water or infected zombies trying to eat me."

"Gotta say," said Richard, "I'm impressed with your spirit, old man. What about your friends and family? Have you heard from any of them?"

"Don't go en call me old man, I'll whoop you if I have to. Call me Clyde. Anyways, my wife passed on a few years back en my children live on Erde where all the big business is at. I retired awhile back en moved out here. Been by myself ever since, for once in my dag-blasted life!" Clyde chuckled at his own words.

"You sure know how to be happy with all this trouble around," said Kelly. "How can you be so relaxed when everything we know is being destroyed and turned upside down?"

"I've seen a lifetime of trouble en it just don't worry me anymore. All of you kids have many many years left to explore, but I'm just sitting back en enjoying what the universe has left me before it comes to take me away. Trouble will pass until it's my time." Clyde jumped up as he remembered the water boiling on the stove top. "Sheesh-ma-geesh! Sheesh-ma-geesh! No wonder why it was getting so muggy in here. I thought it was just because of all of you sweaty bodies. I was boiling the water in case I had to throw it on your evil faces, but now we can use it for something more enjoyable. Anyone want some tea?"

Clyde was a gracious host and made sure everyone was well fed. The tower that supplied fresh water to his home was still intact and they all took the opportunity to bathe for the first time in weeks. As night set in Clyde rested in his armchair and the others gathered around to free their minds by watching some films on his telepod. The small apartment had little more than enough room to sleep them on its floors, but the carpet made a much more comfortable bed than had the cold dirt outside.

The next morning Kozz and Richard repaired Clyde's busted door to pay him back for his kindness. The group was ready to set off soon after and offered to take Clyde along with them.

"Nope nope. Like I said, this is my home en I'ma staying. You all go en carry on with your adventure. Have fun out there en be safe!" He bid them a happy farewell.

"You're a delightful man," said Luciele, giving Clyde a hug goodbye.

"Thank you for everything, Mr. Clyde," said Caleb.

"Thank you for everything, Mr. Caleb," said Clyde. "It's always nice to meet new friends."

They left Clyde's home behind and walked into the sunny streets. The sense of danger that crept in during the night was mostly gone, but the daytime creeps were crawling along the streets again. Caleb stayed close to his mother's side, holding her hand most of the time. They stuck to the main avenues to blend in with the populace and avoided walking down small streets or alleys where they could easily be ambushed.

The number of people walking the streets increased as they moved closer to the heart of the city. They had seen several infected running around and had helped save a couple of people from their attackers.

A young man wandering on his own was adorned with a homemade metal helmet and several sheets of plastic which covered his torso and limbs. He proclaimed to all in earshot that it was armor he created to protect himself from the hordes of zombies that were ravaging the world. He said that he knew one day the zombie apocalypse was going to strike and he had prepared for its impending arrival. Caleb snickered as the young man spoke. Luciele thought that the man was just pulling their legs, he did seem like a smart person after all, but his lengthy professions and undying devotion to his cause displayed a rather sad loss of sanity, probably caused by the amalgamation of tragic events which had taken place. They entertained the man and let him drone on for a bit, but eventually left him to his search and elimination of the "zombie prime" which he felt was the key to ending the zombie rampage and saving humanity.

The day was succumbing to twilight. Luciele wanted to find somewhere to spend the night as soon as possible. Richard agreed and took the lead, but he led the group around a corner where a mass of people was gathering in the street. Kozz took action and turned the group around, but they found themselves surrounded.

All around were people with painted faces. They wore an assortment of clothes and hairstyles, but they all had in common the same facial artwork— a painted pair of white glowing eyes, large and bright in their fluorescent exaggeration. They approached from several streets and alleys at once, closing in on the group of weary travelers. Kozz counted thirty of them at least, but there were still more arriving.

Kozz grabbed Luciele's hand and pulled her towards him as she held on to Caleb. Kelly grabbed Caleb's and Richard's hands and together they marched forward, pushing their way through the tightening group of bodies. None of the people spoke, not even when Kozz yelled and pushed them out of his way.

"This is worse than wiggling through the crowd at a Dusty Flakes concert," said Luciele. "And I thought sweaty teenagers on Erde smelled bad."

Kozz halted when a wall of people startled him. He went to push through them, but they did not move out of the way like the others had. A short man with a black strip of hair down the middle of his head stood at the forefront of the human wall.

"Looks like ya...decided to walk into our territory, bub," said the man. His voice had a strong nasal buzz as if he were talking through his long, hooked nose.

"Move out of our way and I won't have to slug ya," said Kozz. A larger man behind Hooknose stepped forward and rubbed his fist in his other hand. Hooknose held his friend back.

"You guys have...a lot of heavy lookin' bags there, bub," said Hooknose. "Perhaps we can help you lighten your load a bit."

"We're not in need of your help, bub," spat Kozz at Hooknose's face. He reached into his jacket. Hooknose and his friends all flinched, drawing for their weapons as Kozz pulled out a cigar and a lighter. He lit up his stogie and drew in a deep breath. "Calm down," said Kozz as he exhaled the smoke from his lungs, "my gun is at my hip if I was gonna go for it. Now like I said, move out of our way or you're gonna get hurt."

Kozz was stalling. He knew they were in danger and he did not have any plan other than fighting his way out, but that would put Luciele and the kids in too much danger. These people had weapons as well, and they looked like they were itching to use them.

"What's with the circus paint anyway?" said Kozz. "You guys runnin' a clown college or something?"

Hooknose motioned to his larger friend. Kozz knew what was coming and pulled the cigar away from his lips, then he stuck his chin out and smiled. The larger man stepped forward and punched Kozz square in the jaw. Kozz's chin turned bright red, but he kept the smile on his face and slid the cigar between his lips and drew another breath.

"Back off you twerp!" shouted Luciele.

"Hush yourself," said Hooknose. "Anyway, we're Infestation. We've banded together to survive the apocalypse, and our face paint signifies our...respect for the greater power that is causing it. There has yet to be a single member of Infestation who has fallen sick to the disease while we've seen members of other gangs and random people walking down the street...turn to the sickness. We have survived. Together we are strong, and together we survive."

The otherwise silent members of the gang cheered at Hooknose's words. Kozz clapped his own hands and smiled around at the painted faces. Hooknose snarled and the crowd silenced.

"I know you all...didn't ask for help, but I'm a nice guy. I'm going to have my friends here relieve you of your baggage, and as long as there is no trouble we'll send you on your merry way."

"You must be forming a clown college," laughed Kozz, "because you're an awful funny man. All that silly makeup and those goofy stories. You're a riot!"

Hooknose gritted his teeth. Kozz could smell an offensive stink coming from the man, and he felt the heat as the crowd pushed in tighter.

"Smells and feels like a can of sardines," said Luciele. She picked her son off the ground to make sure he did not get crushed.

"They look like clowns," said Kozz, "and stink like fish. What an odd pairing."

"They should call themselves The Clown Fish," said Richard.

Hooknose looked as if he were going to burst with rage. He lifted his arm and stabbed the air in front of Kozz with his pointer finger. "Get them!"

The big man behind Hooknose stepped forward and drew back a fist. Kozz caught the man's punch with one hand and made three quick motions with his arm. Snap, snap, snap. Kozz broke the man's arm in three places and pulled him down. The man dropped to the ground in pain. Kozz turned around to see the others defending themselves and pushing back against the encompassing weight of human bodies. Richard's tent pack was ripped from his arms and someone else was pulling on his backpack. Kozz felt a sting in the back of his leg and turned back to see that Hooknose had stabbed his thigh with a small knife. Kozz spat his cigar at Hooknose and the burning tip hit the small man right in the eyeball, then he kicked Hooknose in the side of the head and the momentum of the hit caused the man to fall on top of his larger companion.

Kozz wailed on other members of the group, smearing their makeup and mixing blacks and blues and reds into their white eyes. Kozz was quickly becoming overwhelmed by the number of grabbing hands and flying fists in the air. He was tiring rapidly and saw that his friends were losing their fights as well. His heart thumped like a galloping horse. The pain began to sink in and he struggled to keep from dropping to his knees. Luciele screamed and fell to the ground with Caleb in her arms. "Mom!" the boy cried. She was hit hard in the face. Kozz used his remaining strength to bulldoze the crowd away from Luciele, and just as he tackled half a dozen painted faces to the ground he looked up and saw a welcome sight barreling down the road.

"All of you drop to the ground!" shouted a gunman on top of a military frontline gunner vehicle. The gunman fired a swift spray of rubber rounds into the crowd. Kozz jumped back to cover Caleb and the others. He was hit in the back by one of the rubber bullets, but he knew it would only leave a welt.

The gunman continued to fire upon the dispersing crowd. Hooknose was one of the last to flee and was pelted by the gunman until he turned down a corner at the end of the road. Kozz stayed in his position until the firing ceased.

"State your business, citizens," said an officer as she exited the vehicle, her weapon drawn but not pointing at Kozz and the others. Kozz stood and turned towards the officer.

"We've traveled a helluva long way to get to the damn quarantine zone. We were just walking down the street when those clowns ganged up on us."

Luciele stood up and lifted her son to his feet as well, her face was beginning to bruise from the hit she took. "All the way from Edgetown for some of us. My son has a fractured rib, and the rest of us are exhausted. Is there any way you can help us get to the quarantine zone?"

The officer considered them for a moment. "Climb aboard," she said. "That's why we're on patrol. We have others seated in the back. You can join them."

"That's awesome!" said Kelly.

"Can you tell us what's going on?" asked Richard.

"No," said the officer. "Classified."

Kozz knew that would be the response. They were going to have trouble getting the truth out of anyone.

The officer led them to the rear of the frontline gunner. The back hatch read 'FROG', the acronym supported by the vehicle's green armor plating and wide shape. Six others were already seated in the back cabin, including two children.

"There won't be much room left in there once you all get in," said the officer, "but we're scheduled to do a couple more hours of patrol. Take it easy and relax for awhile. The seats aren't that bad, and we have some food and water in there for you. Take a nap or something. We'll head back to the quarantine zone in a bit."

They climbed into the vehicle and the officer closed the hatch behind them.

"She was nice," said Caleb, "but she didn't smile at all."

"She's just as exhausted as we are," said his mother. "She's probably been through a lot in the last couple of months like the rest of us."

They introduced themselves to the others in the cabin. A husband and wife with their two children said they were rescued from a homemade bomb shelter they were hiding in. They had just run out of supplies and exited their shelter as the military officers drove by and had no idea the scope of what had happened while they were below ground these last few weeks. The other two occupants were two men who did not know each other, but they found themselves fighting off a couple of the infected together and then were spotted by the roaming military vehicle.

The two children were a couple years younger than Caleb. They were coloring with crayons and invited him to join them. He sat on the ground of the cabin and started to draw the face Sam had made in the sand back in Siletz, but he crossed it out and drew a picture of his house instead. Outside of the house he drew himself, his mother and father, and his grandma.

"I miss dad," said Caleb, "and grandma."

"I know, darling," said Luciele. "Me too."

"At least dad's not infected anymore," said Caleb. "At least he can go to heaven now. Grandma always talked about heaven. She always talked about how wonderful of a place it would be. I'm sure she knew the way there, and she probably helped dad find it too. I wish we could have saved them though."

Kozz listened to Caleb talk, finding a sad comfort in the boy's understanding and acceptance of his father's and grandma's deaths. If only he himself had been able to accept death as easily when his son was murdered, then he would have been able to spend the last decade with his lovely wife instead of all alone on a frozen rock, but Kozz did not want to drown in sorrow any longer. He was glad that Caleb could move on as he himself was unable. Kozz also knew that he had battled his personal demons and, through the help of his new friends, he had defeated them. He was going to find a way to get to Erde, and he was going to find his Priscilla. Nothing was going to stop him.

The hours slipped by as everyone faded in and out consciousness. The seats were comfortable and everyone seized the opportunity to nap while they could. Kozz stared with unfocused eyes out of the small window to his side, drifting in and out of consciousness.

The streets enlivened as streetlights and lamp lit windows illuminated the night and more people walked the broken streets. Occasionally another military vehicle would pass by, and once Kozz would have sworn he saw a personal vehicle drive on the road, but it could have just been from one of his dreams. He was not sure. The lights did get brighter, however, and soon enough he realized that they had made it to the city, and it was still alive. Port Town was still alive.

The officer opened up the hatch and had everyone exit the vehicle. The city should have stood tall and bright in all its glory, but the recent carnage and neglect had ravaged its former beauty, turning it faded and ugly. Countless people roamed about, awkward and afraid. Skittish eyes darted in every direction. The silence was confusing, and the air stank.

Soldiers stood stationed at one of the entrances to the Grand Downtown Arena that towered above them. The arena had been designated as the quarantine zone because of the enormous amount of refugees it could hold. Thousands of people were camped outside the structure. Those who were trying to enter stood in a long line which wrapped around the arena, but it was at a stand still as soldiers checked each and every person for symptoms of infection. Even though the line to enter the quarantined arena was staggering, what was more unbelievable was how the arena was already bursting at the seams with bodies. Slots in the outer walls revealed the tightly packed populace who camped out on stairwells and loading ramps. Conditions were dreadful. People rested around piles of trash and clogged every crevice of the arena with their sweaty, unwashed bodies.

Soldiers were stationed all along the city streets. Some walked the byways with civilians while others perched on ledges and in windows with their sniper rifles. Screams broke out just inside the gateway of the arena and people ran as they screeched about an infected attacker. Soldiers slipped through the runners and shot the glowing-eyed man, but he continued running for a bit longer before he dropped to the ground nearby Kozz and the others. His eyes did not beam and he did not scream. A small dart was lodged in his neck. Three soldiers ran over, lifted the body, and carried it off to some unknown location. The people calmed and moved about their business as if nothing had happened, as if they were accustomed to the situation.

Another set of screams came from a nearby intersection as a hefty old woman with glowing eyes ran after a thin old man. She was hit with a dart as soon as the screams broke out and she slowly collapsed to the ground. Another group of soldiers carried her body away.

"This is the quarantine zone, ladies and gentlemen," said the officer as she closed the hatch. "The arena may be your destination, but I wouldn't recommend going in there. It's a mess, and it isn't any more safe than being out here in the streets. We can prevent anyone showing signs of infection from entering the complex, but that doesn't seem to stop them from turning while they're inside. Even our soldiers aren't safe from the disease, here or on any of the other planets. Your best bet would be to find a hole to crawl in and hide, or maybe you should stay in public light and let the soldiers protect you. Either way, just hope to high heaven that you don't catch it. Whatever it is."

She doesn't know what's happening, thought Kozz, *and she's an officer. Even the soldiers aren't safe. Then there is no cure or way to prevent it, and she just said that it's happening on the other planets as well....* "This is hell," he said.

"Close enough," said the officer. Her eyes looked down towards the ground, "God speed." She turned away and walked back to her vehicle. The driver-side door shut itself as she hopped in and drove off into the night.

"We can't stay here," argued Luciele to no one in particular. Horror took over her face as she scanned the masses of sorry people, those suffering and living in fear all around the quarantined arena. "We would have been better off living back at home in the wilderness."

"Your power wouldn't have lasted much longer without people to keep it running," said Kozz, "and you couldn't have lived off hunting alone. There was nothing left until we came here. No medicine, no food, no people. What would you have done when the warm months passed and the frigid weather returned? There would have been no game out there for you to grab. You know this. You took the only option."

"We could have lasted for a while at least," said Luciele, "but you're right. We couldn't have lived alone out there forever. But this...this is sickening. I can't keep Caleb in a place like this. We need to go elsewhere."

"You can come with us to Quartz," said Kelly. "There has to be some kind of transportation between here and there."

"But who is to say that it will be any better there?" said Luciele. "Quartz is smaller than Port Town and won't have as large of a military presence. There will probably be less protection and aid there."

"That's probably true," said Richard, "but you can stay with our families when we find them. If we find them." Richard turned to his love. "I hope they're alright."

"Thank you both for the offer," said Luciele. "Caleb and I will have to consider it. I don't know what else to do, but we can't stay here."

"What if we go to Erde with Kozz?" asked Caleb. "Maybe it's safer. Maybe they're not infected. We can fly in a spaceship to get there!" Caleb had only been to Port Town twice before with his parents and was still struck with awe at its size and bright lights. He had always wondered what it would be like to go to Erde, a planet that was essentially one enormous city filled with people and buildings and airships. The thought of getting to fly through space to get there was very exciting and was something he had always wanted to do.

"Maybe," said Luciele. She assumed that Kozz had his own plans for Erde and saw the look in his eyes when Caleb mentioned the thought of following him. She knew Kozz cared for them, but she understood that he never intended for them to follow him to Erde.

They stood where they were, not knowing where to go or what to do. They each had their own separate paths to take and knew that they were at a crossroads, but no one knew where to take the first step. They each took the time to absorb the chaos which surrounded them. Military presence was everywhere, on the ground and in the sky. Men, women, and children were scattered all across the streets, staying at a distance from one another in fear that anyone could become infected at any moment. Was there no answer? Was there nowhere safe to go?

As they stood there staring off into the distance a heavy slap hit Kozz across the back. Kozz turned as quick as lightning and was reaching for Red when he stopped in mid-motion, recognizing a face from his past.

"Cosmo you devil dog," said a soldier who was as large as

Kozz, "I never thought I would see your ugly mug ever again." The soldier's attire was more decorated and polished than most of the other men and women in uniform, and he wore a short-brimmed hat rather than an armored helmet. His hair was neat and trim, face clean shaven, and his smooth skin was dark like a stout beer.

"Jammer," said Kozz. "Look at what they've done to you. It's been a long time."

"Cosmo?" asked Caleb.

"And who do we have here," said Jammer. "Did you run off and start a new family?"

"These are my friends. That's Caleb, his mother Luciele, and this is Kelly and Richard. We've been surviving this mess together for awhile now." Kozz stood in disbelief for a moment before he thought to introduce his old friend to the others. "This guy is Jammer, my buddy from a long time ago. We grew up on the streets together."

"And now I'm a commander for the Cooperation," Jammer said, tugging on the chest of his uniform with both hands.

"Nice to meet you," said Kelly.

"You already remind me of Kozz," said Luciele. "You both share the same...charisma, or something to that effect."

"Well like he said," responded Jammer, "we're old buds. We went through a lot together, up until he started working as a bodyguard for that senator. Didn't see him much after that, then one day he just disappeared. Now what is it, twenty years or so later and I find you on this ice block. What have you been up to all this time?"

Kozz sighed. "I have a history that I've been meaning to tell to my friends here, but I've been too scared to share it. I've kept it secret for over a decade now, hiding from my past to protect it. It's not necessary to keep quiet any longer, because it's helping nothing. My friends here have saved me from myself and they deserve to know what they've saved me from. If you have some time, Jammer, I'll share with you what I want to share with them. Is there some place we can go to rest other than that hell hole in the arena?"

"Yeah," said Jammer. "It's about time for me to be relieved for the night anyway. I can get you and your friends into our barracks, give you an area for yourselves to rest and grab some food. The barracks used to be full, but we've lost quite a few soldiers. How about we get over there, grab you guys some dinner, and set everyone up for the night, then we can talk."

"Sounds good old friend. Thanks."

"Thank you, Jammer," said Caleb.

"Thanks man," said Richard.

Jammer led the crew over to the military barracks. Several more infected were taken down by soldiers and carried off.

"What are they doing with those poor people?" Luciele turned to Jammer. "Are they going to be alright?"

"We're trying to save as many people as we can by tranquilizing the infected, rather than killing them. They're carried across town to a military barge that's been converted into a medical storage and research facility. The crazies are being put into medically-induced comas until someone comes up with a way to fix 'em."

"Are they studying them?" asked Caleb. "Are they doing experiments on the infected? How can they help them?"

"They're doing what they can, kid. Someone will find a cure," said Jammer. Caleb tried to pry further, but Jammer ignored him. He turned away from the curious boy and feigned interest in a small conflict down a side street away from the barracks. "Come on. Let's get the bunch of you inside and away from all this trouble." Confidentiality was part of Jammer's position and Caleb was left with more questions than answers.

Jammer greeted the guards at the entrance and gave specific instructions that Kozz and the others were to be granted entrance to the facility as they pleased. He then led the group to an empty area of the barracks and showed them to the mess hall. Jammer warned that armed soldiers patrolled the barracks for infected. He made sure that, as civilians inside a military facility, they understood to remain calm and not make any extreme movements or sounds. Every soldier was instructed to keep their weapon ready at all times and act swiftly if one of their fellow soldiers turned infected.

The military had discovered that keeping a weapon handy at all times was necessary in dealing with the infected. The weapon did not present immediate danger if its wielder became infected because it took some time before an infected understood that they had a weapon and figured out how to use it. It was as if their minds had erased the knowledge of such things and had to relearn them.

They all grabbed some dinner from the mess hall and headed back to their section of the barracks to unpack their belongings and settle in for the night. Jammer went to his own room and changed out of his uniform and into more relaxed military garb. He returned with his pistol still strapped to his side. They sat together on their beds as Kozz collected his thoughts and prepared to tell his story.

"I was fourteen when my parents were killed in a vehicle accident, or at least that's what I was told. It was only a few weeks earlier that my father had given Red to me. He showed me how to use her and how to treat her right. When my parents passed away I was put under the supervision of the authorities who were responsible for setting me up in an orphanage. I had no other family to take me in. They wanted to take Red away from me. She was the only thing I had left to remind me of my parents and I couldn't let her go, so I ran and took her with me. I knew they would look for me if I tried to go back home, so I ran to the streets and lived in the darkened alleyways of Erde.

"I survived on handouts and favors for awhile, but it wasn't enough. I needed more to sustain myself, and that's when Jammer walked into my life. He was a boy about my age, living on the streets, but he told me about the people he worked for and how well they treated him for doing good work. We got along real well together and Jammer took me in one day to see his boss. They welcomed me with open arms and offered me work. I took a job as a delivery boy for some bad people and learned to defend myself in ways my father would have never taught me. It was a harsh life, but the people I worked for rewarded me well. I grew in size, eventually becoming the mammoth you see me as today. When I was first given Red I was barely able to lift her with both arms, but by the time I grew into her I had lived my life as a cold thug, the kind of person people feared to cross. My delivery jobs turned into bigger things, turned into making threats and collecting payments of money or broken bones. Jammer and I did our work together and we became good friends.

"One day, in my early twenties, a senator of the Cooperation representing Erde was checking out the slums of our glorious city. I can only assume that it was a public relations ploy, him wanting to give the impression that he cared about our little shithole. I was relaxing against a building, smoking a stogie one fine afternoon after collecting some late and unpaid debts, when the senator walked by with two sunglasses-and-black-tie bodyguards hugging his sides. The walkway was thin and one of the guards told me to move out of the way as they approached. I stood my ground, too proud to let some suited asshole tell me what to do. I figured they would just move around me, but the one guard came over and pushed me. I didn't move, just kinda smiled and blew a little smoke in his face. He came at me again with the intention of bringing me to the ground, but I grabbed one of his reaching arms, turned his body around and snapped the arm in half at the elbow. I snatched his other arm as the second guard came running over to help his partner and told him to stop right where he was or I would break the guy's other arm as well. The second guard hesitated for a moment and then came rushing towards me. Snap the other arm went and the guy fell to the ground, pleading in pain. The second guard attacked me and I grappled him tight enough to make him useless and at the mercy of my whim. Before I could do anything to him the senator ordered for his guards and I to stop. If the suits weren't going to bother me any longer then I had no problem with them, so I let him go.

"Story goes that he was impressed with my abilities and wanted to hire me as one of his bodyguards. I wound up filling both positions."

"And that's about the time I didn't see you around much

anymore," said Jammer.

"It was time-consuming work," said Kozz. "You know I stopped by the streets as often as I could, but the senator didn't want any media catching his bodyguard hanging out with thieves and gangsters."

"True enough," said Jammer with a smile. "But it wasn't much longer before you disappeared completely. That's when I decided I had enough of being a lowlife and signed up for the military. All those long years passed by and I worked my way up to Commander. Crazy shit. I still don't believe it myself. And now I'm put in charge of the brigade stationed here in Port Town and find your ass running around in all this calamity. I suppose if I should have expected anyone to survive this shit it would be you."

"I can't believe it either, but I'm proud of you, Jammer. You belong in that uniform. It fits you well. But there was a reason why I disappeared, why you haven't seen me in so long. I was the senator's guard for a good six years. It wasn't very satisfying work, but at least it was honest, if only because I was now beating people up to protect a government official. It was during my time working for the senator that I met my beautiful wife, Priscilla. We married a year after we met and had our son Jacob not much later. We were very happy and in love."

"See, now I remember Priscilla," said Jammer. "For a while

there I thought that she was why you left the streets. Figured you didn't want her to know too much about your past, figured you wanted to forget me and all those jobs we did together."

"That wasn't the case at all. I missed your crazy ass ever since we last saw each other, but Priscilla and I were happy and in love. We wanted to get off Erde and live a more rural life away from all the crime in the city and drama in the government, but as you all are aware, it's extremely expensive just to travel to another planet, never mind moving to one and starting a new life from scratch. It was at that time in our lives that a great opportunity came to me, a position as an Enforcer for the Presider of the Cooperation."

Everyone was aghast except for Caleb who looked to his mother, not fully understanding the importance of the position.

"You were a freaking Enforcer?" squeaked Kelly through the hands covering her mouth. "You're the most important person I've ever met!"

"So that's the part of your past you wouldn't tell us about," said Luciele. "No wonder why you wanted to keep it a secret. No one ever knows the identities of the Enforcers."

"That explains why you're such a badass," said Richard.

"What's an Enforcer?" asked Caleb. His mother told him that she would explain it later.

"An Enforcer," said Jammer. "Wow. That's why you just

disappeared. Four Enforcers working directly underneath and for the Presider. The hand of power in the known universe, the Presider its thumb and the Enforcers are its fingers. And you were one of them. A diplomat, a spy, a warrior—"

"An army," said Kozz. He turned his attention to Caleb, wanting the boy to know what he was. "An Enforcer is a sort of bodyguard for the Presider, a bounty hunter, an emissary, and a literal one-man army. There are only four Enforcers at any given time, and none of their identities are known by anyone, even the other Enforcers. The Presider appoints his Enforcers and only a couple of his top advisers are told minute details about their identities. The purpose of the Presider having Enforcers is to help him maintain his presence and authority in the ever-expanding empire of the Cooperation. I would wear this enormous, impenetrable, highly-advanced suit of armor that had all sorts of weaponry and gadgets attached to it. I would make threats to dangerous people on the Presider's behalf. I would perform top-secret and not-so-secret missions for the Presider. I would protect the Presider and his family. I would do whatever the Presider asked of me and I would only take orders from him."

Kozz turned his attention back to everyone else. "It was really the same sort of work I had been doing all of my life, but I was so damn good at it that the Presider wanted me to do it for him, and if I'm doing it for the Presider...the beatings and killings had to be justified, right? My father was a former Enforcer, that fact and my skills are what led me to the position. I didn't even know what my father was until I joined the ranks.

"But I planned on keeping the job for only a couple of years, just long enough to build up retirement savings. Once we had the cash I was going to quit and take my family to a far away place where we could leave all of it behind. The position was too dangerous for me and my family. Turns out I was locked in until the Presider relieved me of my duties. Turns out I was his best Enforcer and he didn't want to let me go.

"The years rolled by, but we were safe enough. Priscilla and I became dulled by the danger of the position and grew too comfortable with it after some time. There was always a bit of worry, but time turned it into just another part of the day. No one knew my identity or the identity of my family and we were living a good life. We weren't out of the city, but at least we were living on top of it, as far as we could be from everything while still being in it. Jake was going to a good school and we were all happy. I eventually stopped asking to leave and I continued doing what I was doing for twelve years.

"That twelfth year I was sent to the Insurrectionist Moon, or the Rebel Moon as a lot of people like to call it. The place is full of high-profile criminals and fugitives, all on the run and hiding from the Cooperation. The moon isn't under

Cooperation control, not that we haven't tried, and wouldn't be a habitable place if several wealthy crime organizations didn't band together to create an underground fortress fit with all the necessities for life. The Cooperation has battled and bargained with those anarchists for over a century, and there's nothing to show for it. It's crawling with villains of the Cooperation—thieves, convicts, terrorists, murderers, and gangs, all the scum of the universe that has found a way to make it out there. The people there knew what I was and who I was going for. I killed many men in the short amount of time I spent on the moon, fighting my way to the Narnkazi family crime lord, one of the wealthiest and most powerful crime lords in history. He had become a major threat to the Cooperation. I wasn't there to kill him, but to threaten him. He saw how powerful an Enforcer could be. How one of us, never mind all four, could break through his walls and tear apart his entire organization. He heard the threat and he heard it well.

"Six months later I came home from a different mission to find my wife in tears and my son, Jacob, lying dead on top of his blood soaked bed. It was Narnkazi. That was the first time I cried since my parents died all those years before. Priscilla and I held each other and wept all night long for our fallen son. The next day I went to the Presider and told him what had happened and that I was resigning with or without his permission, no matter the consequences. He accepted my resignation and told me that his Chief of Global Representatives Robert Densen had only minutes earlier confessed to answering to threats from Narnkazi against his family. He had given away what few details he had known about my identity. Apparently he knew enough.

"Presider Conway told me that he had just dispatched soldiers to warn and protect us from any impending danger, but it was too late. I was going to kill the Densen sonofabitch, but Conway told me that he had already been locked up and relieved of his position. He would be prosecuted like any other person.

"I wanted to go to his cell and rip his head off. Conway ordered me to sit and calm myself before I did something stupid. I had just put in my resignation, but I was too adjusted to acting on the man's every word without question that I just did as he said. I sat in the Presider's chair and I convinced myself that the man, Densen, only did what was required to protect his family, not himself. I couldn't kill him for that.

"I left the office, never intending to return again. I went home to Priscilla. I told her that I love her and held her in my arms again for a little while. Then I explained to her that I had to leave, that I had to leave so that nothing like this would happen to her. I loved her so very much. I cried as I told her this." Tears fell from Kozz's cheeks as he stared at the floor. He was uncomfortable appearing vulnerable to his companions and could not meet their eyes. "She fought against the very thought of it, fought with me. She said she would come with me no matter how far we had to run, but I knew that nowhere would ever be far enough. She didn't understand, but I would not back down. We embraced each other, said things to one another for the last time, shared sweet memories one last time. Then I left, not telling her where I was going. She would be safe with me gone. I failed my son, and I would fail her as well if I stuck around. I couldn't protect her. She would never be safe with me around.

"I didn't know where I was going. I changed my name. I made it impossible for her or anyone else to follow my tracks, and no one ever found me in the last ten years I've spent on this block of ice.

"That's why I couldn't tell anyone about my past. I couldn't tell anyone because I didn't want to risk Priscilla's safety. But now I am telling you, my friends, the first people I have ever truly trusted since I came to this world, because this infection has changed all the rules, because you all have made me a better person, and because I need to get off this planet and go to Erde to find my Priscilla and protect her from whatever the hell is going on. I need to make sure my Priscilla is alright, I need to find her again, and I have to make sure she is safe. That is my story, my story that I have kept inside for too long, my story that has eaten away at my heart."

Kozz was hunched over the edge of his bed, elbows resting on his knees. A small puddle of tears soaked into the concrete floor beneath him.

Caleb left his seat and sat next to Kozz. Everyone else remained quiet, not knowing what to say to the man who had broken his ten-year silence.

Jammer shuffled his feet. The man he used to know like the back of his hand was now almost a complete stranger. His personality was the same as ever, but a lot had happened to the both of them in the twenty years they had been apart. "I saw her," he said.

Kozz lifted his head. His eyes and face were not red because he was not sobbing, he had simply let the tears fall without hindrance. "What was that?" Everyone else in the room looked at Kozz and followed his gaze over to Jammer.

"Priscilla," said Jammer. "We came across each other something like five years ago. We didn't talk for long, you know I never really knew her since it was about the time you met her that you stopped hanging around, but we sure as hell recognized each other."

"Where..." asked Kozz, "how was she?"

"She was doing good, man. Priscilla left the senate offices and was working on some space vessel collecting intel on something. She was a numbers runner, doing some kind of work for the government. She said she just had to get away from Erde.

"Anyway, I thought I would see your ugly face again since I ran into her, but she started asking me about you. I told her I didn't know anything, that I thought you ran off with her. Then she told me about Jacob, and that you had to leave. I had no idea about the Enforcer stuff, she didn't let any important information slip, she just told me that she had been trying to find you for years and hadn't come across a single lead. You're definitely a sneaky motherfucker.

"That was about all we shared. She was so disheartened that I didn't know where you were. Hindsight. Now I can see the glimmer of hope that shined in her eyes when she first recognized my face. I wish I had something to tell her, at least a hint of a direction you were in."

Kozz's eyes had dried and hardened into something fierce and committed. "She's alive."

"Well like I said, that was five years ago. I mean, with everything that's going on right now—"

"She's alive," Kozz said again. "I know she is." Kozz met his old friend's eyes. "I have to get off this planet. Now."

"Well, rest yourself for the night and I'll see what I can do," said Jammer. "You don't still have any of your Enforcer credentials, do you?"

"I still have my voided badge. It's endorsed by the Presider himself. No name, no picture, but it's clearance code used to get me access to any room or ship in the Cooperation. Even voided it should still hold some weight."

"Good," said Jammer. "That'll make things easier. I know that one of our medical barges is leaving for Erde tomorrow to bring the comatose to a better equipped research facility. I'll talk to some people and get you clearance."

"I owe you more then I could ever repay," said Kozz. "Thank you for doing this for me."

"Think nothing of it, but you do own me big." They both smiled.

"Caleb and I were thinking of heading to Erde as well," said Luciele. "Do you know if it's any better there? And is there any way for us to get there?"

"Well," said Jammer, "the crisis is just as rampant there as it is here. It's spread across all of our civilizations. The death toll is higher on Erde, but that's only because the population is so immense. Though, from what I've heard, the military response was much quicker and more efficient than on these fringe worlds. They have more forces to control the outbreaks and more supplies to care for the refugees. You might fare better on Erde than here on Frostarc. I've even heard rumors that the Presider might call in the populaces of the outer worlds to Erde in order to pool our resources and save as many lives as possible."

"The death tolls are that bad?" said Kozz.

"Not yet, but we still don't know how to prevent people from becoming infected. The numbers are climbing and we're slowly running out of the manpower to keep our cities running. We may not be able to provide aid to the fringe worlds indefinitely."

"Then we shouldn't stay here on Frostarc, should we?" asked Caleb.

"Well it's all just rumors for now, but it could really happen at any time. I'm losing soldiers every day to the infection. It'll be safer for you where there are more soldiers to protect you. I can't get you on the medical barge with Kozz, but there is a passenger barge heading to Erde later in the week. We're already bringing people to Erde in mass quantities, so maybe the rumors are more truth than fiction. The barge will fill up quick, but I can make sure you get on."

"That's what we'll do then," said Luciele. "I just don't think it's safe enough here for us, even in the city. I think my sisters are on Erde. Maybe fate will give us another chance to be a family again. Thank you, Jammer."

"What about Kelly and Richard then?" asked Caleb.

The young couple had been silent ever since Kozz started telling his story. They appreciated their new friends, but did not feel a part of their close-knit relationship. They had fought together and survived together, but Kelly and Richard knew that they had their own path to take. They looked into each other's eyes and held a silent conversation in that short moment. They knew what they had to do.

"We're still going to head to Quartz," said Kelly.

"Our families need us," said Richard. "We've got to find them."

"We love you guys." Kelly grabbed Richard's hand. "But Richey and I have to go our own way. We knew this was what we had to do, even before we met you kind folks."

"Quartz is a dangerous place right now," said Jammer. "I just sent a battalion of soldiers over to aid them in their efforts. The gangs are under as good of control as here, but the infected are tearing the place apart. It's chaos."

"But that's where we need to go," said Kelly. "I'm sorry that we have to leave you, Caleb, but it's what we must do." Kelly hugged the boy.

"Yeah man," said Richard. "You guys are great, but you understand. We have to find them."

"We understand," said Luciele, "and Caleb will in time."

"No, I understand," said Caleb. "You have to help them. You have to save them. I just wish we were all going to the same place."

"Well I'm gonna go start contacting some people," said Jammer. "You all make sure to get some rest tonight. I'll see you in the morning."

They stayed up late reminiscing about the adventure they

had shared. That night would be the last night they spent together on Frostarc. Kozz was going to leave the next day to Erde, and Richard and Kelly would be looking for a way to Quartz. Kozz told stories of his past and everyone was most interested in his time as an Enforcer. He told them about his journeys along the four inhabited worlds of the human universe and shared stories about their dark undergrounds. They sat in a circle like they had around their campfires as Kozz told his tales.

Caleb fell asleep at Kozz's side. Luciele let him rest for a bit the way he was before bringing him to his bed and calling it a night. Richard and Kelly prodded Kozz for awhile longer before growing tired themselves. Kozz was the last awake, as usual, and for awhile he watched over his friends as they slept. He had learned more about himself in recent weeks than he had let himself in the ten years he lived on this planet. The friends he had fought for and survived beside had become his family, something he had abandoned years ago, and he knew that they all thought he was the strong one of their group, but inside he always felt that he was the weakest. He had failed to protect so many, but they did not see him that way. They always looked to him for strength and courage when he felt like he had none, but what they did not know was that they gave him his strength. He had run away and hid for a decade, and it was not until they had walked into his life that he had felt brave again, that he felt strong and alive again.

They had all changed him for the better. Kozz rested in his bed, thinking of how much he was going to miss them all, until exhaustion dragged him to sleep.

CHAPTER FIFTEEN

Flight

"Your ride leaves in three hours," said Jammer. He found Kozz and the others in the mess hall. Hundreds of tables and benches were filled with soldiers scarfing down their meals before heading out to their duties. "Sorry I couldn't give you any more warning, bro, but you're in. Just show them your badge at the gate. They'll be expecting you."

That was sooner than Kozz had expected, but he was ready to leave as soon as possible. Kozz caught Caleb's eyes as the boy put his fork down, the child looked like he had suddenly lost his appetite.

"And you two kids," Jammer said, looking at Richard and Kelly. "I have a supply convoy moving out to Quartz in a few days. There's room aboard if you can wait that long."

Everyone was thanking Jammer for his kindness, but Caleb could not help feeling a little resentment towards the man. Jammer was making it too easy for all of his friends to split up and go in separate directions. *Why couldn't he just wait a little while?* thought Caleb, *and why couldn't Kozz wait a few days and come with us to Erde instead of going by himself?* He understood the reasons as to why everyone wanted to go their own ways in such a hurry, they had people they needed to make sure were safe, but he could not help feeling abandoned by them all. Almost everyone he knew was gone, and now his new friends were all leaving him. The only person who was staying with him was his mother. Caleb scooted down the bench to get close to his mother and he latched on to her with a tight squeeze. Luciele was surprised by the sudden affection. She put her arms around her son, knowing that he was upset.

After breakfast Kozz grabbed his already packed belongings and began the trek to the medical barge that would be his home for the next three weeks as it made the journey to planet Erde. It was a bit of a walk to get to the ship and he wanted to make sure he did not miss his flight. Kozz bid farewell to his friend Jammer before leaving the military barracks. Jammer was on duty and could not escort his friend to the ship.

"Thank you for everything, Jammer," said Kozz. "We'll run into each other again, I'm sure. I'm not in hiding any longer."

"I'll find you, big man. You're not gonna run away as easily this time."

"Take care of my friends for me when I'm gone."

"I will man, don't worry. They can stay in my barracks until they're ready to leave and they'll have some guards to protect them while they're in my city."

"You've always been a good man," said Kozz. "Even when we were kids and doing bad things, you were always a good man. Keep yourself alive."

"You do the same."

They shared a handshake and a hug before Kozz walked off. Jammer stayed behind as the rest of Kozz's friends followed him to his ship.

The streets were heavily guarded and full of early morning traffic. It almost looked like the beginning of a regular work day in the city, but the broken windows and occasional outbreak of an infected was enough to keep the reality of the situation alive.

The spaceport was a massive area on the edge of the city. A wall of tall skyscrapers were the border between the city itself and a vast emptiness that lay beyond. No buildings existed beyond the skyscrapers at this end of town because the strong pulses of energy emitted by the spaceships would obliterate anything beneath them. Empty fields were flattened under the massive ships, the grass itself crushed against the earth as the behemoths floated above. Pathways extended from the skyscrapers, giving access to the ships on various levels. One ship in particular nearly touched the ground, its height almost as tall as the two-hundred story skyscraper that served as its loading platform. The black hull was as wide as two of the largest city blocks in Port Town. "Sticks out like a sore thumb," said Kozz. "Just like Jammer said it would."

Kozz and the others entered the skyscraper which served as the docking station for the ship Kozz would embark upon. The staff loading platform was on its roof, and that is where Jammer instructed Kozz to go. The building was unscathed by carnage around it, the outer glass remained unbroken, and inside crystalline statues adorned the floor and hung from the ceiling. The bottom floor was a grand display of light with its ceiling standing a hundred feet high and its walls of clear glass letting in unhindered sunlight from all directions. The sun's rays bounced through the crystalline structures, creating a beautiful brilliance throughout the entire lobby and giving life to the green gardens at all four corners of the floor.

They entered one of the dozen elevators and were crammed into the small space with several other people, all pushing different buttons as they headed towards their own destinations within the building. The elevator shot up ten stories at a time, not stopping at any floor which did not end in a zero. The elevator halted its ascent several times as it emptied out its passengers until Kozz and the others were the only ones left. They flew up the remaining fifty stories at a high velocity and arrived at the rooftop.

The elevator opened to large glass archways and a view of the medical barge which floated outside. Through the archways they could see dozens of other ships docked at other skyscrapers of varying heights. Nearly all of the ships were military, but none were as large as the medical barge. *There sure must be a lot of comatose bodies in the belly of that ship,* thought Kozz. The outermost edges of the archways met either end of the skyscraper. From such a height the city below looked like it should have, as if nothing had changed its usual ebb and flow.

Caleb stuck his nose against the glass as he walked and observed as much as he could, amazed at all he could see from such an incredible height. He imagined how it would feel to be flying high up in an airship, soaring even higher than the Port Town skyscrapers. He jumped up and down, letting free the excitement that coursed through his veins. It felt right for him to be so high above everything else. Luciele, Richard, and Kelly succumbed to a sickening vertigo when they looked down at the streets and so they drifted towards the center of the archway.

Kozz approached the security perimeter and turned to face his friends, putting his bags on the ground. The sudden realization of where they were slapped Caleb across the face. His skyward fantasies disappeared in an instant. The boy ran to his mother's side and sniveled into her leg.

"It's not over little buddy," said Kozz. "Just because I'm leaving doesn't mean it's forever."

"Will you..." Caleb cleared his throat as he pulled his face away from his mother's leg. He wiped his nose on her dress. "Will you wait for us on Erde?"

Kozz's mouth opened to say something, but no words came out. Luciele noticed his hesitation.

"Kozz has important things he has to do as soon as he arrives on Erde, sweetie," said Luciele as she rubbed her son's head. "Our ship might not even be landing on the same side of the planet that Kozz will be on."

"I wish you didn't have to go," said Caleb. "But I know you miss your wife and I know it's been a long long time since you saw her."

"It has been a long time," said Kozz. "Thank you for understanding why I have to leave. This isn't goodbye. I'll find you once I have found my Priscilla."

"I'll be trying to find you the whole time!" said Caleb.

"Good luck trying to catch me," said Kozz. "I'm pretty darn quick."

"Yeah..."

"What's the matter, Caleb?" said Kozz.

"I just still feel bad about leaving everyone else in the camp behind and all the infected people that were killed. I just wanted to save everybody, but I guess I learned that you can't save everybody." Caleb sighed. "I guess with you leaving it makes me think of it all because you saved me. I know you can do it, but now you're leaving and I guess people are gonna keep dying. I thought maybe when we got to Port Town you would find a way to help everyone."

Caleb's mood had shifted from innocent sadness to a mature acceptance of the situation. The boy had grown strong over the short time Kozz had known him. Kozz was aware of Caleb's desire to save people from the infection. Every time his friends fought with the infected Caleb had questioned why the sick people could not be saved.

But it was not that simple. They had to fight to keep themselves alive. Kozz knew that perhaps he could have tried harder to save some of the unlucky fallen, but it was not his highest priority. He had other things to worry about such as protecting his friends and finding a ship to Erde. He desperately wanted to find his wife, but he also kept much of his plans secret from Caleb and the others— mostly because they were just wild ideas, but partly because he did not know if the young boy he had met back in Edgetown was strong enough to understand the scope of the chaos all of humanity was in. Caleb was once an innocent boy, easily brought to tears by a single mention or thought of his deceased father or grandmother. After experiencing all of the destruction and bloodshed that a massive war would have trouble garnering, the young boy had formed a hardened soul and had gained some control over his emotions. He knew the gravity of their situation. He was mature enough to understand.

"That's another reason why I'm leaving," said Kozz. It was time for him to let some of his wild ideas loose. "I want to figure out just what in the hell is going on, and I want to find a way to fix it. I should still be able to locate some of my old connections on Erde, and I know that once Presider Conway hears I'm back in town he's going to want to see me. I want to help the Presider and everyone else battle these demons that are haunting us."

"You mean you're gonna find a way to save everyone?" said Caleb.

"I'm gonna try. I've seen death before, but never have I seen so many innocent people fall so quickly. Whatever is happening is evil and I have a feeling that it isn't natural. I think someone has caused all of this, and I'm gonna make them pay."

"That's a hell of a theory, big man," said Richard. "Do you think getting to the Presider is going to be that easy?"

"Well," said Kozz, "trying to get to him in a civilized manner would be near impossible, but I think I can figure out a way to grab his attention. Once he sees my face or hears my name, I'm in."

"But how do you know he's still alive?" asked Kelly. "I mean, what if he became one of the infected?"

"That's possible, but it's the only plan I have. He's one of the few who knew anything about my identity when I was an Enforcer. To those few I have an incredible amount of authority, but no one else would give a damn about me because they don't know who I am. My gut tells me that he's still alive, and I think Jammer or someone else would have mentioned if the Presider was dead."

"Good point," said Richard and Kelly in unison.

Several men and women exited the elevator and walked through security into the massive ship which hovered outside the skyscraper.

"The ship is departing shortly," announced a woman's bubbly voice over the speaker system. "Last call for all employees and passengers. The gates will be closing soon."

"It's that time then," said Kozz.

Luciele was the first to run over and hug Kozz. The big man put one arm around her in return. "Thank you so much for everything you've done for us. You have no idea how grateful Caleb and I are. I'm going to miss your big head." Luciele kissed him on the cheek. His gray stubble poked at her soft lips. "Good luck. I hope you find everything you're looking for. You're a wonderful man."

"You and Caleb have done more for me than you'll ever know," said Kozz. "I think of you as family now, and I'll never forget you."

Richard walked over and shook the man's hand. "It's been a

journey, my friend. Hope you find your wife, and you know, save the world and stuff." Kozz patted the kid on the back. Kelly sneaked in a hug just as Kozz let go of Richard's hand. "Have a safe trip," she said, "and tell your wife I said hi when you find her. I know she won't know who I am, but you'll have a ton of stories to tell her and you can start off with one about me!"

"You're a couple of crazy kids," said Kozz. "Good luck finding your families. Maybe we'll run into each other again if the Presider calls everyone back to Erde."

Richard and Kelly moved out of the way to let little Caleb through. Kozz bent down and picked up the boy. "Don't worry kid," said Kozz, "we'll be seeing each other again. If we're both hunting around for the other we're bound to wind up in the same place." Kozz saw that Caleb's expression was thoughtful and concerned.

"Did you mean what you said about trying to save everyone?"

"I sure did. I've defeated bad guys before and I'm gonna beat this one too."

Caleb was sitting on Kozz's crossed arms. He bent forward and hugged the man who had saved his life and became his best friend. "Thank you," said Caleb. Kozz heard Caleb sniff, but the boy did not cry. Kozz held him up for a few moments before lowering him back down to the ground.

"Sir," said the woman at the security gate, "are you coming aboard? We're about to close the gate." Everyone else in the rooftop gateway lobby had entered the ship or left down the elevator.

"I love you all," said Kozz. He picked up his bags. "Be safe."

Kozz turned towards the gate and walked away. Luciele teared up and grabbed her son. Kelly and Richard stood each with an arm around the other and waved as Kozz walked up the security ramp. Kozz showed the woman his badge and walked through the gate without hindrance. He looked back to the others and gave a single wave before moving forward into the ship. Two members of security followed him in and closed the gate.

Tears fell from Caleb's eyes.

Jammer's duties let him check in on Luciele and the others sparingly, but he kept his promise to Kozz and made sure they were taken care of while they stayed in Port Town. He set up the ride for Kelly and Richard on board a caravan that was leaving for Quartz and he told Luciele and Caleb that he would walk them into the Erde-bound passenger barge himself to guarantee that they found a comfortable spot on the vessel.

The passenger barge was set to leave five days after Kozz

had departed Frostarc. Luciele and Caleb left early that day with Jammer. Richard and Kelly followed them to their ship and would be leaving with their caravan later that evening. The passenger barge was a further distance down the massive docking bay than the medical barge had been. Instead of climbing a skyscraper to enter the ship at its top, a loading ramp was lowered from the bottom of the floating hull. A line of eager and frightened people had already formed near the ramp and extended down the city blocks as far as the naked eye could see. Dozens of soldiers guarded the ship and were perched high above the populace, ready to snipe tranquilizers at any who turned infected. A trail of dirty tents, torn blankets, and food trash was scattered around the waiting people. Many had camped out, apparently for days, at their chance to find a spot on the massive ship.

"Shouldn't there be plenty of room on that barge for everyone?" asked Luciele.

"There are a lot of people that want out of here," said Jammer, "and I don't blame them, but there isn't as much room on that barge as it seems from the outside. There are several levels on the ship, but they are all designed with lots of space to carry enormous loads of goods from one destination to another. Each level has a ceiling which a hundred feet above the floor. Since the levels are so spaced out, there isn't all that much floor space for the thousands upon thousands of people who want on that ship."

"Why aren't there more ships traveling between here and Erde then?" asked Kelly.

"Because there aren't many left," said Jammer, "or many left who know how to operate them. A lot of trained pilots have fallen to the infection, and some of the ships held by the Cooperation have been sabotaged and destroyed by the infected. It's like they intend to cripple our society and know just what to attack to achieve that goal."

"Scary stuff," said Richard.

"They're smart," said Caleb. "We've seen how smart they are over and over again. I told Kozz that when I was infected there was something in my mind that took control of me, something that pushed my thoughts aside and controlled my body. I felt like I kinda saw it and it pushed against me when I tried to fight back. Whatever it was, it was smart. It wasn't just a sickness."

"I've heard rumors of others who eradicated their infection and described similar stories," said Jammer. "Our top scientists and bio-engineers are trying to figure out how it all links together and how they can cure it. I just hope to God that they put the pieces together sooner rather than later." Jammer sighed. The man always tried to appear optimistic, but he showed signs of fatigue and concern. Experiencing months of carnage and death had taken its toll on even the most courageous of soldiers. "Let's get you guys on that ship."

It was time for more goodbyes. Hugs went around as they shared their last moments together.

"Please take good care of yourselves," said Luciele. "You two are as cute as a couple of ducklings in a pail of water. Stay out of trouble, and good luck finding your families.

"We're so fortunate to have met you guys," said Kelly. "If you didn't come around we would still probably be stuck back on the glaciers with the others. I hope you find a safe place on Erde to stay until this crisis is over."

"I don't know what we're going to do when we get to Erde," said Luciele, "but all I want is for my son to be safe. From what I can tell this is the best path for us to follow."

"I hope it's better than what we've seen here," said Richard. "I'm sure we'll head off to Erde once we track down our families."

"That would be cool," said Caleb. "I'm gonna miss you guys."

"We'll miss you too little buddy," said Richard. "Maybe we'll find you on Erde or something."

"We'll keep in touch once everything is back the way it was and the communication system is up and running again," said Kelly. "I wouldn't dare miss watching you grow up into the strong man you're going to become."

"You guys are awesome," said Caleb. He ran over and

hugged them both one more time.

"Wait for me in that cafe across the street," Jammer said to Richard and Kelly. "I'll be back in a bit."

Jammer walked towards the ship. Luciele waved goodbye to the young couple as she followed, pulling Caleb by his hand. Caleb walked backwards and waved until they approached the long line of people waiting to board the ship. Luciele pulled her son close as Jammer pushed his own path through the line. Luciele diverted her eyes from those she passed, feeling guilty for walking to the front of the line which these people had spent days in, but she marched forward, seizing the opportunity to ensure Caleb's safety.

They approached the security gate at the base of the massive loading ramp. The guards opened the gate for Jammer without him needing to show identification. Luciele and Caleb followed Jammer through the gate as the people waiting in line hollered obscenities behind them.

The loading ramp was a large section of the hull which folded down to allow large vehicles and storage containers entry. Luciele thought the massive ramp seemed both overwhelming and silly at the same time. She felt like they were just three little bugs climbing a very big hill.

Jammer led them into the lowermost level of the ship where parallel rows of lights lined the walls up near the high ceiling and light seeped in through the hundreds of open vents at the bottom of the walls near the floor. Segmented living spaces covered nearly all of the floor space, leaving only thin passageways to travel throughout the level. Each living space was fitted with a bed, a chair, and a small section of cabinets that doubled as a tabletop. The same pattern repeated the full distance to the other side of the barge, only breaking for the occasional restroom compartment and kitchen area. Jammer explained that there would be a few cooks and attendants on board, but most of the food preparation and cleaning was going to have to be done by the passengers themselves as there simply was not enough staff on the ship to go around.

The floors were a rusty brown, as were the walls, but the inside of the ship had been sanded, smoothed, and sealed to make it a safer and more comfortable living space. Many thousands of people would be spending weeks inside the hull walls which were designed for carrying large supply loads from one planet to another.

Jammer led them into a freight elevator. "We're going to the topmost passenger living space. The area is small, but more comfortable. You'll be directly below the on-board crew living space. It's simply been converted from a level of offices to a level of bedrooms, but there's not enough crew on the ship to fill the spaces any longer. We decided that we wouldn't hold this area off to more 'important' passengers. Who all else winds up here with you two will just be from a random drawing. The rest will have to live on the loading levels for a few weeks."

The freight elevator took them up several levels until they reached the uppermost loading area. Each loading level looked similar to the one below it. The only difference with the uppermost storage level was a second elevator which was required for passage up to the remaining levels of the ship. The rusty brown of the storage areas was contrasted by the steel blue color scheme of the office level Luciele and Caleb would be staying in. The ceiling on their level was only a few feet above their heads, and the walls were a smooth, cool metal.

Though the area was a cold and professional atmosphere, its cleanliness and quietness comforted both Luciele and Caleb. Not much had seemed this pristine and normal in a long time.

A large office with glass walls had been converted into a kitchen, the only one on the level. There were several hallways with at least a dozen rooms down each.

Jammer led them to a room at the end of one of the halls, one that looked just like any other, but it was right next to one of the security offices on the level. Jammer went inside the office and instructed the two guards inside to take special care of Caleb and Luciele.

"Well this is it," said Jammer, "your home for the next few weeks. They'll start letting people in about an hour from now.

You can use that time to explore the area here or just set yourselves up."

"Thanks so much for all of this, Jammer," said Luciele.

"Not a problem, Luce." He smiled at the scrunched face Luciele gave him. "Just fulfilling a promise to an old friend and taking care of a lovely lady and her son while I'm at it."

"You remind me a lot of Kozz," said Caleb. "You two must have been good friends."

"We did grow up together," said Jammer. "You remind me a lot of him too, when I first met him. He was a shy but determined little kid. He grew big quick, and the streets made him the brute he is today, but he was a lot like you when he was younger. Remind him that he owes me a drink for taking care of you guys." Jammer looked around the room, nodding to himself. His eyes went to Luciele and he smiled. "On second thought, I did hook you up pretty good— make that two drinks."

"But we might not..."

"You'll run into him again." Jammer did not let Caleb finish his thought. "I'm sure of it. He's not the kind of guy to forget his friends."

Jammer bid them farewell and left them in the hands of the officers on board. Luciele left their belongings in the room and decided to take Caleb on a walk around the level before it filled with people.

"What do you really think about all of this, Richey?" Kelly had not touched the cup of coffee she had ordered. Her nerves had tensed her body and mind. Her new friends had all left and she was unsure what it would be like when she and Richard arrived in Quartz. "Do you really think we'll find them? I mean, alive and well? Who knows what could have happened."

"We can only try, Kell." Richard grabbed his girlfriend's shaking hands. She tried to steady them by wrapping her fingers around her cooling coffee mug. "There's no way to know what happened. We just have to see if they're alright. Whatever happens, we still have each other."

"But what if..."

"Then we move on," Richard interrupted. "I don't want to think of anything like that. There's a good chance that they're all just fine. They have to be. I'd travel across the galaxy to make sure you were alright, just like Kozz is doing for his wife. We need to know so that we can help them if they need us."

Jammer pushed open the cafe door. Kelly looked at him with frightened eyes. *They're still just kids themselves,* thought Jammer. *They haven't given up, but they feel lost.* "Come on now. We're gonna get you two where you need to go."

A FROG with speckles of dried blood splattered across its matte-black front waited for them on the street. An officer sat inside, barely visible through the hardened, tinted windows.

"This is your ride," said Jammer. "Inside is Officer Daube. She's one of the finest FROG drivers I've ever known. She'll bring you to the military caravan that is leaving for Quartz later this evening and will be joining the caravan with this vehicle and you in it."

"You're the man," said Richard. "Seems like you got all the hook ups."

"We owe you so much," said Kelly.

"You owe me nothing. Kozz asked me to take care of you all and so I've done so to the best of my abilities. You're great kids. Good luck out there."

Jammer opened the back hatch and let them inside, closing the door behind them. A mesh fabric separated the back benches from the front seats. The bright sunlight had trouble piercing through the tinted windows and was absorbed by the black interior. It was difficult to see where they had placed their bags.

"Greetings and salutations," said the driver. "I am Officer Daube. Welcome aboard the Blackbull, my personal warbeast and transport vehicle for the last six years. Located above your heads is a dial, please turn the dial in a counter-clockwise manner if you wish to see the hands in front of your face."

"Ah!" Kelly turned the dial which controlled a dim set of lights in the back of the vehicle. "Thank you!"

"We'll be joining with the rest of the team shortly," announced Officer Daube. "I sure do hope you enjoy your ride. Be aware that Blackbull's suspension isn't what it used to be and that we might encounter some bumpy terrain along the route!"

"This is going to be fun," said Richard.

Kozz was greeted by a guard and led to his room. He took mental pictures of the signs and guide maps he passed as the guard led him down numerous white corridors. The elevator had enough buttons for fifty floors, but Kozz knew that there had to be even more. The living level was furnished like a city home with modern furniture and warm colors. They passed other people as they walked around, everyone giving friendly nods like they were neighbors in a cozy community.

The guard led Kozz to the end of a long hall filled with closed doors and showed Kozz to his room. Inside was a plush bed with a steel frame and enough desk space to accommodate any of the scientists or engineers on the ship. The guard left him where he was and said that the ship's captain would send a representative down to welcome him aboard.

Kozz dropped his belongings in his room and grabbed his room key, locking the door as he set out to explore. At the end of the hallway, next to his room, was a lounge area with a telepod, a sofa, several reclining chairs, and a steel table with a neat stack of magazines. He flipped through the pile, pushing most to the side. Many of the magazines were from several months ago, all he had already read, but he found two copies which were recent. One of the covers displayed a horrifying scene of a gang of infected attacking a city bus on the streets of Erde, and the other was a picture of Presider Conway standing at a podium with an elbow resting on the lectern and his face buried sorrowfully into his hand. Kozz's thirst for knowledge enticed him to sit down and read the articles inside. The magazines might provide some insight into the cause and scope of the horrors taking place in the galaxy, but he felt that there was more pertinent information to be discovered on this medical barge. He could not relax, not yet.

The elevator dropped down to the top level of the loading docks, he thought. *There are more loading levels for sure, and I bet that's where they are keeping the comatose bodies of the infected.* Kozz believed that they had to be performing research on the comatose. Finding a reason or a cure for what was happening to humanity was more important than the ethics behind it. They would have a database of information down there, not only from the findings of the staff on this ship but possibly the cumulative research of the Cooperation. Kozz had to get down there and sniff out what he could.

Better to jump the gun now before everyone around here has seen my face. Kozz headed straight for the elevator, deciding that now was the time to act. He tracked back through the many corridors the guard had led him through after they had exited the elevator and found his way without taking a wrong turn. He pressed the glowing yellow button to request the elevator. It turned red as he heard the box travel through its shaft and come to a rest at his floor. Kozz stepped forward as the doors opened, but he was blocked by a tall woman with coffee-colored hair tied back into a ponytail.

"Mr. Cosmo?" asked the woman. She was nearly as tall as Kozz, but skinny as a twig. Her striking blue eyes demanded attention, standing out like stars in the night against the motor oil color of her skin.

"Maybe."

"My apologies, but I was never given a last name."

"Kozz is just fine."

"Kozz. I like it. Reminds me of the old action movies I used to watch with my father when I was a child." She was holding a clipboard and flipped through the papers it held as she spoke. "There is a seating area just behind you. Let us sit and discuss your presence on our ship." The woman stood in Kozz's way, not giving him any other option. He decided that it was too soon to be causing trouble, so he walked back to the armchairs and the woman followed. "I am Personal Compliance Officer Marissa Batoon. Apologies for the formal introduction, but I was instructed by the captain to make you well aware of my authority on this ship. I'll be your attendant for the duration of this trip."

"So word has gotten around about my high-level security clearance card then."

"Indeed it has. The captain fears that you will run amok on our ship without heed of our authority. I was told to inform you that in such uncertain times as we are experiencing right now, and with the nearly paralyzing lack of staff we have on hand, we will grant you no command on this ship. You are simply a welcomed guest and you are expected to abide by our rules."

"Oh really? And what would those be?"

"The current level we are on is the topmost of three living levels. The floor directly above us is the wellness, activity, and nourishment level. These are the only levels you are permitted to roam. Everywhere else is off access."

"This level is already big enough to get lost in," Kozz smiled at the woman. Even with her impersonal black pantsuit and the stern look her rectangular glasses gave to her face, Kozz couldn't resist Marissa's elegant charm. "I'm sure I'll have enough elbow room."

"Good. There is a page button located in your room next to the door. It is directly synced to my personal communicator. If you require any assistance or have any questions, feel free to contact me."

"Wow. That's better service than I would get on a passenger ship. Your captain must really want you to keep your eyes on me."

"He does. Your high-level security clearance, though voided, is extremely rare, as I'm sure you're well aware. He doesn't know who you are or what you're up to, but he wants you to know that this ship is his. Now, if you don't mind me asking, Mr. Kozz, where were you heading off to? You only just arrived. I would have thought that anyone would spend at least a few moments getting acquainted with their room and immediate surroundings." She smiled at him.

"I was just looking for the pisser," Kozz said in a whimsical tone, letting Marissa, and more so her captain, know that he knew he would keep up a charade if he needed to. "I just couldn't find it with all these hallways and doors everywhere."

"Well then, let me show you to the restroom located only a few doors down from your room. I'll play along if I must."

Kozz chuckled as they both stood up. Marissa walked a step behind Kozz, letting him lead her back to his room while she kept an eye on him.

"There we are," said Marissa with a boatload of sarcasm hidden behind her rigid face. "Only a few steps away from your door. So silly of you to have missed it."

"I can be a silly man sometimes."

"Alright, well I'll leave you alone for now." She continued speaking as she walked away. "And don't worry about your safety. All of my guards have been told of your presence and are well aware of your clearance level, both on and off the ship. I'm sure you will have no trouble finding a guard if you need one as I have instructed them to pay close attention to your care and safety." She winked and then turned down another hall.

Kozz stood outside his door, looking in the direction Marissa had walked away. "Breathtaking. What a doll."

Kozz sat down in the lounge. His name had already been passed around like a bottle of liquor at a New Year's party. Quick action was not going to work. He had already noticed several guards pass by his room, all glancing inside, taking swift inspection. He was going to have to put forward a more subtle effort now. He did not know if he could get to the loading docks and inspect the database without getting caught. There were not as many staff members or guards on the ship as there should have been, but they were all keeping an eye out for him. Kozz decided that he was just going to have to do the best he could before they found him out. *What's the worst they could do anyway? Throw me off the ship?*

He opened up the magazine with the infected on the cover. Inside was a lengthy report given by a man who had explored the streets of Erde as soon as the carnage started and recorded every bit he could with his camera. The article did not describe much more than the horrific scenes he had witnessed, and it was filled with a dozen page-length images of men and women with glowing eyes rampaging through the streets. Other sections of the magazine highlighted the many politicians and celebrities who were known to have died since the "outbreak", as the magazine called it. To Kozz's relief, Presider Conway was not on that list. Smaller articles speculated about the cause of the crisis and placed estimates on the damage taken place and when or if the Cooperation would ever be able to suppress the "infection". Kozz felt that it had to be something else, something more controlled and evil than a sickness. He put down the magazine and picked up the other with Presider Conway on the cover.

Inside the magazine was more of the same garbage as the first, but this one had an exclusive interview with the Presider himself. Kozz's interest flared.

> **Interviewer:** Reports show that the current state of this infection has wiped out at least fifteen percent of humanity in less than two weeks. Presider Conway, do you believe the Cooperation will be able to find a cure before our species

comes to an end?

Presider Conway: We as a people have endured many hardships throughout our existence. Hurdles have been placed in our path, and we have jumped over them. Trials have been set at our doorsteps, and we succeeded them. Unfathomable problems have been solved by our intelligent and creative minds.

This may be the most difficult of situations we have ever been placed in, but we will survive. Many of us have suffered, and many more will suffer, but we will survive. Our most brilliant minds are exploring all aspects of this unheard of crisis and will find a solution. In the past we have proven that impossible is nothing more than a word, and now we will do so again.

Interviewer: You never mention the words "infection" or "disease" in any of your statements. Is there a reason for this? What have your researchers discovered that you have not told us? If you do not believe that this is some sort of disease or virus then tell us what it is.

Presider Conway: There is reason to my choice of words. From the start I did not believe that a simple bacteria or virus could be the cause of such widespread death and aggressive behavior.

Our scientists have discovered connections between the abnormal aggressive behavior and a microscopic parasite living within the brains and bodies of those afflicted with the abnormalities.

The species of toxoplasma was discovered over a century ago when our forefathers were first settling the planet of Frostarc. The toxoplasma was found in the water and ice of the planet. It was studied and found to be absolutely harmless to humans and has remained so ever since, until these recent events. Since then the toxoplasma has been carried around by our interplanetary travelers and has spread to the water supplies of every inhabited planet within the Cooperation, including the Insurrectionist Moon.

Our scientists are certain that there is a link between the parasite and the affliction, but there is as of yet no solution to the problem. We are working as hard as we can to find a cure, of somehow ridding our people of the parasite, but there is not yet a way to do so safely.

Interviewer: Astonishing. Is there any word on the percentage of the population that carries this parasite? What about other species? Could our pets or wild animals succumb to this affliction?

Presider Conway: We're certain that one-hundred percent of the population carries this parasite within them. We need to find a cure now.

When introduced into the bloodstream of an animal the parasite always finds a way out. It has been found to survive just fine in the climate of another species' body, but it refuses to stay. The parasite will leave a non-human host and will either die or return to a water source where it will repeat the cycle over and over again until it transfers into a human body.

It is all utterly bizarre and baffling.

The article spiraled downward into an unimportant debate between the Presider and the interviewer about the experiments being performed on the comatose. *Desperate times call for desperate measures they always say,* thought Kozz, *and no one's gonna convince Conway otherwise.* Kozz closed the magazine and tossed it back onto the table.

"Damn."

Kozz had found more than he thought he would in a simple magazine, but the new found knowledge did not solve any of his problems and only raised more questions in his mind. He had to find out more. The database on this medical barge would provide him some of the answers he needed, and now that he had some understanding of the problem he could pinpoint paths of information to follow, skipping right over all of the bullshit and running straight for the answers.

He needed to know what was happening. Answers would help him find a way to stop whatever was causing the chaos, and getting to Conway would give him the means he needed to take action. He had to do all of this while trying to find his wife. He needed to protect her. He needed to solve this problem for her. He needed to solve it for Caleb, Luciele, Kelly, and Richard. He needed to save everyone. That's what Caleb wanted him to do. That's what Jake would have wanted him to do.

The next step was getting to that database of information located somewhere in the belly of the ship.

CHAPTER SIXTEEN

Uncertainty

Voices floated through the air as the barge filled with people from all walks of life. Luciele and Caleb had taken the opportunity to explore before the living spaces filled, but when passengers started to enter their level they thought it best to stay out of the way.

Men hauled large traveling cases full of clothes and personal belongings while women carried crying children through the halls. A dozen people at a time exited the elevator and clamored for claim to a room. The guards forced entire families to use no more than a single room to themselves.

Several hours passed as more and more people piled into the barge. Luciele was surprised at the amount of people they were allowing on the level and knew it must have meant that the large loading levels were even worse. She and Caleb organized their belongings and did as best as they could to make their small room a home for the next several weeks. She kept the door ajar to keep an ear out for what was going on out in the hall, yet shut enough to keep prying eyes from looking.

Caleb heard children's voices in the next room. He asked his mother if he could go over and meet them, but she told him to wait until everyone was settled in.

More people packed into the nearby rooms, parents yelling and children screaming. It scared Caleb. Luciele explained to her son that everyone was frightened and on edge, that they all had to abandon their homes and travel to a far off planet which most of them had probably never been to. The guards did what they could to maintain order, but there were too many refugees for the small security force to handle.

"Scuse me, but could y'all tell me if this room here is taken?" Luciele's heart sank when she heard that familiar voice outside her door. Caleb looked over to his mother's wide-eyed face, checking to see if she noticed the voice as he had.

"Yes sir," said the guard stationed outside his office, "but the room across is still empty. I would grab it now if I were you."

"Thank ya much," said the voice.

Luciele stood from her seat and walked to her door.

"Mom," said Caleb, "do you think that's..."

"I hope not." Luciele pulled her door open a few inches to peek into the room across the hall. A man had his back turned to her as he dropped his baggage onto the floor. He put his hand on his lower back and bent backwards to stretch his muscles. His wide-brimmed hat hid his face from her, but she knew. He turned and his eyes met hers. She shut the door.

"Dammit," said Luciele. "It's Tim." She did not know why she felt scared. The man had never actually harmed her or her son. She had never been afraid of him before, but she certainly did not enjoy his company. He was always a little odd, and he had a strange obsession with Caleb ever since discovering that he was once infected, but he had never done them any harm. She decided to open the door again.

He stood just outside the door as she opened it.

"Well look who we have here," said Tim. Bags rested under his eyes and he had not shaved in some time. "Looks like y'all made it just fine. Where's the big fella and those two lovebirds? They in a differnt room?"

"Hello Tim. Surprised to see you here. We've all parted ways, it's just Caleb and I now."

"Ah, the boy. How is he? Turn back into an infected yet?"

"He's just fine. You don't need to worry yourself with him."

"Yeah, leave me alone fuckwad," said Caleb. He got up and stood next to his mother.

Luciele 's jaw dropped. "Caleb!"

"What?" said Caleb. "That's what Kozz would have said to him. I don't want him bothering me anymore. I thought he was gone forever."

"Haha!" Tim laughed as Caleb stared at him with angry

eyes. "That boy of yours needed some spunk. Looks like the big fella rubbed off on him some." Luciele was relieved that Tim brushed off her son's outburst. "I reckon I'll have to make sure to inform the guards of his...history, however. Don't want him surprising me in the middle of the night with a bite to the neck or something equally as monstrous."

"You do not have to tell them," said Luciele. "I will. They would be likely to jump in here with guns drawn like a couple of angry cowpokes if they heard the way you would spin it."

"Haha, you're probably correct in that regard. Alright then, I'll stand aside if you take care of your responsibility."

"Yeah, don't worry about it." Luciele rolled her eyes. The man enjoyed causing trouble, but she figured it would be best to be as friendly as possible in order to make their voyage more comfortable. "Anyway, where are Daryll and the others? Did all of the old folks make it? It sure was difficult crossing those glaciers."

"Oh no, they're all dead." Tim spoke as if it were merely a matter of fact. Luciele's eyes widened and Caleb's angered face morphed into disbelief. "Well I know Daryll is anyway, and I assume the rest are."

"Samuel...?" Caleb whispered.

"I don't know, kid, but he was with them when I left them behind. Didn't have much hope for any of them."

"What happened?" asked Luciele.

"We got to that glacier and all hell broke loose. Daryll and I knew that we would have a heck of a time gettin' them old folks up and across the glacier, and there was no chance for the mules. Without mules to carry the supplies those old folks wouldn't have survived long anyway. Daryll wanted to turn back and find another way 'cross the sea, but I just wanted to move forward with the healthy of us.

"He wouldn't have any of it, that bastard, and he tried to force me to turn back with him and the others, sayin' that he needed my help. Damn guy pulled his gun out on me and so I blasted him square in the head in front of everyone. Shot him b'fore he shot me. Felt like shit doin' it but he wasn't goin' to let me go.

"So I told all them folks to head back to Blackwater with their supplies, but no one wanted to go back. I climbed up the rope y'all left behind and stood on top of the glacier. I said to them that any of them that could make it up with me on their own could come with me. None of them even tried, and the other healthy, young folk wanted to stay with the old ones.

"So I yelled at them. I hollered at them to go back and die if that's what they wanted. No one moved so I started shootin' at them and then they started to run. I grabbed my bag and crossed the glacier all on my lonesome.

"Now I'm here and so are y'all. We survived because we're the strong ones."

"You bastard!" Tears leaked from Luciele's grizzly eyes. She had not been friendly with many of those people, but she knew them all. At first she may have disliked both Daryll and Tim, but in the end she had thought they were good men who were going to lead the others to safety, despite their character flaws. Caleb ran to his bed and started bawling. Luciele took a step forward, meaning to go out the door, but Tim did not move out of her way. "I'm going to report you to the security guards!"

"Report me?" said Tim, chuckling to himself. "I did what I had to in order to survive, little missy. And b'sides, what evidence do ya have about a gunfight that happened next to a glacier on the other side of the sea? They won't arrest me just because of hearsay."

He was right, and Luciele hated him for it. She stepped back into her room. "You stay the hell away from me and my son."

"That'll be kinda hard seein' as we're neighbors and all, but I'll try my best. Don't want to get too close to your sickly boy anyhow. Good thing we're allowed to carry our weapons during this crisis in order to protect ourselves. I might be needin' mine for self-defense if the kid starts acting weird."

"Don't ever come to our room again!" She slammed the door in his face.

"Don't forget to tell the guards about his past!" yelled Tim through the thin metal door. "Y'all have a good day now!"

Luciele walked over to the bed to cry with her son. Caleb sat up and tried to dry his eyes.

"We could have saved them if we stayed with them, mom. We could have saved Samuel and the others."

Luciele did not know how to respond. She and Kozz had tried to explain to Caleb that saving everyone was impossible, but he always refused to believe it. They left the others in order to save themselves. She could not bring herself to say anything uplifting to her son. "Yes, we could have."

Together they let their tears fall for the fallen they had left behind. Screams broke out in the hall, shouts of a person turned infected attacking the masses. "Papa!" cried a young boy. The man had fallen to the infection, but swift action from the security guards quieted the situation. The man fell to the ground with a tranquilizer in his back.

The event in the hallway only made their sadness worse. Caleb's tears for Samuel and the others had become tears for his father, Harold. Luciele's thoughts coincided with her son's, and they comforted each other as they let their sorrows and fears pour out in the privacy of their room.

They were on a journey to a world which they barely knew and they had no idea where they were going to go once they got there. Harold, father and husband, had fallen. Their friends had left them. They were all alone, but at least they had each other.

The nourishment level was a mess of people gallivanting about the food courts, dining halls, and bars. Kozz could have easily been lost in the crowd, guards and personnel unable to pinpoint him in the masses, but it was too soon. He wanted to wait until night when there would be fewer people walking about, when Marissa would be in bed.

He grabbed a bite to eat, some sort of meat in tube form—lord knows what it really was. Kozz sat down at a table with his snack. Marissa found him. She brought over a plate of greens.

"May I join you for dinner?" she asked.

"Sure, toots."

"So, Mr. Kozz," she propped her elbows on the table and intertwined her fingers, resting her chin on her conjoined fists, "tell me, who are you? Where are you going?"

"Does your captain say I'm required to answer these questions?"

"No. I just wanted to chit chat. I'm curious as to who you are."

"Well, who I am is a secret. You should understand from my clearance level that not many people know who I am."

"Indeed. But your secrecy intrigues me, and I am not easily intrigued."

"I'm just a guy on my way to Erde, just like everyone else on this ship, as far as you're to be concerned. There are people I need to see."

"What kind of people, Mr. Kozz?"

"We've all suffered one way or another during these trying times, haven't we, Marissa? We all need to see our families, need to make sure they're alright. I've been away from my family for awhile. It's time I paid a visit. I just used my old clearance card to get me on the ship that was leaving the soonest."

"You used your clearance and your friend the military commander. You have connections that the average man does not acquire."

"I've lived a long time and made a few friends along the way." Kozz was uncomfortable with all of the questions, and he finished his meal. It was time to leave. "If you'll excuse me, doll. My belly's full and I'm all worn out. It's time to hit the sack."

"Yes, I should sleep soon as well. I have early hours on the ship." She picked up her fork as she prepared to eat. "I'll be seeing you soon, Mr. Kozz." Marissa sat in her chair and watched Kozz walk away. She eyed the gleaming scarlet weapon at his side. Her fork punctured several leafy greens and she took a bite. She chewed her food without interest, her eyes intent on Red. She had seen that gun before.

Kozz went back to his room, closed the door, and waited for the hours to pass. His plan was to go for the database in the middle of the night. He heard the other residents of his level talk the evening away with each other, several spending time in the lounge until the late hours. The voices dwindled away, one by one, until there was not one left. Doors closed and latches locked. The only sound in the hall after that was the soft steps of a patrolling guard.

For several hours Kozz listened for any sound, only hearing the guard as he walked by. Kozz timed the man. His patrol brought him past Kozz's door every half hour, to the minute.

Kozz knew he needed a security card to reach the loading levels, and he had to avoid detection at all costs. He let the guard walk by one last time before Kozz opened his door and hid himself in the corner next to the doorway, concealed from anyone who would glance inside from the hall.

Pressed against the wall, Kozz waited for the guard to patrol by at the half-hour mark again. He heard the soft steps approach and stop outside his doorway. The guard looked inside and saw that Kozz's room appeared empty. He walked in to search for Kozz, and he found him.

Kozz leaped from his position. He clasped a hand to the man's mouth and brought him down to the ground. The guard reached for his weapon, but Kozz punched the man's hand into the floor and shattered the bone inside. The guard tried to scream, but Kozz used his punching hand to chop at the man's throat, temporarily cutting off his air supply.

The guard gasped on the floor. Kozz was going to knock the man out with a swift blow, but he realized that the guard's weapon was loaded with tranquilizer darts. Kozz grabbed the dart gun and shot the man in the leg. A moment later he was asleep.

Kozz closed the door and lifted the man on to the bed. A quick search of his body led to a security card. Kozz took the card and the dart gun, knowing that it might do better in a stealth situation than Red would.

Kozz crept down the hallways and corridors, avoiding the other patrolling guards with ease. There were not many, after all. Half of the lights in the halls remained on, but it was still too bright for him to be completely hidden. If he were seen the guards would have no trouble recognizing him. He would have to be cautious. Cameras monitored the passageways, but they were placed more for general observation and had many blind spots for Kozz to sneak through.

Getting to the elevator was simple, but using it would create a distinguishable noise through all the levels. Kozz hoped that use of the elevator was common enough at night to not attract attention. He entered the elevator car and selected the lowest floor, the uppermost loading level. A voice requested his security card and he shoved it inside of a blinking slot. A machine inside the elevator scanned his card and granted him access. The car was lowered to the levels below.

Anxiety gnawed at Kozz's nerves. He hoped that his elevator would not stop on the way down for another passenger requesting a ride. Luckily, it continued its descent without interruption.

When he reached the loading level the elevator stopped and the doors opened. A guard stood just outside the elevator doors, but he did not turn right away to see who was exiting the elevator. Kozz reached for Red on impulse, then consciously forced his hand back to the dart gun. He fired a tranquilizer as the man turned and the dart hit the man underneath his chin. The guard's eyes fluttered and he sank to the ground before he could signal an alarm.

Kozz spotted another guard in the distance, but the loading level was enormous and the other guard had not seen what had taken place. The entirety of the room was filled with comatose patients held in medical care incubators. The distant guard walked slowly through the rows of sleeping patients.

Kozz dropped low and dragged the downed guard behind one of the incubators. Inside was a young girl, not more than six years of age. Kozz watched her for a moment. She was breathing softly. A tube was inserted down her throat, and Kozz was able to see the nutrients that were being fed into her system. Several monitors were placed on her head and torso. The outside of the glass incubator held a series of digital numbers and he could see her heart rate, neurological signatures, *and a bunch of other stats that don't matter*, he thought. All that mattered to him at that moment was that she looked like a beautiful little girl, sleeping the night away and dreaming of whatever little girls usually dream about, but he knew inside was a terrible demon that was tormenting her. He had to find out what was going on. The little girl needed him.

Kozz crept over to the loading freight elevator and near it was a small map showcasing the three freight loading levels. He was currently on the third level. The first level looked the same as the third, but the second level had a large section bordered off on the map that was labeled as a lab. That was his destination.

Kozz pushed the button for the freight elevator and listened as the beast roared its engines and clanked its way up the shaft. He looked around to see if the distant guard was heading his way, but he seemed to pay no attention to the elevator and continued on his route through the incubators. Kozz would not have long before one of the guards he had taken down was discovered. He needed to move fast.

Kozz entered the freight elevator. There was enough room to fit more than one hundred men of Kozz's size. He felt like the lone turd in an otherwise empty litter box. Someone had to have noticed him by now.

The elevator dropped and the accordion-style door opened to another loading level which was just as big as the one he had left. Thousands of occupied incubators carpeted the floor, but at the dead center of the room was a lightly walled off lab which Kozz could see was filled with computer terminals and large machinery.

Two guards standing at either side of the elevator saw Kozz as he exited the elevator. They raised their dart guns and commanded him to halt, but he smacked the man to his left in the face hard enough to drop him to the ground and then Kozz fired a dart into the forehead of the woman to his right. Before the guard he smacked could recover from the blow, Kozz fired a dart into the man's thigh.

A guard amongst the row of incubators called for assistance on his communicator and fired his darts spasmodically. Metal tipped needles clinked on the metal wall behind Kozz. He reached inside the elevator and slammed the back of his fist into the controls, sending the freight car to the level below. They were on to him now, and the bulk of the guards would be coming from above. Their delay in getting the elevator would give him a few more seconds.

Kozz ducked behind an incubator. The guard reloaded his weapon and continued to fire at the area where he thought Kozz was hiding. Kozz ran like an ape on his hands and feet from one incubator to the next, making his way towards the frazzled guard. Kozz sneaked up on the man from behind and shot a dart into the back of the man's calf. The guard dropped like a rock, Kozz catching him by the arms to soften his fall.

The chaos of the moment had quieted. Kozz's heart pounded, and it ached only slightly. He had not taken his medication in the last few days. Something within him had grown stronger. He felt young again, like he did when he was an Enforcer, taking down evil crime lords and punishing those who threatened his Cooperation. He crept through row after row of unconscious infected. The room lights gave the rusted metal of the loading level a red glow, but the cool blue lights from within the incubators highlighted Kozz in purple as he dashed towards the lab area.

Thin sheets of cork-board wall sectioned the lab off from the rest of the level, but it was not a completely walled off room. Two rows of computer terminals, ten or so in each, lined the north and west borders of the lab. The south end where Kozz had entered was full of file cabinets and tables with papers scattered all about. In the center of the lab were two large machines.

In one machine a man stood with the assistance of a harness and was surrounded by four glass walls. He was completely naked other than the opaque black bowl which surrounded his head. His body moved in slow motion. The man was either awake or being controlled by his harness, but either way the movements seemed unnatural. Wires attached to the crest of the bowl spiraled up into the large machine which reminded Kozz of a giant microscope.

In the other contraption an unconscious woman rested on top of a bed much like those in the incubators. Her body was covered with a heavy, black tarp while her head was surrounded by the bulk of the machine. Inside the hollow where her sleeping head rested two metal plates spun at varying speeds, slowing and quickening at seemingly random intervals.

Both machines were faced towards a large computer terminal at the east end of the lab where a young woman had fallen asleep in her chair. Kozz saw that she was the only person within the lab at this late hour. She was leaned back in her chair, snoring the night away with a large pair of headphones wrapped around her head.

Kozz hustled over to the woman and fired his last dart into her exposed neck. She jostled at the pressure of the needle penetrating her soft skin, but she never woke from her sleep. Kozz wheeled her out of his way and accessed her terminal. The six screens had all gone into rest mode, but fortunately she had not chosen to log off before taking her nap.

Kozz slipped the headphones off of the woman's head and put them on his own. A jumble of noises entered his ears, making no sense to him at all. It sounded like decelerated static noise that jumped and dropped in pitch every second or two. He found a graph on one of the screens that coincided with the noises, recording them as they went along. Kozz took off the headphones. The noise was starting to hurt his head.

On another screen Kozz found the woman's message system. He opened up the list of recent transmissions and scrolled through a few documents that were sent to colleagues. One of the files was a thorough description of a parasite, the same one as was discussed by Presider Conway in his interview. The bug looked like a microscopic tick. Discussed in the report was the parasite's "perfect cellular and DNA structures" which were both "unlike any seen in other living organisms". The report also described an "antenna" that was placed on the bug's underside. It used the antenna to hold its location on its host, but it also acted as a receiver for an "extremely high-speed electromagnetic frequency".

The article continued to discuss the advanced tools the scientists had used to slow down the frequency, making it so that they could listen to its intricacies. "At first we thought it was an unintelligible mess," said one of the researchers. "The waves are impossibly fast, many times faster than the speed of light. The waves seem to be propelled by some sort of unreadable energy, an empty force which surrounds them. After decelerating the waves in our recordings, and repeatedly listening to them, we discovered patterns within the frequencies. In fact, after breaking down the patterns into smaller bits, the recordings were found to have sound structures that were unique to each pattern, but when layered together they created a sort of code.

"We separated these codes into their own categories, labeling them as 'values'. Each value was found again in future recordings we listened to, but the values had their own unique variants each time they were found in a different recording.

"An even smaller structure was found within them that again could be found repeated in future recordings, but unique unto itself in the smallest of ways.

"These recordings have been found to be too structured to be created under a natural setting."

The freight elevator was in motion. Kozz found the information fascinating, but it was not enough for what he needed. He had to move on. "So the damn things are being controlled by someone?" he asked himself. "Is that what they mean by not natural? But who?"

Kozz scrolled through more messages, finding more interesting pieces, but none provided him an answer. Then he came across a message sent to 'The Office of the Presider' entitled 'Preeminent Hypothesis: Top-Level Security Locks in Place'.

"So this young broad snoozing away on the job has some

important responsibilities and high clearances, eh?" Kozz shook his head as he opened the transmission, "Guess she'll be losing her job over this one."

The freight car opened. Kozz heard one guard commanding others. They were moving his way.

"This message is for Presider Conway's eyes only. All others who attempt to breach the electronic locks in place will be prosecuted." The document was opened before Kozz's eyes. The sleeping woman had to have been the one to send the message to the Presider.

"Over here!" shouted a guard from the south entrance. "Raise your hands and drop to the floor!"

Kozz threw his empty dart gun at the guard. The man fired a dart and then ducked behind the wall, hiding from what he thought was a dangerous weapon heading in his direction.

The dart hit Kozz in the foot. Drowsiness sunk into him and his head felt like it was full of lead. He focused all of his remaining attention on the computer screen. The transmission only contained one short paragraph.

"Presider Conway," it read. "The scientific community hired to solve this infestation has unanimously agreed upon a hypothesis. Attached are all of our current findings." More guards approached the north and south entrances to the lab. Kozz found Red in his hand and he raised her into the air. An ocean of water slashed in his head, its currents rocking his mind from side to side. Red fired into the air, her deafening blast echoing throughout the level. The guards backed away for a moment more. "In the reports listed below are the reasons behind our conclusions. We hypothesize that the parasite responsible for the abnormally aggressive behavior has been created by, and is being controlled by, an outside source. The unfathomable scope of complexity surrounding the parasites leads us to believe that this cannot possibly be man made. Humanity is centuries away from the complete understanding of femtotechnology, or beyond, required to create such a unique and structured life form. Therefore, we hypothesize that the parasites are under the control of a more advanced sentient society. We believe this is out first contact with intelligent alien life forms."

Kozz had enough time after reading the report to inhale a deep breath before the guard who scaled the wall behind him fired a dart into the back of his neck. Kozz slumped forward over the terminal and stared into the screen until his eyes closed and his head sank into his folded arms.

Kozz awoke in his room. His belongings had been ransacked, and much was missing. Red was gone as well. *Feels like a dump truck slugged me across the face.* He stood up and opened the door to leave his room. Two guards waited for him outside.

"You're not going anywhere, big man," said one of them. They were both almost as large as he was.

The other guard raised his communicator. "He's awake," he said, then directed his attention towards Kozz. "Get back in your room. Officer Batoon will be with you shortly."

Kozz did as he was told because he did not have the strength to put up a fight at the moment. He pondered his thoughts on what he had experienced, trying to separate the reality from the drugs. *I know what I saw. It was real. Conway was informed, and he must be taking action. I have to get to him. I have to be a part of this. I can't let bugs or aliens or anything else threaten the people I love.*

And that message was dated only days ago. That means Conway is still alive. Maybe they've found a cure.

But what if there is no cure? Aliens, really? Are we under attack?

It looks like we're in the middle of a war we didn't even know we were fighting.

"Lord, I could use a stogie right now. Shitheads took those from me too."

Thin, beautiful, merciless Marissa opened the door. Two guards followed her in. Kozz stood to respect her presence, but one of the guards ordered him to sit down.

"You are good, Mr. Kozz." She stood tall, knowing she was in charge of the situation. The woman demanded attention with her bright eyes, but their intensity kept Kozz from staring for too long. "Getting all that way, knowing that this entire ship was keeping an eye on you, and all on your first night! Marvelous."

"Yeah, thanks. Now where's my gun and smokes?"

"We have them. Do not fret. You will get everything back once our trip is at an end. Well, maybe I'll let you have your cigars a little sooner if you behave yourself."

"So am I under arrest then? I saw what I was looking for. I don't need to go prowling around for anything else."

"Under arrest? Oh, no. You are not under arrest. We simply request that you remain in your room for the duration of the trip. Your clearance level is too high for us to simply arrest you, even if it is voided. It just seems that you are too important of a person, Mr. Cochran."

Kozz's body tensed. He shot a glare at the woman. "How do you know my name?"

"Guards," said Marissa. Her proud demeanor did not change. "A little privacy, please? Don't worry. I'll be fine." The guards left the room and closed the door. "I know more than just your name, Cosmo. I know all about you. I wasn't sure it was you when we first met at the elevator, but the expertise you displayed last night proved who you are. I have been searching for you for a long time. A little over a decade, in fact."

"Narnkazi," said Kozz. Her eyes revealed everything she knew. Her confidence was manifested in the fact that she had finally found the prey she had been hunting for the last ten years. "You killed him."

"Him? Oh, you mean your boy? Goodness no, I've never killed anyone. I simply ordered it to happen. You destroyed most of my father's organization and killed many of his men. Don't you think he deserved the retribution?"

"I'm going to fucking strangle you!" Kozz lurched forward and grabbed the woman's thin throat. "You killed my son! You killed my beautiful Jake!" He squeezed her throat, twisting his hands back and forth to make sure she felt the pain. His rage tightened his face and swelled his muscles. The guards outside heard the noise and burst through the door. They raised their weapons and ordered Kozz to stop, but he would not.

"Priscilla," squeaked Marissa. She mouthed the name again. "Priscilla."

Kozz read the name off her lips and released her. The guards swarmed around him and tackled him to the ground. "What about her?" he yelled. "What have you done to her? You better not have fucking touched her!"

Marissa muttered something no one could hear. She tried to speak several times, but Kozz had squeezed hard. She managed to make a sound. The guards did not understand her at first, but she repeated herself. "Leave us!" she demanded. The guards did as ordered and closed the door once more.

"Where is she?" demanded Kozz.

"We have her. We've had ever ever since you abandoned her. She's been at my father's side since the day you left her. She's been our slave and our whipping board for the last ten years."

She was lying, and Kozz knew it. He did not let it show. He played along. "I told her to run away. I told her to change her name. I told her how to lose herself in the crowd so that you would never track her down."

"And we did anyway! She ours, Mr. Cochran. Mr. Enforcer. My father is holding her, knowing that you'll one day come to her rescue. He wants you to come. He wants you to try and save her. He wants you to watch her die as he watched his companions die on the day you invaded our complex, and then he will kill you. Painfully. Slowly. Then he will send both of your heads to the Presider, letting the galaxy know to never challenge Narnkazi! We have rebuilt since your attack, and we are stronger than we ever were before, especially with the current weakened state of the Cooperation. If you want to find your wife, you are going to have to let me live. I will be your guide."

"And if I kill you right now?"

"Then she remains my father's slave. He enjoys her company, and my brothers love using her for a punching bag. Keep this in mind. I'll give you instructions at the end of our journey to Erde."

"You're a fucking bitch."

"Compliments are unnecessary, Mr. Cochran. Enjoy the next three weeks in your room. The guards will keep you company, and your meals will be brought to you. If you are lucky I will check in on you from time to time. Farewell."

She closed the door behind herself. Kozz thought about what she had said. *She lied. Jammer had run into Priscilla a few years ago and she was fine. That means they don't have her. Marissa wouldn't have lied about having my beautiful wife for so long if she had her at all. They found me and they want me to lead them to her. They still hold their grudge after all of these years.*

I thought that it had been long enough. I thought they would have forgotten about me. I thought we were more safe now in the midst of all this carnage happening in the galaxy, but I was wrong. They'll never stop hunting Priscilla, and they'll never stop hunting me.

It's time to stop running. I'm going to have to end Narnkazi once and for all. I'm going to take him and his entire organization down, and I'm going to make sure Marissa is there when all hell breaks loose.

But I still have to get to Conway and help him solve this crisis. Priscilla is only one of many people I have to protect. Caleb and Luciele are depending on me, as are Richard and Kelly, and all of humanity is under threat.

I have to do what I can. I have to stop anyone else from suffering. I have to save everyone, for Caleb. For myself.

Good thing I have three weeks in solitary to plan out what I need to do.

"Guards!" shouted Kozz. "How 'bout throwing me a damn magazine or something. And where's my razor? I need to shave."

About the Author

Arthur McMahon is an independent author of fiction and non-fiction, publisher, and outdoor adventurer.

Arthur's passion for writing began as a child when he found that he preferred writing essays to taking exams. Having graduated from the University of Oregon with a bachelor's degree in journalism, Arthur enjoys recording the world which surrounds him. His backpacking journeys and other escapades have been recorded in numerous articles and in his own published trail journal, Adventure and The Pacific Crest Trail.

Fiction never loosens its hold on Arthur's thoughts, especially the realms of science fiction and fantasy. Frostarc is Arthur's debut novel, and his Silhouette novellas are set in the same space-pioneering universe. Reviews have praised Arthur for his suspenseful writing and exciting action.

As a self-proclaimed nomad and traveler, Arthur will always have new stories to tell. His latest work, Silhouette, can be found in print or as an ebook on Amazon. You can stay up to date on Arthur McMahon's latest projects at ArthurMcMahon.com or follow him on Twitter and Facebook.

Thank you for reading!

www.ingramcontent.com/pod-product-compliance
Lightning Source LLC
Chambersburg PA
CBHW030546200626
46812CB00022BA/1897